"We'll get married," he blurted. "Right away, as soon as you want."

The declaration caught him completely off guard and he added, "You can move to Chicago. I'll take care of you and the baby and…"

Horrified didn't come close to describing her expression.

"What?" he asked.

"Oh, gee, Jack. We hardly even know one another, for one thing."

"Emily, we've known each other for years."

"All right, then," she said. "What's my favorite color?"

He looked her up and down, as though her wardrobe might offer up a clue. "Yellow?"

"Wrong. What's my middle name? When's my birthday?" she asked, relentlessly hammering her point home.

Again, he had no idea, none whatsoever.

"See? You don't know anything about me, but you think getting married is a good idea. You think I should walk away from my family and my job and everything I've ever known, follow you to Chicago, waiting for you to get unbusy enough to be a husband and a father?"

"I don't know, Emily. We're going to be parents, and I'm trying to do the right thing."

Dear Reader,

Welcome to Riverton, Wisconsin! This (fictional) small town, steeped in the culture of America's Heartland, is home to the Finnegan sisters—Emily, Annie and CJ—and I'm delighted to introduce them to you.

I grew up in a close-knit family, always knowing there was someone there to celebrate the good times and to offer support when the going got tough. I cherish all the memories of afternoon picnics and Sunday dinners, so it's no surprise to anyone who knows me that those are the things I love to write about.

To Catch a Wife is about coming to terms with the past, learning to cope with an uncertain future and discovering that love is all about the compromise. This is middle sister Emily's story, and I hope you enjoy it. I love to hear from readers and invite you to visit my website at leemckenzie.com, where you can send me an email, sign up for my (mostly) monthly newsletter and find out about my other books, including future books in this series. Happy reading!

Warmest,

Lee

HEARTWARMING

To Catch a Wife

—

Lee McKenzie

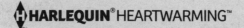

Recycling programs for this product may not exist in your area.

ISBN-13: 978-0-373-36790-0

To Catch a Wife

Printed in U.S.A.

From the time she was ten years old and read *Anne of Green Gables* and *Little Women*, **Lee McKenzie** knew she wanted to be a writer, just like Anne and Jo. In the intervening years, she has written everything from advertising copy to an honors thesis in paleontology, but becoming a four-time Golden Heart® Award finalist and a Harlequin author are among her proudest accomplishments. Lee and her artist/teacher husband live on an island along Canada's west coast, and she loves to spend time with two of her best friends—her grown-up children.

Books by Lee McKenzie

Harlequin Heartwarming

The Parent Trap

Harlequin American Romance

The Man for Maggie
With This Ring
Firefighter Daddy
The Wedding Bargain
The Christmas Secret
The Daddy Project
Daddy, Unexpectedly

For Johanna Raisanen, editor extraordinaire

Acknowledgments

Many thanks to Melanie Backus for entering my Name This Furry Friend contest and suggesting the name Tadpole for Emily's hamster. It was a hands-down favorite with the judges.

CHAPTER ONE

EMILY FINNEGAN SETTLED onto the middle stool at the big kitchen island, sliding comfortably into her place as the middle sister. No matter what was wrong with the world—floods, famines, personal freak-outs—here in the heart of the Finnegan family farmhouse, everything felt right.

Her younger sister, CJ—Cassie Jo as their father affectionately called her—sat on the stool to Emily's right. CJ was dressed for the stables in dark jeans and a faded denim work shirt, her long blond hair pulled back in a high ponytail.

Across the gleaming white Formica countertop, Annie, eldest of the three sisters, stood with carafe in hand. "Coffee?" She angled the pot over Emily's mug. If the kitchen was the heart of the home, then Annie was the life force that kept it beating.

"Sure. Oh, wait. No." Emily hastily withdrew her cup. "Only if it's decaf."

CJ clapped a hand to Emily's forehead.

Emily ducked away from it. "What are you doing?"

"Checking to see if you're running a fever. Since when do you drink decaf?"

A good question for which Emily didn't have a good answer. Yet. "I haven't been sleeping well, so I thought I'd cut back on caffeine, see if that makes a difference." Only partly true, but at least it wasn't a lie.

"It's ten-thirty in the morning," CJ said.

Emily shrugged.

"Not a problem," Annie said. "I'll make a fresh pot of decaf. It'll be ready in a few minutes." She looked amazing in a slouchy yellow pullover and crisp white slacks. Given everything she would have accomplished since getting up before sunrise—gathering eggs from the chicken coop, making breakfast, vacuuming, laundry—Emily had no idea how Annie kept herself looking fresh as a summer daisy.

While her older sister turned to the coffeemaker, Emily tried to ignore her younger sister's scrutiny. Ever since CJ had been little, she'd had a talent for sniffing secrets and wheedling information out of the secret keeper.

"You're being weird," CJ said.

"I'm always weird."

"Weirder than usual."

"Don't bug your sister." Annie, ever the mom, filled CJ's mug, then her own.

The coffee smelled like a little piece of heaven to Emily. How would she make it through nine whole months without coffee? Although, if the secret thing that had been keeping her up at night turned out to be true, it was now closer to seven months.

Annie set the carafe on the counter next to a basket of muffins. "These are blueberry," she said. "They should still be warm. I baked the oatmeal-raisin cookies yesterday. I had to send something for the school bake sale, so I made extra."

"Mmm. Yummy," CJ said, biting into a cookie. "What are you raising money for this time?"

"A field trip to the geology museum in Madison. Isaac is over-the-moon excited because they're going to see 'real' dinosaurs."

"He knows they're just a bunch of bones, right?"

"He does. He also knows the scientific name of almost every dinosaur that ever existed, how big it was, whether it ate meat or plants. Thanks to the set of books you gave him for Christmas, Em, dinosaurs are a very big deal for my little boy."

"Pun intended?" CJ quipped.

Annie grinned. "Of course." She poured Emily a mug of decaf coffee. "You seem awfully quiet this morning."

"I'm always quiet."

"Okay, quieter than usual."

Emily shrugged. She didn't like to keep things from her sisters—hated it, actually—but there was no point in saying anything about this particular *thing* until she knew for sure. If it turned out to be a false alarm, then they'd be none the wiser.

Time to change the subject. "Where is my favorite dinosaur-obsessed nephew this morning?"

"Dad drove him into town to shop for a birthday present for his friend Matthew. The party's this afternoon. They'll be home for lunch, and then Dad will run him back to town for the party. I'd take him myself, but I have a guest checking into the B & B this afternoon, and I need to be here when she arrives."

"Where's she coming from?" CJ asked.

"Chicago."

"Will she want a trail ride? Maybe a riding lesson or two?"

"I don't know. She booked online and didn't request it, but I'll be sure to ask when she checks in."

While her sisters discussed the anticipated

guest and what her needs might be, Emily's thoughts drifted, as they often did when the three of them were together in the kitchen, in search of one of her few and fleeting memories of their mother. Few because Emily had barely been four years old the last time they'd seen Scarlett Finnegan, and fleeting because that's what twenty-five-year-old memories tended to be.

What came to mind was an image of her four-year-old self sitting on the lap of a gaunt-looking woman with dark, soulful eyes and long chestnut hair the same color as Emily's. Her sisters were blue-eyed blondes like their father, but she had taken after their mother. As always, the memory was tinged bittersweet. Was it real? Or was she simply conjuring the moment that had been captured in the framed photograph on her dresser? She would never be sure. The picture had been taken in this kitchen on Emily's fourth birthday, only a few weeks before her mother had gone away.

The kitchen island hadn't existed in those days. She and her mother had been sitting at the long butcher-block table that had filled the middle of this room for three generations. After Annie married her husband, Eric, and he had moved in, she'd converted the family farmhouse into a bed-and-breakfast. Now recently widowed, and in spite of the family's insistence she take a break, Annie had decided to carry on with the business. She needed to earn a living, and she also didn't want to disappoint her clientele. They were devoted, and had increased her business by posting amazing online reviews and telling family and friends about her B & B.

"Emily?" Annie's question hauled her thoughts back to the present.

"Hm? Sorry. Daydreaming."

"I said you look nice today," Annie said. "Is that a new top you're wearing?"

"Oh, yes, it is."

"The color really suits you."

"Thanks. I thought I'd try something other than my usual black and beige." Truthfully, she'd chosen the deep marigold patterned top more for its style than its color. The soft gathers falling from the U-shaped yoke added some flare to the hemline and enough fullness to disguise the fact she was no longer as skinny as her jeans.

Annie studied her seriously but, in typical Annie fashion, kept her thoughts to herself.

Something CJ seldom did. "I told you something's weird. You're quieter than usual, avoiding caffeine, jazzing up your wardrobe. What's up with you?"

Emily glared at her little sister. "Nothing. Everything's fine." That's what she desperately hoped for anyway.

"So, Em. What have you been working on these days?" Annie asked, switching subjects as though she had somehow gleaned what was up with Emily and was intentionally trying to distract CJ.

"Oh, this and that." She sipped her coffee. "The mayor has called a special session of the town council on Monday afternoon—says he has some big announcement—so I'll be covering that."

"A big announcement? In Riverton?" CJ's tone was tinged with derision. "Don't tell me the mayor's finally decided to fix that rusty old stop sign at Main and Second, the one old man Thompson ran into when his truck skidded on a patch of ice last winter."

"I certainly hope not. They'll have to raise our taxes if they do that." Annie chuckled at her own joke. "I'm betting someone has an overdue library book."

"No, I've got it," CJ said. "Another garden gnome has gone missing."

Emily laughed at their lame attempts at humor, knowing her sisters loved their hometown every bit as much as she did. "Come on, you two. Riverton's not *that* sleepy. Besides, my sources tell me the mayor's going to announce that Chief Fenwick is retiring from the Riverton Police Department at the end of the month, and he's looking for a replacement."

CJ wasn't buying it. "Yes, Riverton is *that* sleepy. And excuse me, but…you have *sources*?"

"I do."

"Let me guess. Becky Wilson?"

Becky, who ran the only beauty salon in town, was an avid participant in and a regular contributor to Riverton's rumor mill.

"No, it wasn't Becky," Emily said. "She never gossips about anything interesting. Fred told me when we had lunch yesterday. Mayor Bartlett was in for a haircut that morning and happened to let something slip."

Annie smoothed a hand over her short blond bob. "Maybe I should get Fred to cut my hair. Everyone jokes about the beauty parlor being a hub for gossip, but I never hear anything worthwhile at the Clip 'n' Curl. Did the mayor say who he's planning to appoint?"

"No." Emily sighed. "Just that he's casting a wide net." She liked to think she'd make an ace investigative journalist but in fact spent far more time writing obituaries and reporting on town council meetings. "I haven't had a chance to talk to him and wheedle it out of him. I've been a little preoccupied."

"With…?" Annie's scrutiny once again had her on edge.

"Oh, you know. Work, writing my blog, stuff like that." Emily slid off her stool and loaded her mug and plate into the dishwasher. CJ stood, too, and crossed the big kitchen to open the French doors and let Chester outside. The old retriever ambled across the plank porch and onto the sprawling back lawn.

Emily gave her older sister a hug. "Thanks. This has been great."

"We do this every Saturday."

"I know, but I really needed some sister time this morning. And a muffin." She had eaten two.

"Want to tell me what has you so out of sorts?"

"Nothing," she said, lowering her voice even though her nosy younger sister was out of earshot. "And I'm not 'out of sorts.' I'm fine."

Annie held her by the shoulders and gave her a long look. "I know you, Em. And I know you'll tell me in good time. Promise me you'll call if you need to talk?"

She appreciated her big sister's restraint. "I promise. You're the best, you know that? Will you give Dad and Isaac my love? Tell them I'll be around for dinner tomorrow night?"

"Of course."

Emily heard her phone ringing from inside her bag, which she had left on the bench by the doors to the veranda.

"I'll grab it for you." CJ reached for Emily's tan leather satchel.

"Sure, thanks." Oh. No. Oh, no! "I mean, never mind. Just leave it. It's not important."

But CJ had the bag open and was staring at the contents. "What on earth?" she gasped, and pulled out a box. "A pregnancy test. What's this for? I mean, I know *what* it's for, but who is it for?"

And then both sisters skewered her with their attention.

"Emily?" they chorused.

Her face burned. "I might not be. I mean, it's just a precaution. You know, to be sure. One way or the other." Busted, Emily babbled like a kid caught with her hand in the cookie jar, a D-minus science test buried at the bottom of her school bag and one foot out the window at midnight on her way to meet friends. Guilty, on multiple counts.

"There's a 'one way or the other' chance you're having a baby? I didn't even know you were seeing anyone." The disappointment in

Annie's voice was reflected in her eyes. "Why haven't you said something before now?"

"Because if I'm not..." She placed her hands on her belly. "If I'm not, then no one needed to know there was a chance I might be." She ignored Annie's reference to seeing someone because it was mortifying to admit she wasn't. She shot an accusatory look at CJ instead. "And no one would know if it hadn't been for a snooping little sister."

"Hey! I was not snooping. I was looking for your phone. I thought I was helping. How'd I know I was going to find—" she brandished the box "—this. But if you are, that means... holy moly, Em. If you're going to be a mother, then who's the father?"

"He..." Nowhere near ready to admit the truth, Emily did something she was sure to regret. She lied. "It's Fred."

Her sisters gaped at her for a full five seconds, and then they both burst out laughing.

CHAPTER TWO

THE JANGLE OF his cell phone made Jack Evans hastily sweep his desk, shoving aside papers and lifting files to check beneath them till his phone slid out from inside one of the folders—the Scarlett Daniels homicide. She was the third victim of Chicago's most recent serial killer, the South Side Slayer, as the media had dubbed him. Scarlett's murder was arguably the grizzliest of his three victims.

"Evans here," he said, managing for once to answer his cell before the call went to voice mail.

"Jack, Brett Watters. I found the daughter of your murder victim."

"Rose Daniels?" Finally. "Alive?"

"Living and breathing."

"Where is she?"

"We got a ping off her driver's license. She was pulled over for speeding near some hole-in-the-wall in Wisconsin."

Huh. He'd figured if the girl was still among the living, she was running from something, more likely *someone*, but he hadn't expected her to make it that far out of Chicago. "Does this place have a name?"

He could hear the sound of his colleague tapping on a keyboard. "Riverton. That ring any bells?"

A whole cathedral full of them. "That's my hometown, so, yeah, it sure does."

"Huh. You don't say. Want me to give the Riverton PD a call, have them ask her some questions?"

Jack opened the top drawer of his desk and plucked a business card out of the pencil tray. He'd put it there almost two months ago, the day he'd returned to Chicago from a rare visit to his hometown to attend his friend Eric Larsen's funeral.

He'd looked at the card every day since.

Emily Finnegan, Reporter.

The *Riverton Gazette*.

Beneath that, her phone number and an email address.

He thought about her every day, too, even when he wasn't looking at her card. He hadn't wanted to. Simply hadn't been able to stop himself. He'd thought about calling her but had decided against it. What would he say?

Thanks for a good time? Too tasteless.

See you next time I'm in town? Too vague.

Better to let it be. With some regret, he was now wishing he had given her a call.

Years ago, they had been paired up as maid of honor and best man at Eric and Annie's wedding. Tall and reedy, a glossy-haired brunette with a brown-eyed gaze that didn't miss a beat, Emily had returned home for the big event from Minneapolis, where she'd been studying journalism. Quiet, though not so much shy as watchful and reserved. It would have been a cliché for the best man to hook up with the maid of honor, so he hadn't tried. But he'd wanted to. The next time he'd seen her was at Eric and Annie's son's christening. He and Emily were godparents, and a post-baptismal hookup would have been even tackier. Again, he'd let it go.

Eric's funeral had been a game-changer. A change driven by grief, the raw emotion of the day, the sharp reminder that life could be unexpectedly short. As a homicide detective, Jack knew about death, had seen it up close and personal in a way few did. He possessed intimate knowledge of all the gruesome ways people could die. What he didn't know, he'd realized the day of Eric's funeral, was how they lived. He had no idea how *he* needed to live, and he'd discovered just how clueless he was as he'd helped carry his friend's casket to the waiting hearse and later stood on the sidelines, watching a young widow with her family, each of them grieving the loss of a man they had loved. They should have been angry with the world, with the unfairness of losing someone so young. They were mourning their loss, of course, but they were also honoring their loved one by moving on with their lives and caring for one another. By living.

After the funeral, Jack had spent a polite amount of time exchanging platitudes with people he barely knew, drinking bitter coffee and eating several crustless triangle sandwiches that were a church-hall staple. He had spoken briefly with Annie and then left. He had encountered Emily dashing out of the coatroom with her jacket slung over her arm. He had done the gentlemanly thing and helped her put it on. They had walked out of the church and into a deluge, so he'd offered her a lift and suggested they go for coffee. That had segued into dinner. He had assumed they'd have nothing in common. The energy of city life pulsed through his veins, and she was a small-town girl through and through. So when he'd taken her home, he shouldn't have stayed. But he had.

"Evans? You still there?" Brett's voice dragged his attention back to the business at hand and the card between his fingers.

"Yeah. Sorry. What were you saying?"

"Should we have the Riverton PD interview the Daniels woman for us?"

"No." Jack set the card next to the stack of reports on his desk. "I'd like to talk to her myself. If I leave now, I can be there in five hours. Could you ask them to—"

"She's not going anywhere. They've given her a twenty-four-hour suspension, and her car's been impounded. She's been drinking."

Jack checked his watch. Seven-thirty. An early start by anyone's standard. He knew Rose had been raised by a drug addict and spent a lot of years in and out of foster homes. The Chicago PD wanted to know more about her relationship with the suspect they had in custody, and to what level, if any, she was involved in the homicides. Also, were they the reason she was on the run?

"Could you give them a call, let them know I'm on my way? I'll talk to her when I get there." By then, she should be sober enough to answer his questions.

"You got it."

Jack closed the files on his desk and shoved

them into a drawer, scrolled through the list of contacts on his phone and hit the one called Home.

"Mom, Dad," he said after their voice mail beeped, glad he hadn't woken them. "I need to be in Riverton for a few days. See you tonight."

He picked up Emily's card, debated whether or not to call her, too, let her know he was coming to town. No. He'd surprise her. Smiling at that, he slid the card into the pocket of his leather jacket.

"I might be late," he added to the message he was leaving for his parents. "Don't wait up."

HER SISTERS HAD insisted that Emily take the pregnancy test immediately, so she had reluctantly barricaded herself in the second-floor bathroom, alone. The result was positive, as her gut instinct had been telling her for the past week.

Now what? The only thing she knew for sure was she wasn't ready to venture back into the world, and she wasn't ready to face her sisters.

Why had she lied? Telling them she was having Fred's baby was the dumbest thing she'd ever done. What must they think? What had she been thinking? Fred had been her best friend since first grade, the closest thing to a brother she'd ever had, and just about the last person in the world she could imagine making a baby with. Fred? The very idea made her cheeks burn. Now she wouldn't be able to face him, either.

Then there was Jack Evans, the real father of this tiny human who had taken up residence inside her. No need to worry about how to face him. After one night with her, he had hightailed it back to Chicago, never to be seen or heard from again.

She would have to get in touch with him, tell him about the baby. She wasn't ready to go there, though. Not yet. This news was too new, too unsettling, too overwhelming. Jack was not part of her life, never had been, not in any real or meaningful way. And he never would be. *Don't think about him*, she told herself. *Not now.*

Besides, she had more pressing concerns. Her sisters were waiting downstairs. They would pepper her with questions, most of which she wasn't ready to answer. She needed to figure out something to tell them, though. Aside from Fred and her father, of course, they were the two people in the world who always had her back, and now she was going to need their support more than ever.

CJ would be this new little person's irrepressible, fun-loving aunt, the one who took him or her kite flying and horseback riding. She'd teach him or her how to blow bubble-gum bubbles. The farm was as much a part of CJ as her free spirit. According to her, she had a perfect life—teaching riding lessons, taking B & B guests on trail rides, boarding horses for several families in town, and operating a successful therapeutic riding program. CJ would welcome this baby with arms as wide as the world.

Annie, the world's best mom, knew all about raising a child on her own, but at least she'd done things in the proper order. Marriage first, baby second. The recent and unexpected death of her husband had been beyond her control, but she was coping as only a natural-born supermom could. She carpooled to softball games, helped with homework, baked the most awesome bake-sale cookies on the planet, all while single-handedly keeping house, running a business and making it look easy. Annie's huge heart was brimming with all the care and attention this newcomer would ever need.

Fred, too, would be great with the baby.

He'd be a sort of surrogate dad, as soon as he got over the shock—no, make that horror—that she had told her sisters he was the father. Once he was over that, he would always be there for her and—Emily ran her hands over the almost indiscernible curve of her belly—whoever this was.

But for now, it's just you and me, kid.

Her heart rate amped up, and she realized she had been standing at the bathroom window, staring unseeingly through the white lace drapery. She pushed aside her panic along with the delicate fabric and focused her attention on the familiar scene below. The grassy backyard gave way to the soon-to-be-planted vegetable garden with its deer-proof fence and the chicken coop with its fox-proof enclosure. Beyond those, a stand of poplars, their branches studded with new buds. The stables, still visible through the trees, would soon be obscured by a trembling, leafy-green curtain. Emily had committed every square inch of this place to memory, could picture it clearly in any season. She loved the farm as it was now, sun-warmed and fresh from the late-spring rains. Summer would arrive any minute, and she would always associate it with the long, lazy days of school holidays. Then the sudden burst of autumn color would gradually fade to the monochrome that was a Wisconsin winter, then it would be Christmas, and after…

The baby would be here, and she'd be a mom. A fresh wave of panic rolled over her. Truthfully, she didn't know the first thing about being a mother, never having had one, or at least, scarcely able to remember a time when she had.

Emily swung away from the window and faced herself in the bathroom mirror. She had been only four years old when her mother left them, and she had been waiting for her to come back ever since, a silly childhood fantasy she had never outgrown. She stared hard at her reflection. No matter how the future unfolded, she would figure this out, and she would always be there for this little one. Always, always, *always*.

"And, please, be a girl," she whispered. She didn't know anything about boys, and at that moment, she didn't like them much, either. At least not the ones who stayed the night and never called.

She looked down at the plastic pregnancy stick and wondered for the umpteenth time how she could have let herself get so caught up in the moment. Because it had been *the* moment, she reminded herself, the one she had fantasized about since she'd started high school and her hormones had kicked in. She had been an underdeveloped fourteen-year-old. Jack Evans had been sixteen and in lust with Belinda Bellows, the knockout who had been crowned queen of Riverton's Riverboat Festival, with the requisite physical assets needed to pull it off. Emily had been invisible back then, and she had stayed invisible, as far as Jack Evans was concerned, until her brother-in-law's shocking death had put her on a collision course with the heart-searingly handsome Chicago PD detective.

During a cozy dinner conversation about pasts and futures—his and hers and Riverton's—she had been surprised to learn they had things in common. A lot of things, actually. They both preferred dogs to cats, marinara to alfredo, red wine to white. Regrettably, they had shared a bottle of wine over dinner. Red, of course. And then he had walked her back to her little apartment above the newspaper office...and *that* was how she'd ended up here, two months later and too many weeks late, holding this stupid stick with its two colored lines. She hadn't heard from him since. No phone calls, no emails. Not even a lousy text message. Calling him would have made her seem desperate, so she hadn't.

The shuffle of footsteps in the hallway was followed by a light knock on the bathroom door.

"Emily?" Annie asked. "Are you still in there?"

"Be right out." She tossed the remains of the pregnancy test into the trash and unlocked the door. As her father had often reminded her when she'd landed herself in trouble, it was time to face the music.

CHAPTER THREE

AFTER A RIDICULOUSLY tearful conversation with her sisters, during which Emily extracted promises they wouldn't breathe a word of her pregnancy to anyone, especially not their father, it was now almost lunchtime, and she was back in town. Standing in front of Morris's Barbershop, she closed her eyes and took a deep, steadying breath. She opened them again and yanked on the door handle before her courage fled and dragged her away with it. The bell jangled, and the open sign clattered against the glass. No turning back now.

Fred was sweeping the worn black-and-white tile floor as he always did after finishing up with a customer. She had been anxiously watching from the newspaper office across the street, waiting for Elroy Ferguson to leave. Fred was alone now, whisking Elroy's salt-and-pepper hair clippings into a tidy pile. Her best friend's familiar, slightly lopsided smile should have made her feel at ease. He glanced at the big clock above the door.

"You're early. Is that lunch?" he asked, eyeing the brown paper bag she carried.

She nodded and managed a weak smile. She set the bag on the counter. "I need to talk to you about something."

"What's up?" he asked, bending his tall, lanky frame to brush the sweepings into an old metal dustpan, its yellow paint chipped from many years of service.

She flipped the lock on the door, turned the sign to Closed and pulled down the roller blind, its frayed edges barely covering the glass. She was a little misty-eyed by the time she turned back to face him. More tears? Seriously, what was the matter with her?

"Wow, must be important," Fred said, dumping the hair clippings into the trash bin. He leaned the broom in a corner, hung the dustpan on a hook next to it, and then he looked at her, really looked at her. His amusement turned to concern. "Emily? What's wrong? Is it your family? Your dad?"

She shook her head. Her throat had squeezed shut, and the words wouldn't come.

Fred crossed the floor in a flash and pulled her into a hug. "Hey. Whatever it is, it's going to be all right. Just don't cry, okay?"

"O-o-kay," she hiccupped, but now that the waterworks had started, she couldn't stem the flow. What was wrong with her? She never cried.

Fred didn't say anything more. He simply held her, letting her tears soak into his shirt, patiently waiting for her to compose herself.

He smelled like shaving soap and styling mousse. His shoulder, more bony than muscular, had always been available for her to lean on. They were best friends. She had known him forever. He knew her better than anyone else ever had or ever would.

Dear, sweet Fred. Loyal, down-to-earth, dependable. He'd make a great dad. Perfect, really. He would always be there for his kid, just as her dad had been for her. Steady, patient, reliable. Exactly what every child needed in her life. Or *his* life, since there was only a fifty-percent chance she was having a girl.

After she stemmed the flow of tears, she gripped his upper arms, tipped her head back and stared up at him.

"You look awful," he said.

"Gee, thanks. Just what a girl wants to hear. I'm glad I ruined your shirt." The crisp white cotton was smeared with dark mascara and tan-colored eye shadow.

"That's okay. I have a clean one in the back."

Of course he did.

"Just in case," he added.

This was the Fred she'd always known. Mr. Just-in-case. Mr. Always-prepared.

Why couldn't he be her Mr. Tall-dark-and-dreamy?

She gave him a long look, taking in his wavy sand-colored hair, unruly eyebrows, gold-flecked hazel eyes and nicely shaped mouth. For the first time in all the years she'd known him, she wanted to feel something when she looked at him, that special something for that one special person. But she didn't. It just wasn't there.

What was wrong with her? How could she feel all fluttery for someone like Jack, someone who would never be there for her, when she already had this great guy in her life? Fred would make a perfect father and a wonderful husband...for someone. Not for her, though.

"Em?"

"What?"

"You're kind of scaring me."

"Sorry."

"What's going on?"

She took a deep breath, held it, exhaled in a rush. "I'm pregnant."

Fred stared at her, opened his mouth, closed it again, leaving his first thought, whatever it was, unspoken.

She waited.

"Um, wow, I…" He stepped back, looked her up and down, his gaze finally coming to rest on her midsection. "You…you're having a…"

She nodded. "A baby."

"Jack Evans's baby."

Now it was her turn to stare. "How on earth did you figure that out?"

"The day of Eric's funeral, I closed the shop for a couple of hours so I could go. Later that afternoon, I came back here, and it was business as usual. Before I closed up, I saw the two of you going into the café down the street. What was that, two months ago? And now you're…"

Having a baby. Fred seemed unable to say the actual words out loud.

"What did he say when you told him?"

"Well, that's the thing."

"You haven't told him?"

She shook her head.

"Em! Why not?"

"Because I only found out this morning." Because the thought of telling Jack terrified her, and because some secret little part of her hoped she wouldn't have to. She hoped having her family and her best friend to support her and this new little person would be enough, even though in her heart she knew it wasn't the right thing to do.

He hugged her again. "So I'm the only person who knows?"

She shook her head against the soggy mess she'd made of his shirt. "My sisters know, too. CJ found the pregnancy test in my bag, and they made me take it while I was out at the farm this morning."

"That must have been interesting. How did they react when you told them it was Jack's?"

"I didn't tell them."

"Your sisters didn't ask? Didn't try to pry the truth out of you? That's hard to believe."

"They did. I kind of lied."

Fred leaned back and stared down at her, momentarily confused. "You told them it was somebody else's?"

She glanced up at him but couldn't bring herself to confess. She didn't have to.

He let go of her and abruptly stepped back. "You didn't. Emily, tell me you didn't tell your sisters that this…"

She lowered her head and fixed her guilty gaze on the toes of her beige ballerina flats.

"You did. You told them… You told them…" His voice had risen a full octave. He stabbed the fingers of both hands through his hair, held them there. He had a tendency to blush when he was embarrassed or angry. Right now even his ears were crimson, and he was looking a little wild-eyed, too. "You told them it was *mine*? That I…? That *we*…? Why would you do that?"

Her sisters would find out the truth soon enough, but since she had humiliated her best friend in the whole world, she owed him an explanation now.

"I don't know. It was all so unexpected. I drove over to Wabasha early this morning and went to the pharmacy there." If she'd bought the test in Riverton, half the town would know by now that she might be pregnant.

"On my way back to town, I stopped at the farm for my usual Saturday-morning coffee date with my sisters. I had no intention of actually doing the test while I was there. I was going to wait till I was alone at home, but then my phone rang and CJ opened my bag to look for it and…surprise."

Fred's color was gradually returning to normal, and he'd stopped pulling at his hair. Now he stood, arms folded, silent and waiting.

"I was hoping I wasn't pregnant," she continued. "I was hoping I was late, you know? It happens a lot, but I've never been this late—"

Fred's color deepened again. "Stop. Too much information. I don't need to know how late or how often you're… Geez, Em. That's just…"

"Okay, okay, I get it." *Too much information*. She was feeling woozy all of a sudden, which made no sense, and she reached for the back of one of the barber chairs for support. The chair pivoted away from her, and she lost her balance.

Fred caught her.

"Can we sit down?" she asked. "I brought lunch, remember?" She pointed to the brown bag on the counter. Maybe she'd feel less light-headed if they were having this conversation on a full stomach.

"You thought you could butter me up with lunch?"

"Annie made sandwiches. Ham and Swiss on rye, with extra mustard."

He narrowed his gaze, but she could see she had his attention. It was one of his favorites. "She sent some of her apple strudel, too."

His features softened a little. "You sort of had me at extra mustard, but no sane person ever turned down your sister's strudel."

Emily smiled. Given Fred's appetite and the universal appeal of Annie's pastries, she'd known the strudel was her ace in the hole.

"Come on," he said. "We can sit in the back

office. Just don't think that one of your sister's killer lunches gets you off the hook."

Fred led her into the cramped office-slash-storage room off the back of the barbershop and sat her in a chair. He unpacked the sandwiches and two generous slices of strudel and set them on the narrow wooden table, then pulled two bottles of water from the mini-fridge.

Emily found the small, familiar space vaguely reassuring. She'd always liked this little room, couldn't begin to count the number of hours she and Fred had spent in it over the years—playing Go Fish when they were kids, working on high school assignments, catching up on town gossip during her brief visits home from college. These days they usually met for lunch at the Riverton Bar & Grill down the block, but today's conversation was not for public consumption.

Fred sat across from her, peeled the plastic wrap off Annie's signature sandwich, bit off a mouthful and slowly chewed while he studied Emily through narrowed eyes.

She didn't know what to say, and Fred was in no hurry to fill the awkward silence. This must be how a criminal felt, sitting in an interrogation room, trying not to squirm beneath the steely gaze of a hardened detective.

Like Jack. He would be cool and collected, in spite of feeling disillusioned about his job. Over dinner that night he had told her being a homicide detective was taking a toll on his work life, his personal life…his *life*. Still, he had been surprised when she'd asked if he had considered making a change. Never, he'd said. He had known since he was a kid that he was going to be a big-city cop. He had invested everything in his career. Change wasn't an option.

Well, Jack Evans was in for a surprise. Emily Finnegan, the one-night stand who hadn't been interesting enough or attractive enough to warrant so much as a phone call, now had some news that would change his life forever. Forget calm, cool and collected. Jack Evans was going to go ballistic.

"So here's what I don't understand," Fred said. "After all this time, you finally got what you wanted, but you didn't say anything to anyone. Not me, not even your sisters."

"What are you talking about? I've never, ever said anything about wanting a baby." She'd never said she didn't want one, either. Having a baby had always been one of those someday things that would happen eventually. Someday.

"I'm not talking about kids. I'm talking about Jack Evans."

Emily's face heated up. "I had a crush on him in high school."

"And now?" Fred challenged her with his unwavering gaze.

She shrugged. "He has an interesting job. He's smart and he's…"

"Hot?"

That made her laugh. "Yes," she conceded. She could always be honest with Fred. "No one's going to argue with that, but for me he's always been…you know. Haven't you ever felt that way about someone? Your head is telling you this person is completely wrong for you, but your heart goes all wobbly, and your brain turns to mush every time you see her?"

He solemnly shook his head, and her heart broke for him a little. He was a great guy, and he deserved to find a woman who would fall completely head over heels for him. "It'll happen," she said.

"In Riverton?"

"Stranger things have."

"I suppose. And nice try, by the way."

"What did I do?"

"Shifted the subject from you to me. You do that all the time."

It was true. It was the reporter in her.

"Sorry." And she was, sort of, as she gave him a long look. Really looked at him, willing herself to feel something more than sisterly affection. Fred was a nice guy, and he'd be a great dad. They'd been best friends for such a long time. It could work, maybe. Couldn't it?

"Em?"

"What?"

"Don't look at me like that."

"Like what?"

"Like you're going to try to talk me into being part of whatever crazy story you told your sisters." He was blushing again. "Not going to happen."

She dropped her gaze, nibbled at the crust of her sandwich.

"You know I'm here for you," Fred said. "Always have been, always will be."

She tipped her head back and took a sip from her water bottle, then hastily dropped her gaze, so Fred couldn't see her eyes getting watery. More tears? This was getting ridiculous.

"You should be happy, Em. You deserve to have someone special in your life, too."

Tears rolled down her cheeks. "He isn't *in* my life. He went back to Chicago the next day, and I haven't heard from him since."

"You're joking." Fred handed her a paper napkin to stem the waterworks. "You mean he…? And he didn't…? I think he and I need to have a talk."

"No, you don't. I'll talk to him myself, I just have to find his phone number."

"You can't pick up the phone and call him."

"Why not?"

"Why not? Em, this is huge. We're talking life-changing huge. You owe it to him to break the news in person."

"I was thinking I don't actually owe him anything. He didn't call me, so apparently he doesn't think he owes me anything, either."

"He owes you eighteen years of child support, but that doesn't let you off the hook. This kind of news must be delivered in person."

"He hardly ever comes to Riverton."

"Then you'll have to go to Chicago."

"I don't know where he lives."

It sounded lame as she said it. Apparently, Fred thought so, too.

"Ever heard of a little thing called the internet? Or you could ask his mother."

She had already tried the internet and hadn't come up with anything, not that she'd tried terribly hard. And there was no way she was going to ask Norma Evans—her baby's grandmother!—for her son's phone number. She would demand to know why Emily wanted it. What would she tell her?

Hi, Mrs. Evans. Remember me, little Emily Finnegan? Your son and I hooked up a while ago, and now... Oops... I'm having his baby.

"I am not asking his mother."

"Fine, don't. I'll ask her. I'll even go to Chicago with you." Fred made a fist and hit the palm of his other hand to indicate how he intended to handle the situation if called upon.

Emily couldn't help rolling her eyes. "You know you can do some serious time for assaulting a police officer, right?"

Fred grinned. "How you handle this is up to you, but if he doesn't do the right thing, then I'll have something to say."

"I appreciate the offer, but I don't need anyone to fight my battles. And this is something I need to do alone, as soon as I figure out what I'm going to say to him." Then she'd need to think about the future, one for which she was completely unprepared. "But no matter what he says or does, I'm scared," she whispered, finally finding the courage to confess what she truly felt. "I have no idea how to be a mother."

"Sure you do." Fred reached across the table and took her hands in his. He was the only person who knew her secret wish, that after all these years her mother would finally come home and *be* a mother. "You have Annie. She's a great role model."

True. Problem was, Annie made it look easy. What if she, Emily, was a total disaster like their mother had been?

"Don't go there, Em. You've always been great at everything you've ever chosen to do. In school, at the university, your work for the newspaper, your *Small Town, Big Hearts* blog."

She knew he was trying to buoy her, but this was different. Raising a child wasn't like writing a newspaper story or a blog. She had chosen to do those things, but she hadn't chosen to become a mother. Motherhood had chosen her.

They were interrupted by the rattle of the barbershop door.

"My next customer. Lunchtime's over already." Fred sounded reluctant to wrap up their little tête-à-tête, as though she might not be able to move forward on her own. "You going to be okay?"

"Of course. I'll be fine. I have to get back to work, too." She needed to finish her article about this week's town council meeting, put the finishing touches on centenarian Sig Sorrenson's obituary and check her blog for comments. She waved Fred out of the back room. "Off you go. I'll tidy up in here."

Emily slipped out of the shop several minutes later, avoiding eye contact with Fred as he swirled a black plastic cape around the shoulders of his first customer of the afternoon. When she stepped onto the sidewalk, she narrowly missed a head-on collision with Mable Potter, her former high school English teacher and Riverton's favorite octogenarian. The woman was struggling with her oversize purse, a large bag of groceries and the leash of her energetic mutt, Banjo.

"Hi, Mrs. Potter. Here, let me give you a hand."

"Oh, could you, dear? I didn't realize how many things I had in my shopping cart until it was rung through the checkout. I was getting low on milk, and I needed a dozen eggs and another bag of flour because my daughter, Libby, is coming all the way from Minneapolis tomorrow, and she loves my red velvet cake. I always bake one for her when she visits."

"Your daughter's a lucky lady." Everyone in Riverton had sampled Mable Potter's delicious dessert at one time or another, and everyone loved it. Emily shouldered her own bag and settled Mable's grocery bag on one hip, surprised by its heft. "Come on, I'll carry this home for you."

"Thank you, dear. You're good girls, you and your sisters. I ran into your father at the post office the other day, and he was telling mc about what you've been up to. He's awful proud of the three of you."

Emily walked with Mrs. Potter, dawdled, really, for a block and a half down Main Street, then three blocks along Second Avenue. The route took them past Jack's parents' place, one of several stately two-and-a-half-story red-brick homes, complete with carriage houses that were a throwback to Riverton's horse-and-buggy days. She kept her head down and her eyes averted, praying Jack's mother didn't appear. There'd be no avoiding a conversation. To her relief, they were able to slip by and make their way to Cottonwood Street, where Mrs. Potter lived.

As the dog sniffed every light standard, fence post and hydrant along the way, Emily only half listened to Mrs. Potter's chatter about the weather, her daughter's impending visit and Sig's funeral. Luckily, the woman didn't expect a response, which was just as well because Emily was now preoccupied with thoughts about her father. She adored him, and the prospect of telling him about her current situation was almost as terrifying as telling the baby's father. In the absence of a mother, she had always looked to her dad for encouragement, support and validation. Jack was not going to be happy with this news, but his anger would pale in comparison to her father's disappointment.

CHAPTER FOUR

JACK FELT A sense of ease the moment he saw the Welcome to Riverton sign. Its billboard proportions, depicting an old Mississippi paddle wheeler plying the waterway while a pair of majestic bald eagles soared overhead, might be disproportionate to the size of the population, but never its allegiance. Even people who'd left for the bright lights and busy streets of cities like Chicago were proud to call Riverton, Wisconsin, home.

Jack swung his Jeep onto Main Street. The two-story, redbrick buildings flanking the wide thoroughfare were as familiar today as they had been when he'd worked Saturdays as a stock boy at Henderson's Hardware, bought sodas at Baxter's Pharmacy and had his hair cut at Morris's Barbershop.

He'd eaten his share of burgers and fries at the Riverton Café, which still existed, but was now under new ownership and called the Riverton Bar & Grill. He'd made that discovery the last time he'd been home because he and

Emily Finnegan had gone to the restaurant for dinner. And there, in the back row of the Big River Theatre, he'd made it to first base for the first time with…? Huh. He'd been sixteen or thereabouts. She'd been hot, blonde, that year's Riverboat Queen, if memory served. Why couldn't he remember her name?

Did it matter? Not even a little bit. What mattered was this unexpected homecoming gave him a chance to see Emily again. He slowed as he drove past the *Riverton Gazette* office, glanced up at the windows of her second-floor apartment and told himself he was being an idiot to feel disappointed he didn't see her.

He shook his head. "What? You expected her to be standing by the window, waiting for you?"

Now that he was here, he deeply regretted not calling her. In some ways, it seemed like a lifetime ago. In reality, it had been—what?— six weeks. Or was it longer? Maybe eight? Too long to expect her to simply pick up where they'd left off. She probably thought he was a first-class jerk.

Would she understand when he explained how he'd been catapulted into the most bizarre triple-homicide investigation of his career, sometimes working more than twenty-four hours before realizing he hadn't slept? And when he did nod off, usually for just a few hours, his dreams were crowded with images of three innocent people, their cold, bruised flesh cut so deep, he wished they'd already been dead by the time the wounds had been inflicted.

Slapping cuffs on the killer should have provided some satisfaction. It hadn't. Instead, he had hoped the guy would resist arrest, give him a reason to pump a couple rounds into his chest. Jack hated himself for wanting that, but not as much as he'd hated the narcissistic sicko who had held his head high and smiled widely, preening for the TV cameras on the day of his arraignment. That's when Jack knew. He was bitter, burned out and he needed a change. He wanted a normal life. He wasn't sure what that was, but he wanted a woman like Emily Finnegan to be part of it.

She was bound to be irate with him for not calling and he couldn't fault her for that, but he would make it up to her. As soon as he finished interviewing Rose Daniels this afternoon, he would take Emily out for dinner. Pasta with marinara sauce, coffee and a lemon meringue tart for dessert. He never forgot details like that, and he remembered other things, too. The way she'd smiled when he'd reached across the table and covered her hand with his. The way she'd sighed after their first kiss, the way that kiss had led to another, and another, and...

He remembered, all right, and he would put those memories to good use tonight. He grinned at his reflection in the rearview mirror, ran a hand over the stubble on his jaw. He should probably get cleaned up before he interviewed this witness. From what he'd read in Rose's file, he had a better shot at getting her to open up if he used his good cop routine. His current five o'clock shadow and too-long scruff were more in keeping with the bad-cop version of Jack Evans. Besides, the longer this witness languished in a cell, the more likely she'd be to spill the details once he had her sitting in the interview room.

He had a hunch that Emily preferred the good cop, too.

He swung right on Second Avenue, circled the block and angled into a parking spot in front of Morris's. Again, he glanced up at Emily's apartment across the street, relieved this time she wasn't by the window. Better to wait and catch her unawares. He would use the element of surprise to get her attention, apologize and then tell her about the case that had consumed him for the past however many weeks.

Jack strode between the red, white and blue striped poles that flanked the barbershop door, wondering if Chicago had any old-fashioned barbershops like this one. It must have, but he couldn't remember having seen one. He certainly hadn't looked for one. Morris's was... normal. Familiar.

Fred Morris sat in one of a pair of ancient barbershop chairs, facing the mirror, reading a newspaper. Jack pushed the door open, the sound of the bell causing Fred to glance up. There was no mistaking the flicker of deer-in-the-headlights surprise in the man's eyes, but it was gone by the time he swiveled around and stood up.

"Jack. Ah, good to see you. What...ah... what brings you to Riverton?"

The guy was a bundle of nerves.

"A case I'm working on."

"Right, right. So...ah...what can I do you for you?"

Seriously? "Shave, haircut."

"Right, of course. Here, sit." He moved around to the back of the chair and held it while Jack shrugged out of his jacket. "Here, I'll take that."

After he sat down, Fred swung the chair to face the mirror, and Jack watched the man's reflection as he scurried about, stuffing his hastily folded newspaper into a wall-mounted magazine rack. He hung Jack's jacket on an old coat tree.

Jack didn't know Fred well, admittedly, but he didn't remember him being this jumpy, acting as though he had something to hide. Besides, what could he be hiding? Come to think of it, Fred was a longtime friend of Emily's. Would she have told him about the night she and Jack had spent together?

Awkward. Not to mention unlikely. He was jumping to conclusions for which he had no evidence. He watched Fred take his cell phone out of his pants pocket, tap out a quick message and put it back.

"Okay. A shave and a haircut." Fred, suddenly all business and apparently recovered from his case of nerves, shook out a black plastic cape and draped it over Jack's chest and shoulders.

MABLE POTTER LIVED in a quaint one-and-a-half-story house on Cottonwood Street, in the middle of a block of identical dwellings. Over the years, the homes had been personalized with a picket fence here, a glassed-in veranda there, window boxes, skylights and paint colors that spanned the rainbow. The clapboard of Mrs. Potter's house was salmon pink, the trim snowy white. In the back corner of the yard was a garden shed. Mable's husband, who'd passed away more than a decade ago, had designed it to look like a miniature version of the main house, capturing every detail right down to the lace-curtained windows.

As a child, Emily had daydreamed about playing house in the Potters' garden shed. Today, her current reality made her wonder how in the world she was going to manage a baby on her own in her cramped one-bedroom apartment over the newspaper office.

Emily followed the elderly woman through the gate and up the steps. Mrs. Potter opened the front door and stooped to unfasten the dog's leash. Instead of going inside, though, the scruffy, wiry-haired dog of indeterminate breed let out a yip, raced back down the steps and disappeared around the corner of the house, a black-and-white blur in pursuit of a squirrel.

"I don't know why he chases them," the woman said. "He's never caught one. And I think they come in the yard on purpose, simply to torment him."

Emily laughed at the idea of a ragtag scurry of squirrels plotting to outwit a hapless predator. Possibly something she could work into a story for her blog. "Where would you like me to put the groceries?" she asked.

"Would you mind carrying them into the kitchen for me?"

"Of course not." Emily noticed Mrs. Potter hadn't used a key, which meant she hadn't locked the door when she'd left the house to go shopping. Not usually a big concern in Riverton, especially during the daytime. Still, the woman did live alone, and things around town had mysteriously started to disappear. "Did you forget to lock the door when you went out?" she asked, deciding to play it low-key.

"Oh, I never bother. This is Riverton, after all, and Banjo's a good watchdog."

"I'm sure he is." Except Banjo hadn't been here, and Emily suspected his watchfulness extended only to keeping small rodents at bay. Still, everything in the house looked as it should, not a doily out of place.

Emily set the bag of groceries on the kitchen table and glanced through the window to the backyard where the dog ran in circles around the trunk of an oak tree, tormented by the squirrel chittering at him from an overhanging branch. Instinctively, she pulled her camera from her bag, zoomed in on the scene and snapped a series of photos.

"Are you going to put those pictures in the newspaper?" Mable asked.

"No, but I'd like to post them on my blog if that's okay with you."

"A blog? I don't know what that is, but it's fine with me."

Emily watched with amusement and mild curiosity as the woman carried the kettle to the sink, filled it and then put it in the refrigerator.

"Would you like to stay for tea?"

"Ah…" Emily did her best not to laugh out loud. "I'd love to stay, Mrs. Potter, but not today, thanks. I have to get back to the office and catch up on a few things." Now that she had talked to Fred, she needed to set her sisters straight and then plan an unwelcome trip to Chicago. "But I'll be happy to drop by early next week," she was quick to add, noting the woman's disappointment. The weekly edition of the *Gazette* came out every Wednesday morning and she always had a little breathing room after that.

"That'll be nice, dear. I'll save you a slice of my red velvet cake."

"I wouldn't miss it." She left Mable to put away her groceries, wondering how long it would take the poor woman to figure out why it was taking so long for the kettle to boil. Outside, the standoff between dog and squirrel continued to play out in the yard. Not able to resist, she followed the stepping-stones that meandered from the back porch to the garden shed and walked up onto the narrow veranda. The lace curtains were drawn in the shed's windows, and the interior was dark. Emily wasn't sure why, but she reached for the doorknob. It was locked. Interesting. Well, no one would be able to steal the old woman's wheelbarrow and watering can.

Her cell phone buzzed as she was making her way around the side of the house to the front gate. It was a text message from Fred.

The jig is up. Get over here. Now.

What? How? Had one of her sisters gone into the shop to talk to Fred, even though they had both promised not to utter a word about this to anyone? Or had one of them told their father? If anyone had blabbed about this, it would be CJ. Ugh. The little busybody. Emily was going to wring her neck. As for her father, was he at the barbershop now? Annie had said he'd be driving Isaac into town for a birthday party that afternoon. Emily shoved the phone into the side pocket of her bag and set out for a brisk walk back to Morris's. Time to face the music, again.

SOME OF THE tension that had knotted in Jack's neck and shoulders during the drive from Chicago loosened a little.

"How long are you in town for?" Fred asked.

"A couple of days."

"Nice. You'll see your family, I guess."

"Plan to."

"Your dad was in for a trim last week." Fred tucked a towel around the neckline of the cape. "Haven't seen your mother in a while, though. How's she doing?"

"Oh, you know, she's the same as always."

Jack didn't actually know that, although it's what he assumed. Norma Evans would always do the things she'd always done. Keeping the house where he and his sister had been raised, which was far too big for her and his father, as neat as a pin. Reminding his father that salads were good for him and pipe smoking was not. Volunteering at church bazaars and literacy book drives, organizing care packages for troops in Afghanistan and Iraq.

Walter Evans was retired from his lifelong career as maintenance supervisor for the Town of Riverton. It used to be his job to keep the fire trucks, police cars and snowplows running and on the road. Now he spent most of his time in his workshop at the back of the garage next to the house, tinkering with his twenty-year-old Ford F-250, fixing bicycles and repairing broken appliances and old lawn mowers for everyone in the neighborhood. The shop was the only place where Walt could listen to NPR uninterrupted and puff on his pipe without censure.

Jack stared up at the tin-tiled ceiling as Fred applied pre-shave cream to his face. The question about his parents was a harsh reminder that Jack had been doing a lousy job of staying in touch with them. He needed to figure a way around the tunnel vision he developed every time he worked a major case.

"And now for the towel," Fred said.

Jack heard the steamer open, then gave an inward sigh as Fred placed the hot towel on his face. The heat seeped along his jaw, up his cheeks and across his brows.

"There we go. Give that a few minutes, and then we'll get started."

Jack's thoughts drifted from his family to the interview he needed to do this afternoon and then to Emily, to seeing her again, to holding her, to…

The clang of the bell on the barbershop door cut into his thoughts.

EMILY WAS BREATHLESS by the time she returned to the barbershop. Fred met her at the door and shushed her with a quick finger to the lips as he escorted her across the floor and sat her in an empty chair. The other chair, she noted, was occupied. Fred unceremoniously returned his customer to an upright position, peeled back the towel and swung him to face Emily.

"Jack?"

He blinked, clearly as startled to see her as she was to see him. "Emily."

She blinked back.

"You two need to talk," Fred said. And then he walked out and locked the door behind him.

CHAPTER FIVE

JACK HADN'T REALIZED how much he'd been looking forward to seeing Emily until he opened his eyes, and there she was. Glossy dark hair, intelligent brown eyes behind the black, square-framed glasses she sometimes wore instead of contacts, a perfectly shaped nose with a dusting of freckles, luscious lips that appeared to be calling out for a kiss.

Or maybe not. She did not look happy to see him, not even a little bit. He had meant to have the element of surprise work to his advantage. Instead he found himself at a distinct disadvantage, and he hated that. He snatched the towel from around his neck and used it to swipe the pre-shave off his face, then cast it aside along with the cape.

He had planned to show up at her place later that day, unannounced. He knew she'd be surprised and most likely a little—or a lot—ticked off that he hadn't called. He had a knack for picking up on a person's emotions, for reading their body language, and right now, Emily was both surprised and irritated. He hadn't expected this third emotion, though, something akin to fear.

"How did you know I was here?" he asked, sitting up straighter. It was a dumb question, a question he wouldn't have asked, and in a tone he wouldn't have used if he felt more in control.

"I had no idea you were here." She narrowed her gaze. "Why are you here?"

Wasn't it obvious? "A shave, a haircut."

She rolled her eyes. "Here in Riverton."

"Oh. I have to interview a witness at the police station this afternoon."

"Okay." She looked as though she didn't believe him.

"What are you doing here?" he asked.

"I live here."

His turn for an eye roll. "Here, in the barbershop, not here in Riverton."

"Oh…I…um…"

But he already knew the answer. "Fred texted you I was here, didn't he?"

Emily shook her head. "He didn't say anything about you. He just said I needed to get over here."

Jack did not like the sound of that, not one bit. "Why would he do that?"

She started to say something, seemed to think better of it and closed her mouth.

"Why did he say the two of us need to talk? Did you tell him about us?"

She was blushing furiously and looking guilty as all get-out. He could understand that she'd maybe talk to a girlfriend or her sisters about their night together. He knew women shared those kinds of details, but would she talk to another guy about them?

Unless…for a few seconds, his doubts got the better of him. Were she and Fred more than friends? Or was Fred more of a girlfriend type of friend? Not that Fred's relationships were any of his business, but there was obviously something going on here that involved Jack, and that *was* his business. There had to be a reason the guy had been so jumpy when Jack had walked into the shop. He planned to find out what it was.

Jack stabbed his fingers through hair that was evidently not going to get cut after all. "Why would you do that? And how many other people know about us?"

"Us? There's an *us*? Huh. You could have fooled me." Her tone was defensive, and he could hardly fault her for it.

Not only had he started out on the wrong foot, now he'd made her mad. Who was he kidding? She had probably been mad for weeks. Now there was every chance he'd messed up a good thing, possibly the best thing that had happened in a long time. To make matters worse, if she had talked to Fred about their night, she would have told her sisters, too, and possibly any number of other people. This might be all over Riverton by now. No. It couldn't be. If it was, his mother would have heard about it, and then he *really* would have heard about it.

At this point, it didn't matter who knew and who didn't. He needed to come clean with Emily, make her understand how intense this triple homicide investigation was and explain he was an idiot who wanted a second chance. Maybe grovel a little.

"Look, I'm sorry," he said. "Not calling you was a stupid move. Or maybe lack of a move is a better way to describe it. I meant to call, wanted to see you again. I never meant to take this long to get around to it."

"Technically, you still haven't."

Ouch. She was more composed now. She wasn't going to make this easy for him, and he could hardly blame her.

"That's true, but I was going to." To prove his point, he jumped up and crossed the shop to where his jacket hung and then returned to the chair with her business card in his hand. "I was planning to call this afternoon, as soon as I finished my interview."

He glanced at the wall clock. He was going to have one antsy witness on his hands by the time he finally made it to the station, but this thing with Emily couldn't be rushed.

"You were?"

"I was. I..." He considered his options before he continued. Pour on the charm? Shoot from the hip? Knowing she would see right through the first option, he decided on the second. "Look, the truth is, I'm not very good at being in a relationship when I'm working a case."

Her eyes widened at his use of the *R* word. Confident he was on the right path, he continued.

"Really lousy at it, actually." He'd been hauled on the carpet by several former girlfriends, and one had used far more colorful language than that to describe his single-minded absorption with a case, but this was not the time to share those kinds of details with Emily.

"Within a few days after Eric's funeral, there were three murders in Chicago. Different parts of the city, different times of the day over three days. Three victims who at first seemed to have no connection to one another. The only similarity was the MO. All three victims were stabbed multiple times and with the same knife."

Emily paled. "I remember reading about them. Didn't pay attention to the details, though. Those kinds of news stories give me the willies, which is why I prefer human-interest stories. You had to investigate the murders?"

"I did."

"I'm sorry. "

He shrugged. "It's what I do. It took some time, but we eventually figured out the connection. A social worker, a foster parent and a street person, all with a past connection to a young woman."

"She killed them?" Emily sounded incredulous.

"No, her boyfriend did, and then she disappeared. He's in custody now, but he's not talking. Until this morning, we had no idea if she was dead or alive."

"And that's who you're here to interview?"

"That's right."

"Why would she come to Riverton?"

"I guess I'll find out when I talk to her." He checked the clock again. He really needed to get to the station, ASAP. "Anyway, none of this is an excuse for not calling you. It's just how I am when I get caught up in a case. Until it's solved, it's 24/7. And since it looks like I'm not getting that shave, I need to get to the station and get this interview over with. They're holding her on a suspected DUI, but they can't keep her there forever."

Emily studied the card he held. He couldn't tell if she was avoiding eye contact or if she had something else on her mind. She took a deep breath, let it out in a rush. "There's something else."

He had no idea what she was about to say, but he had a pretty good idea he wasn't going to like it.

"That night when we were…together. Something sort of…um…unexpected happened."

An uneasy sensation pooled in his gut.

"What do you mean by something un—" But his question wasn't even fully formed when the answer hit him like a commuter train. Emily didn't say anything. She simply waited as his scattered emotions became a single, coherent thought.

"Are you saying you're…?"

She nodded.

Pregnant? His ability to think rationally had disappeared. No way. Not possible. It had been one night. One night. They'd been careful. *He* had been careful. These things were not supposed to happen to people who were careful.

"You're sure?"

Another nod.

He walked to the door, taking in the street, the buildings, the people he knew so well. Everything *looked* as it always had. Perfectly normal. He swung around and took a long, hard look at Emily.

"Completely sure?"

"One hundred percent."

Just this morning he had thought Emily Finnegan was the kind of woman he could possibly, someday, maybe fall in love with. Now she was having a baby. *His* baby. He was going to be a father. And then his mother's unwelcome voice penetrated his thoughts. *A father who isn't married to the baby's mother. What do you think people are going to say about that?*

"We'll get married," he blurted. "Right away, as soon as you want." The declaration caught him completely off guard.

Emily gaped at him. "Married? Are you out of your mind?"

"What did you expect me to say?"

Emily sprang to her feet. "I don't know. 'How did this happen?' 'What are you going to do about it?'"

He couldn't help himself. He grinned. "I know how it happened. I was there, remember?" Then he sobered. Why would she think he would ask what she was going to do about it? Unless...no. He moved toward her, but she ducked out of reach.

Okay, not exactly the response he would have liked.

"Are you planning to do something about it?" he asked.

She nodded. "Have it, raise it."

Her declaration was meant to be defiant, but it had him breathing a little better. She might not make this easy, but he had to do the right thing.

"Okay, then. We'll raise it together."

"Right." Emily rolled her beautiful brown eyes. "That'll be easy for two parents who live three hundred miles apart. Easy, until the next big case comes along, and you forget all about us for months on end. Yeah, that's going to work."

"Come on, Emily. I'm sorry I didn't call. I know you think I'm a thoughtless jerk, but I'm not. Give me a chance to prove it."

"And how do you plan to do that?"

He couldn't believe he was about to say what he was about to say. "We'll get married.

You can move to Chicago. I'll take care of you and the baby and…"

Horrified didn't come close to describing her expression.

"What?" he asked.

"Oh, gee. Let me see. There is no way I'm moving to Chicago, and we hardly know one another, so I am not going to marry you."

"Emily, we've known each other for years."

"We've been *acquainted* for years. Big difference."

"They're basically the same things."

"All right, then," she said, offering up a challenge. "What's my favorite color?"

He looked her up and down, as though her wardrobe might offer up a clue. "Yellow?"

"Wrong."

"What's my middle name?"

Hmm. Should he know this? Had it been mentioned during her nephew's baptism, when the two of them had become godparents? Emily…? Emily…? He had no idea.

"When's my birthday?" she asked, relentlessly hammering her point home.

Again, no idea. None whatsoever.

"See? You don't know anything about me, but you think getting married is a good idea. You think I should walk away from my family and my job and everything I've ever known, follow you to Chicago and sit around in an apartment…or a house or wherever you live… waiting for you to get unbusy enough to be a husband and a father?"

"I don't know, Emily. We're about two minutes into a conversation I never expected to be having. We're going to be parents, and I'm trying to do the right thing."

"A marriage between two people who don't know one another is not the right thing, so it can't possibly be the best thing for the baby."

Was she serious? "What do you suggest?" he prompted. "I ask you out on a date, so we can 'get to know' each other?"

"That would be a start."

She was serious. "You want me to take you out to dinner and a movie? Drive you home? Leave you at the front door with a good-night kiss?"

She sucker-punched him with her smile. "That's as good a place to start as any."

Oh, man. She was dead serious. Women. Heaven help him. He would never understand them.

"Fine. We'll do this your way. I'll pick you up at six o'clock."

"Tonight?"

"Tonight."

"Oh, okay."

"It's a date." Lamest idea ever, but if this was how she wanted to play it, then this was how they would play it, because in spite of her objections, he was going to convince her to let him do the right thing. Case closed.

EMILY PACED BACK and forth across her apartment's tiny, cluttered living room. In Riverton's early days, these second-floor spaces above the storefronts on Main Street had mostly been used as offices. This one, above what had long been home to the *Riverton Gazette*, had at various times been the office of a barrister, a land surveyor and an accountant. About twenty-five years ago, it had been converted into an apartment by removing most of the partitions to create an L-shaped living/dining/office area, separated from the single bedroom by a minuscule galley kitchen and an even smaller bathroom.

Emily had fallen in love with the place the instant she saw it. She was close enough to her family that she was never, ever homesick, and far enough away to feel like the independent career woman she had imagined being.

"What were you thinking?" she asked, her cell phone pressed to her ear. "You should not have texted me to come to the shop without telling me he was there."

"I'm thinking you should be grateful," Fred said.

Grateful?

She stopped in front of the hamster cage that sat on a low bookcase next to her desk, and tossed in a peanut. Tadpole pounced on it, grasped it with tiny paws, her black, beady eyes bright with anticipation, and attacked the outer shell with her incisors.

"Why should I be grateful, Fred? I wasn't expecting to see him, and I sure wasn't prepared to tell him about the baby."

"And you were going to be prepared…when exactly?"

He had a point.

"Still, you could have given me a heads-up."

"Right. And given you a chance to cook up an excuse to avoid seeing him."

Fred knew her too well.

"So? How'd he take it?"

"Better than I expected." Jack had been kind of amazing, actually, but he might not be so accepting once the shock wore off and he had time to think things through. "He even said…" No. She wasn't ready to say that out loud, either.

"He said…?"

Emily watched Tadpole break through one end of the peanut shell and stuff the first nut into her cheek pouch. Life for a hamster was so easy. Eat. Run on your wheel. Sleep. Get up and do it all over again. Boring, but easy.

"Come on, Em. You're killing me here."

She sighed, knowing Fred wouldn't let this go. "He said we should get married right away."

A moment of stunned silence was followed by stammering. "He... Seriously?"

"Hey! Why so surprised? I'm a total catch."

Fred laughed. "Of course you are."

"I am!"

"I'm agreeing with you."

"No, you're not. You're being patronizing."

"Sorry, Em. I figured he'd be more freaked out, that's all. Do the typical guy thing and carry on about how you were trying to trap him."

She had half expected that reaction, too. Now she didn't know what to think. Since taking the test that morning, she had roller-coastered through every emotion imaginable. This minute, she was a wreck.

With the phone still to her ear, she stepped into the kitchen and filled the electric kettle for tea. "Under that cool-as-a-cucumber exterior, I'm sure he is freaking out, but he didn't go ballistic." Which was what she had expected.

"Good. When's the big day, then?"

She switched on the kettle. "There isn't going to be a big day. I said no."

Another moment of silence. "You said no? Em, are you sure? You've had a crush on this guy since we were kids."

Being best friends with Fred for most of her life meant he knew pretty much everything there was to know about her. Sometimes that was a good thing. Other times, like now, it was definitely annoying.

She eyed a package of coffee longingly before shifting her attention to an assortment of teas. Mint, which Annie had once recommended for an upset stomach and was mildly palatable with a spoonful of sugar. Echinacea, for the time she'd come down with a cold last winter. However, all it did was make her tongue tingle. Red rooibos, which was supposed to be good for everything and tasted worse than all the rest put together. Mint it was, she thought, dropping a bag into her favorite coffee mug and returning to the living room to wait for the water to boil.

"I had a crush on Jack *when* I was fourteen, not *since* I was fourteen. Either way, that's no reason to rush into anything."

Fred made a big production of clearing his throat.

"Don't you dare say it." She could read him

like a book. "I did not rush into this thing with Jack. It just happened, and now I'm being rushed into motherhood, and I'm not ready for it, so I'm not rushing into marriage."

Tadpole cracked the remaining shell, crammed in the second nut, one cheek pouch bulging, and sniffed around the cage for more. The little critter's face, now comically distorted, made her smile.

"Your two-wrongs-don't-make-a-right analogy is all well and good," Fred said. "But what about your family, Jack's family? Everyone will have something to say about this."

Everyone in town would have plenty to say about plain-Jane Emily Finnegan having Jack Evans's baby. Maybe she should move to Chicago. "Trying to avoid gossip is not a good reason to rush into marriage."

"Fair enough. I hope you've talked to your sisters. I still can't believe you told them I was the father."

"Not yet. I need to do that in person."

"You can't call them?"

"No way. They'll want to know who the real father is, and I'm not explaining that over the phone." With her free hand, she pulled her laptop out of her bag and set it on her desk beneath the window overlooking Main Street.

"You can't run out there this afternoon?"

"No time. I have to get ready for my—" Hmm. She hadn't meant to let that slip.

"Ready for your...?"

Fred would find out sooner or later. Probably sooner, since it seemed the barbershop was the hub of Riverton's rumor mill. "Jack and I are going out for dinner."

Fred let out a long whistle. "A date. Interesting."

"It's not a date. We have things to talk about, stuff to figure out." Fred did not need to know about the getting-to-know-each-other portion of the evening.

"And you plan to do that at the Riverton Bar & Grill? Gee, that won't attract any attention at all."

"That's not where we're going." And if Jack suggested that's what they do, she would veto it.

The whistle of the kettle drew her back to the kitchen. "I have to go," she said, filling her mug and inhaling the fragrant minty steam rising from it. "I'll call you tomorrow."

"Right after you've straightened out this mess with your sisters."

"I'll call you. Goodbye, Fred." She disconnected before he thought of another reason to prolong the conversation. She should work on an article for the paper and update her blog.

Most important, she needed to figure out what
to wear tonight. She hadn't wanted to admit
to Fred that it was a date, but it was. Jack had
said so.

CHAPTER SIX

THE RIVERTON POLICE STATION was attached to the back of the new town hall building, just east of the historic downtown district. Technically, the low, sprawling complex wasn't that new, having been built in the eighties, but it was significantly newer than the original town hall, which had been constructed more than a hundred years before that. That particular building, a more imposing two-story redbrick structure, still stood at the corner of First and Main and housed the town's library and the county museum.

Jack swung his Jeep into the lot and parked next to a patrol cruiser. In spite of being much later than he had planned to be here, he sat for a moment and stared at the Visitor Parking sign on the cinder block wall in front of him.

A quick shave and a haircut. That's all he'd stopped for. He'd ended up with neither. Instead…instead…unbelievable. Un-be-lievable. He fast-forwarded through the events of the past hour and a half, hitting pause at a few critical moments.

In no way, shape or form had he been prepared for Emily's appearance at the barbershop. Judging by her reaction to finding him there, the feeling had been mutual. Flustered and evasive at first, she had finally confessed to what had her on edge. She was having a baby, and the baby was his.

Over the years, he'd known several guys who had found themselves in this situation, but he had always been responsible, taking precautions to make sure it never happened to him and the woman he was involved with. He could recall several instances in which those guys felt they were being trapped into a lifetime commitment they weren't ready to make. One had even suspected he was being manipulated into taking responsibility for somebody else's child.

Jack locked gazes with himself in the rearview mirror. Why wasn't he feeling any of those things? Why was he accepting this at face value, acknowledging the child was his? Because in his heart, he knew Emily was telling the truth, and he knew she hadn't planned this any more than he had. Their share of the blame was an even fifty-fifty split, and so was their responsibility.

She thought he didn't know her. But he knew *about* her, and he knew her family. Emily Finnegan was as transparent as Wisconsin sunshine on a cloudless spring day. She had flatly rejected his hasty suggestion they get married—and honestly, what had he been thinking? If he hadn't made the unexpected trip home, if he hadn't given in to impulse and dropped into the barbershop, if Emily's friend Fred hadn't already known the secret and engineered their meeting, he wasn't completely convinced she ever would have told him.

He plucked Emily's card from his jacket pocket. He had intended to call her as soon as he'd wrapped up this interview, or possibly drop by her apartment and surprise her. He had been fairly certain she would have been furious he hadn't called or surprised he thought she cared. Either way, after flatly refusing his offer of marriage, she had agreed to have dinner with him tonight. He should be in denial, panicking, freaking out. Instead, he stared at her business card and cursed himself for being the jerk who had slept with a woman and never bothered to call. Now she didn't trust him, probably didn't believe a word he said. And he couldn't blame her. Convincing her otherwise meant he had his work cut out for him. Good thing he was never one to back away from a challenge. This time was no exception. He slid Emily's card into his pocket and headed into the station.

"Hey, Doug," he said to the young officer manning the front desk. "Sorry to be so late. Something came up, and I had to deal with it." Talk about an understatement.

"No problem. How was the drive from Chicago?"

"As long as ever. How's my witness holding up?"

"Ticked off we're keeping her here 'against her will,' but we weren't letting her go till you got here."

"Appreciate that. Thanks."

The door of Chief Fenwick's office swung open. "Detective Evans, as I live and breathe. Good to see you. Who'd've figured you'd be here on official business instead of just paying us a social visit."

Jack crossed the room and accepted the man's firm handshake. He always made a point of dropping by the station when he was in town, and over the years he and Gordon Fenwick had forged a close working relationship. In his early days with the Chicago PD, Chief Fenwick had been the person Jack looked up to the most, a mentor, a father figure of sorts, even though he had a close relationship with his own dad. As Jack's responsibilities and experience with vice and then the homicide unit expanded, their friendship had been on a more equal footing. From time to time, Gordon would call and ask for his opinion and advice on a police matter.

"Chief, always good to be here."

"You got a minute?" Gordon asked. "There's something I'd like to run by you."

"Sure. I can spare several, actually." Rose Daniels was getting antsy, but a few more minutes weren't going to kill her, he decided, and followed the man into his office.

Chief Fenwick closed the door. "Have a seat," he said, settling himself into the chair behind his massive desk.

Jack sat, expecting to hear about a new case or perhaps field a few questions about the young Daniels woman. "What's up?"

"I've decided to retire."

"Seriously?" Chief Fenwick was a Riverton institution, and Jack couldn't imagine the town without him.

"Not many people know about it yet, including my team here, so I'd appreciate you keeping it under your hat. The mayor's going to make the official announcement at the town council meeting on Monday."

"Of course. I have to say this seems awfully sudden."

"Been mulling it over for the past couple of months. The missus had surgery back in February. Not sure if I told you about that."

"My mother mentioned it." Jack's mother and Eleanor Fenwick had known each other for years, and Norma Evans had been beside herself when her longtime friend was diagnosed with breast cancer.

"She's been going into the city for radiation treatments. Now that that's done and she's starting to feel more like her old self again, the docs are saying the prognosis is excellent."

"I'm happy to hear that."

"So are we, son. So are we. And it's been one of those wake-up calls for us. Eleanor would like to spend more time with the grandkids. We both would. They're all over the map these days—Pittsburgh, Fort Worth, Seattle— and Eleanor's always talked about spending the winter in Florida. So we're thinking about getting ourselves a motor home and discovering America, so to speak."

"Then you should do it." Jack wished his own parents would get around more. His sister, Faith, who lived in San Francisco, was constantly after their parents to fly out for a visit, but their mother hated leaving the house to sit empty, and their father wasn't fond of big cities. "The Riverton PD won't be the same without you, though."

"Oh, I don't know about that. Everyone's replaceable."

That might be a sound philosophy in many cases, but Jack wasn't sure it extended to Chief Fenwick. The man had a reputation for remaining calm during a crisis and for inspiring his staff to rise to the same high standards he set for himself. Finding someone to fill those shoes wouldn't be easy.

"That's what I wanted to talk to you about," Gordon continued. "Last time you were in town, I got the impression working homicide was starting to take a toll, that you were starting to feel burned out."

The man knew him almost as well as he knew himself, but where was he going with this?

"I've been considering a change," he admitted. There were only a handful of people Jack felt comfortable confiding in, and Gord Fenwick was one of them. "Maybe back to vice, maybe something completely different. I've worked hard to get where I am, though, and I don't want the department to think I can't take the heat anymore."

Gord tilted back in his big black leather

desk chair, making Jack the sole subject of his intensely thoughtful gaze. "Looking for change doesn't make you a bad cop. I've seen lots of guys—good cops—happily walk the same beat their whole career. Others, like you, quickly rise up through the ranks. I've seen your track record for cases solved, and it's a lot higher than most. So, no, feeling restless doesn't make you a bad cop," he repeated. "It makes you one who's ready to take on a new challenge."

Jack studied the man on the other side of the desk. He had a hunch he knew what was coming next, and he wasn't sure he was prepared for it.

"I've told the mayor I want to step down as soon as he can find a replacement, so he asked if I had any recommendations." Chief Fenwick had a direct way of looking at people, as though he was challenging them to sit up straighter. That's how he was looking at Jack right now.

Jack adjusted his posture accordingly.

Gord straightened his chair, picked up a gold pen off the desk and, holding the ends in the fingers of both hands, rolled it thoughtfully. "I told the mayor I knew only one person who could step in here and take over tomorrow." He glanced away from the pen and back up at Jack. "That person is you. You know the town, the people. You already have a great rapport with everyone here in the department. This opportunity would take your career in a whole new direction, give you a fresh outlook on police work. I hope you'll give it some serious consideration."

Two hours ago, Jack might have brushed the offer aside, laughed at it, even. Chief of Police? Practically unheard of for anyone at this stage of their career. "I don't know what to say, Chief. I'm flattered, of course, and honored, but this isn't something I've ever aspired to. I've never seen myself behind a desk, being the one in charge. And, yes, I've been feeling a little burned out, but I love what I do, being on the street in the thick of things. I don't think I'm the right guy for the job." He debated whether or not to tell Gord about the baby and his plan to convince Emily to move to Chicago with him, then decided against it. Emily still needed to share the news with her family, and he would need to figure out a way to tell his folks, too. His father would be disappointed in him, but he was pretty sure his mother would bust out the knitting needles and get started on the baby's first wardrobe.

"How long have we known each other?" Gord asked.

Jack pondered the question. "Almost twenty years?" Since that fateful night when he and his friends Eric Larsen and Paul Woodward had foolishly let themselves get drawn into a Halloween prank instigated by Jesse Wilson and his loser friends. They'd spent the next four Saturday mornings at the station, washing and waxing police cruisers.

The man nodded. "Even then I knew there was something special about you. Then, years later, after you'd graduated college and told me you were going into the police academy, I was as proud as I'd have been if you were my own son."

Jack smiled at the recollections. "You do remember why I was here in the first place?"

Gord grinned. "Could've made a lot of omelets with all those eggs you boys were tossing around town."

Not to mention the numerous rolls of toilet paper they'd used to festoon the trees lining the street in front of the high school.

Jack shook his head sheepishly. "You let us off pretty easy."

"Let the punishment fit the crime, I always say. You and your buddies learned your lesson."

"We sure did."

"Wish the same was true for Jesse Wilson, but it seems some fellows never grow up."

Jack glanced at his watch and stood. "I appreciate the vote of confidence, Gord. I'll think about it, I really will, but right now I have a witness to interview."

Chief Fenwick stood, too, and extended his hand across the desk. "You do that. Just don't take too long. Mayor Bartlett has assured me the job belongs to the person I recommend, and I'm recommending you."

They shook on it. "Give my best to Eleanor, will you?" Jack said as he left the chief's office.

On his way to the interview room and his waiting witness, the events of the past few hours swirled in his mind. A family in the making, Emily's reluctance notwithstanding. An incredible career opportunity, albeit one he had no intention of taking. Sitting at his desk that morning, which now seemed a lifetime ago, he'd felt deflated by a job that had become a drain. Now, instead of freaking out, he was energized by the prospect of change. Was he being naive? He didn't think so.

EMILY GRIPPED THE edge of her desk. She couldn't breathe. She pulled in a quick breath, then another, then another and another. Her heart raced. The images on her laptop monitor blurred. The room tilted from side to side, and her stomach followed. Her face warmed, and she could feel her forehead getting damp. With her fingers still clamped to the edge of the desk, she squeezed her eyelids shut and tried to force herself to stop panting.

Calm down, she told herself. *You know how to get through this. Breathe slowly. Breathe in, two, three, four. Out, two, three, four. You can do this.*

By degrees, she relaxed her death grip on the desk and slowly opened her eyes. She forced herself to focus on the words on her computer screen. Her heart still felt as though she'd run a marathon, but it was no longer hammering its way out of her chest.

"You need to keep it together," she said out loud after she was more or less breathing normally again. Would panic attacks be bad for the baby? They probably weren't good.

She pushed back her chair, stood shakily, wobbled unsteadily into the bathroom and leaned on the sink. These episodes left her drained and weak, physically and emotionally. She hated them. They'd started while she was away at college, pushing herself to keep her GPA high enough to maintain her scholarship, knowing her family was enormously proud of her while she missed them desperately and wished more than anything she was back in the big old farmhouse, being bearhugged by her dad, dining on one of Annie's sumptuous meals instead of eating cafeteria food, and even enduring CJ's endless attempts at one-upmanship.

Emily had come home for Thanksgiving with a prescription for antianxiety medication, and her father had sat her down for a heart-to-heart. He had warned her against taking them and advised she find another way to cope. Following the debilitating injuries he'd suffered during the Gulf War, he'd found himself relying heavily on medications to relieve the pain and trauma he'd experienced. Taking them had been easy. Stopping had not. Not wanting to disappoint her father, Emily had flushed the pills. When she returned to school, she had made an appointment with a counselor on campus who'd taught her breathing techniques to control the hyperventilation. He had also recommended more exercise and less caffeine. She had done everything except give up coffee. The techniques had worked, and after moving back to Riverton, she was seldom bothered by the attacks. Now they were back.

Jack Evans had proposed to her, and she had turned him down. Had she done the right thing? She stared at her reflection in the bath-room mirror. Of course she had. Technically, it hadn't been a proposal. He hadn't asked, "Will you marry me?" He had hastily stated, unequivocally, "We'll get married."

Just what every girl dreamed of. Not.

She was convinced he hadn't meant it any-way. He was probably in shock and blurted out the first thought that popped into his head, the thing that was considered the right thing to do. Emily sighed. She hadn't known what to expect when she told him about the baby, but she hadn't anticipated that. He had asked her out to dinner, which made tonight a first date, a prospect that should have her filled with anticipation, not trepidation.

"Why can't you be normal?" she asked her reflection in the mirror.

Her father had always said her tendency to march to the sound of her own drum was part and parcel of being the middle child. She shud-dered to think what he would say about this, and she was in no hurry to find out. Fred, with whom she had shared her most secret hopes and dreams, claimed her at times unorthodox behavior was on account of her mother leav-ing when Emily was so young. As she became older and learned how to talk herself out of doing the wrong thing, she realized both her friend and her father were probably right.

And when she considered her sisters' place in the birth order—Annie, the oldest, having to be the responsible one, and CJ, the youngest, a little flaky and a bit too self-centered—Emily decided she was better off being the one in the middle.

Feeling more in control, she splashed cold water on her face and returned to the living room. Tadpole had given up her search for another peanut and was running on her lopsided wheel. Emily found the intermittent squeak, squeak, squeak oddly comforting. It meant she wasn't alone in the apartment.

She sat at her desk, eased her feet out of her shoes and wriggled her toes. She opened the file with Sig Sorrenson's obituary. She read and reread the first paragraph three times, realized the futility of trying to edit without the ability to concentrate. She couldn't do justice to this man's long life while she was completely absorbed in her own, so she closed the document and logged into her email instead, scrolling up the list and deleting coupon offers for a spa treatment, an oil change and a two-for-one brunch special at a pancake house in Madison. She read a message from her boss reminding her about the town council meeting on Monday afternoon, and she checked her calendar to be sure she had entered the correct time. She had three new followers on Twitter and a reminder that two new comments had been posted on her latest blog entry. The sender of the most recent email nearly caused another panic attack.

From: Norma Evans

Why would Jack's mother send her an email? Surely, he hadn't told his parents about them yet. No, he wouldn't. She was sure of it. They needed to get to know each other first.

Subject: Missing garden gnomes, etc.

"Okay, breathe. This is about the blog, not the baby." She opened the email and started to read.

Dear Emily,
I thought you would be interested to know that along with all the other things that have gone missing around this lovely little town of ours, my garden trowel has disappeared. And before you ask, I can assure you I did not misplace it. I was using it yesterday afternoon in one of my flower beds, the one right outside

the front door, because with this lovely weather we're having, I'm getting ready to plant my marigolds. Some say it's still too early for them, but those flowers are hardy and can hold their own against a late spring frost. When I went in to make dinner, I stuck the trowel in the ground and left it there on purpose because I was planning to finish the flower bed this afternoon.

Well, you can imagine my surprise when I went out after lunch today and my trowel was gone! My first thought was Walt had put it away, but when I asked him about it, he said he never touched it. So this must be the work of the Garden Gnome Bandit, don't you think? There's really no other explanation. I called the police, but they don't seem to be taking these thefts seriously. We need someone like my son, Jack, on the Riverton PD, don't you agree?

I hope your family is doing well. Tell your father hello from us, and remind your sister Annie I'll see her at the Hospital Auxiliary's bazaar and rummage sale in a few weeks. I'm looking forward to sampling some of that strudel of hers.
Yours truly,
Norma Evans

Emily let out a long breath, realizing she'd been holding it while reading through to the end of the message and waiting for the penny to drop. Norma Evans was nothing if not long-winded, but she had given no indication she knew anything about her impending grand-parenthood. The disappearance of her garden trowel coinciding with the appearance of those two pink lines was purely coincidence.

Welcoming the distraction, even though it had come from Jack's mother, she pushed away from her desk and stood to look at the Riverton street map she'd pinned to the bulletin board above the bookcase. She plucked a pushpin from the box on the top shelf and stuck it into the map to mark the location of the Evans's family home.

The missing items now totalled nine, and the location of the red plastic ball on the head of this pin fit the pattern that had been slowly emerging. Every item had been taken from a nine-square-block residential area a little to the north of the historic downtown area. The one outlier was Gabe's Gas 'n' Go on the highway, but that was only two blocks to the west. Next, she scanned her list of things that had been stolen.

Three garden gnomes, one welcome mat, a pair of black rubber boots, a garden stake with a hand-painted sign reading Weed it and Reap, and now one garden trowel. And of course the window-washing squeegee from Gabe's.

The boots had disappeared on two consecutive nights from Ferguson's back door, and Emily had resisted the urge to ask why the remaining boot hadn't been put away after the first one went missing.

The trowel fit the pattern. It was small and the sort of thing a person would intentionally place in a garden or accidentally leave outside because who would bother stealing it? She fetched her camera from her bag, snapped a photo of the updated street map. The rhythmic whirring of the hamster wheel, punctuated by its *squeak, squeak, squeak* stopped abruptly, and Tadpole gazed up at her, dark eyes filled with anticipation. Emily opened the door and lifted her out, holding the warm little body close to her heart while she contemplated the map for a moment. After a few seconds, she settled Tad into the little red plastic box on the corner of her desk that served as the rodent's home away from home and gave her another peanut. Then she uploaded the new photo to a folder on her desktop and logged into her blog.

CHAPTER SEVEN

WITH ONE HAND on the doorknob of the interview room where Rose Daniels sat waiting, Jack paused long enough to clear his head of babies, job offers and Emily. Yes, even her. Every interview demanded focus and control, this one more than most because there was a possibility this young woman had been more than an innocent bystander to three murders. The grizzly stabbings that had occurred on three consecutive days, in three different parts of Chicago, to three women who appeared to have nothing in common. In spite of that, Jack had been convinced they were connected.

There had been no sign of robbery—even the homeless woman was found with two pieces of ID, fourteen dollars and change, and her next fix in her coat pocket. All three victims were fully clothed. There had been no physical assault and no sign of a struggle, which suggested the women had either been skillfully ambushed or they had not felt threatened by their assailant. Jack's gut told him it

was the latter and that there was a single perpetrator. He'd learned to go with his gut, and
it almost always paid off.

The common thread had turned out to be
Rose Daniels. Daughter of the drug addict,
former client of the social worker, former foster child of the housewife. Rose had recently
worked as a waitress at an all-night diner in
the Rogers Park area, and she had been on
duty at the time of all three murders. Rose's
boss, a sinewy woman with bad teeth and
tobacco-stained fingers, along with her gum-
chewing coworker, a handful of late-night reg-
ulars and tedious hours of grainy surveillance
footage had provided Rose with a rock-solid
alibi. Problem was, by the time Jack had connected the dots, Rose had vanished. He hadn't
known if she was dead or alive, but now here
she was in his hometown, of all places. He adjusted his posture, pushed open the door and
strode into the room.

Rose lounged carelessly in a chair designed
for anything but comfort. Jack closed the door,
and she barely glanced up from the purple
polish she was picking off her thumbnail.
Her dark brown hair, which had been long
in all the photographs and video he'd seen,
had been shorn into a short pixie cut. Long,
purple-streaked bangs were swept to one side,

covering one eye. Rose's visible eye was black rimmed and bloodshot. She wore faded, distressed jeans and scuffed combat boots. Her black-and-white T-shirt sported a cat's face with a thought bubble above its head. "Meow."

Jack set a bottle of water in front of her, then pulled the other chair away from the table and dragged it around so he could sit facing her without the table between them. "Hi, Rose. I'm Detective Jack Evans, Chicago PD."

"Took you long enough." She didn't look up.

He ignored the quip. "I need you to know I'm going to record our conversation." He placed a recorder on the table, in plain view, pushed the record button and said his name again.

"I need you to state your name, please, and spell it." She complied. Rose Marie Daniels.

"Thank you, Rose," he said. "I'm sorry for your loss."

She made eye contact then, briefly, warily, then shrugged and looked away. "Whatever."

So this is how it's going to be. He had pored over her police file and her mother's, had spoken with several social workers and former foster parents at length, so he understood where the attitude came from. He was a patient man, and he had all afternoon, his anticipated rendezvous with Emily Finnegan notwithstanding. Given the tremble in Rose Daniels's hands and the way her gaze darted around the small room, she didn't have that luxury. She needed a drink.

"Can I get you anything besides water?" he offered. "A soda, maybe?"

"How 'bout a smoke?"

"Sorry. That'll have to wait till we're done here."

That earned him another shrug.

It would be interesting to see how long the cold shoulder would hold up against the young woman's need for another drink, a nicotine fix or any other substance she craved.

"So, Rose, Riverton's a long way from Chicago. What brings you here?"

She brushed flecks of purple polish off her jeans and started chipping away at the other thumbnail. "Vacation."

Sure, because Riverton was right up there with Disney World and Vegas. "I get that," he said instead. "I'm sure you needed a break from working at the diner."

Rose flicked him a glance.

"Oh, wait. You quit that job, didn't you? Or are you on a leave of absence? Your boss wasn't sure."

"I got bored."

"Fair enough. How long do you plan to stay here?"

"A few days. A week, maybe."

"Where are you staying?"

"At some bed-and-breakfast place."

Interesting. The only B & B in town was operated by Annie Finnegan, who also happened to be Emily's older sister. This was either one very weird set of coincidences, or it wasn't.

"That would be Finnegan Farm," he said, careful not to make it a question. "Out on River Road." The more Rose believed he already knew about her, the more likely she'd be to spill the details he didn't.

She looked startled. "Yeah."

"Tell me about your mother."

"She was lousy at being one."

According to social services, Rose had been in and out of foster care for most of her childhood. Six different homes in all. She'd been returned to her mother's care five times—after Scarlett Daniels had done a stint in rehab, promising every time she was clean for good. Those periods had been brief, lasting anywhere from three to six months. Scarlett would end up back on the street and Rose in yet another foster home.

"So I've been told," he said. "I've also heard

she tried to turn her life around, more than once, but the drugs always got the best of her."

"Yeah, those and the stupid, loser boyfriends."

"Do you want to talk about them?"

"Not really."

"What about you? Do you have a boyfriend?"

She looked up, and this time challenged him with a direct stare. "What do you think?"

"I hear you've been hanging around with a guy named Jason Caruthers. I hear he's pretty crazy about you."

Rose huffed and then rolled her eyes in a way that was meant to show her disdain. However, it wasn't quick enough to mask a wave of panic.

"I hear he'd do pretty much anything you asked him to do," Jack said.

The girl's reaction was swift and forceful. "I never asked him to do anything for me. *Never.*" She practically spat the last word before regaining a smattering of self-control. "Anything he did—*if* he did anything—it was all his doing."

"Oh, he did some stuff, all right. As for acting alone, that's not what Jason's saying." He leaned closer. "I'm going to level with you, Rose. You could be in a lot of trouble here.

Three people who were close to you are dead. Your boyfriend's DNA was found at each crime scene. He's up on murder one charges on all three counts, and he's implicated you as an accomplice."

"He's *not* my boyfriend." She reached for the bottle of water and, with shaky hands, struggled with the cap.

Jack took it from her, broke the seal and handed the bottle back to her.

She unscrewed the cap, gulped the water too quickly, coughed and sputtered, set the bottle on the table, and swiped her mouth with the back of her hand.

"He's not my boyfriend," she said again. "It was never like that."

"Okay." He wasn't sure he believed her, but he needed her to believe he did. "If Jason wasn't your boyfriend, then how about you start at the beginning and tell me what it was like? I can't help you, Rose, unless I have all the facts."

She gave a quick head toss that flipped the too-long bangs away from her face, momentarily revealing the distrust and indecision in those dark, black-lined eyes. He watched her roll the bottle lid back and forth between her fingers, glad she'd finally stopped picking at the scabby remains of her nail polish. She remained silent.

Jack leaned back a ways, confident he had more staying power than she did.

Rose continued her nervous fidgeting until the lid unexpectedly spun out of her fingers. He deftly caught it in midair and returned it to the startled girl.

"How old are you, Rose?"

"Twenty."

"You spent a lot of time in foster homes. How long have you been on your own?"

"Coupla years."

"Don't kids in Illinois stay in foster care until they're twenty-one?"

"Yeah, in sleazy group homes," she snapped, her voice dripping with disdain. "I can look after myself."

Right. Everyone knew how well that turned out. But he would let it drop and try penetrating the tough-girl attitude with a different line of questioning.

"Have you ever been in prison?"

She gave him a sharp stare. "No."

"Just that one stint in juvie," he reminded her.

"Right." The single word was barely audible.

"What was that?"

"Right," she repeated, this time with force.

He leaned forward again, forearms on his thighs, and wove his fingers together. "Compared to a maximum-security prison, juvie's like a walk in the park, summer camp, all fun and games." He gave her a few seconds to absorb that before he continued. "If someone accused me of some bad stuff I didn't do…I'd be doing whatever I could to avoid doing time. You know what I'm saying, Rose?"

Eyes downcast, she responded with a one-shouldered shrug. Over the years, he'd met a lot of kids—young adults, he reminded himself—like Rose. They'd grown up in the system but had pretty much raised themselves. Street smart, yet socially inept and immature, a thin veneer of tough-guy attitude barely masking their vulnerability.

Rose swallowed. "I never asked him to hurt anybody. I swear I didn't."

Finally, a chink in the armor. "Okay. Tell me about Jason. How did you meet him?"

"At the diner. He'd come in for coffee. At first, he'd sit at a table near the back. He always had a tablet with him, and the diner has Wi-Fi, so sometimes he'd hang out for quite a while."

"Did you ever see what he was doing online?"

"Not really, but I'm pretty sure he has a Facebook page."

The reality was he had several, each created with a different identity. He'd used the tablet to surreptitiously take photographs of Rose and post them on his *All-night Diner Guy* page. The captions showed a creepy obsession with the young woman he referred to as *My Caffeine Fix*. Using a host of additional fictitious identities, he had also frequented numerous online chat rooms where the topics of discussion were dark and disturbingly morbid.

Better to withhold this information, Jack decided. Give Rose a chance to tell her story, her way. If she was as innocent as she claimed to be, they might be able to use her to get a confession from an unsuspecting Jason Caruthers.

"So he'd just sit at the back of the diner and drink coffee?" Jack asked.

"Yeah, at first, anyway. Then he started talking to me once in a while."

"What did you talk about?"

Rose furrowed her brow. "Nothing, really. He'd ask stuff like how long I'd worked there, where had I gone to school and where did I live. Stuff like that."

Jack sat back and waited for her to continue.

"One day he sat at a table closer to the front and then the next time he came in, he sat at the counter where we could talk when I wasn't waiting on other customers."

"Did your conversations change, get more personal?"

"I guess." Rose sipped some water. She seemed a little calmer now that she was finally opening up. "He asked questions about my family, about what it was like growing up without a dad, about the foster homes. He asked a lot of questions, actually."

"Did he ever talk about himself?"

She shook her head. "Hardly ever. He told me he was from New York, and his parents were still there. He talked more about the future, how he planned to go back to the city and be an actor."

Jason Caruthers was from New York state, but not the city. He'd grown up in Albany, upstate. Jack suspected the lie was intended to impress Rose, and it seemed it had. Nothing about his background suggested an interest in theater. He was quite the actor, though.

Now that Rose was on a roll, she kept talking. Jack let her continue without interrupting. She appeared to know nothing about Jason's own experience as a kid who'd been abandoned by his parents and raised, not in foster homes but by an elderly grandmother. By all accounts, she had taken him into her home out of some misplaced sense of duty. Worse still, she had ignored and then subsequently denied the indicators her grandson was struggling with mental illness. The forensic psychiatrist who now worked with Jason had diagnosed him with borderline personality disorder.

"Jason was one of the few people who ever really listened to me," Rose said. "He wanted to know about my mother, the foster parents I had over the years, the social workers."

"What did you tell him?"

Head down, she absently picked at the frayed threads on the knee of her jeans, expanding the gaping tear. "I told him everything. How bad it was with my mom, how the social workers would show up with the cops in the middle of the night…"

She hesitated, shot him a quick, wary glance.

Jack responded with a nod, hoping she could see his sympathy was genuine. In his early days with the CPD, he'd been present at a lot of child apprehensions. Too many. Every single one of them a heartbreaker.

"I told him how much I hated moving into some stranger's house, how I never felt like I belonged there, or anywhere. Do you think that's why he…?"

Murdered your mother? Words best left unsaid for now.

"We don't know what motivated him. Can you remember anything else he said about his own life?"

She shook her head, slowly. "I can't think of anything."

"Did you ever meet him away from the diner?"

She hesitated, obviously startled by that question. "Um…he asked a couple of different times if I wanted to go someplace with him after work. I always said no. My boss was, like, superstrict about us 'fraternizing with the patrons,'" she said, punctuating the sentence with air quotes. "A couple of months ago, I started running into him, though. Once at the Laundromat near my apartment building and another time at the convenience store on the corner. He told me he lived in the neighborhood."

Believing him had been her first mistake, but it was easy to understand why she had. Rose wore her neediness like a neon sign. Jason Caruthers had likely zeroed in on that before she'd served him his first cup of coffee.

Jack shook his head. He needed to be honest with her. "Jason didn't live in your neighborhood. He had a room near the Loop down-town."

Rose's overly made-up eyes narrowed to slits. "So, what are you saying? Was he, like, stalking me or something?" A possibility she obviously hadn't considered at the time.

"All I can tell you for sure is he didn't live anywhere near your place."

"That's creepy."

He agreed. "To be clear, Rose, you used to see Jason pretty well every day at the diner, you ran into him a few times in your neigh-borhood, but you never went anywhere with him? No dates, no meet-ups anywhere?"

"Never. I already told you that."

"You did, and I appreciate your honesty." And his gut told him she was being honest. Still, he needed to keep stripping away the lay-ers of this particular onion until there weren't any left.

"When was the last time you saw your mother?"

"About two months ago. She had my cell number, and she called out of the blue."

"Did you get together with her?"

Rose gave a wistful nod.

"How was she?"

"She sounded good on the phone. Like she had it together, you know?"

"Did she come to the diner?"

"No way. I never told her where I lived or where I was working. I met her downtown. Turned out the place she suggested was close to a shelter where she used to hang out, so I figured she must've been staying there again."

"The Helping Hands Women's Shelter?"

"Yeah, that's the place."

"How was she when you saw her that day?"

Rose lifted one bony shoulder, let it drop. "Okay, I guess. I bought her lunch, and she asked for money. She doesn't call very often, but when she does—did—that's always what she wanted. So I gave her my tips from the shift I'd worked the night before, and then I left."

For the first time since the interview started, he let his thoughts extend beyond the interview room. Compared to this poor kid, his upbringing had been decidedly normal. He would guess Emily's was, as well. Her parents had been divorced for years, and he'd never heard much about her mother, come to think of it. She and her sisters had been raised by their father—a wheelchair-bound paraplegic who was something of a local hero in his own right—on the family farm. Thomas Finnegan could often be seen chauffeuring his grandson around in his specially equipped minivan. Last summer, Jack's mother had raved about him being the marshal, on horseback no less, of the Riverboat Days parade. Jack would make a point of learning more about Emily's family over dinner tonight.

He turned his full attention back to Rose. "Giving your mom some money, that was a nice thing to do."

"Not really. I mean, she is—was—my mom and everything, but I knew she was going to use it to get high."

"Do you use drugs, Rose?"

"No way."

"Just booze, then."

She had maintained eye contact throughout the exchange about her mother, but she quickly lowered her gaze when he mentioned the drinking. "Sometimes."

He let that drop. "Did you tell Jason about getting together with your mother?"

"Yes," she whispered. She swiped at her eyes with the back of one hand. For the first time since the interview had begun, her emotions were raw and gut-wrenchingly genuine.

Jack slid a box of tissues across the table and leaned back in his chair, watching her closely. Rose dabbed at her eyes, scrunched the damp, black-smeared tissue into a ball and formed a fist around it.

She's grieving, he reminded himself. *Give the poor kid a break*.

She snagged a second tissue, did a little more damage to the eyeliner, blew her nose.

"I know this is hard," he said, "but I need to ask a few more questions. Take your time and let me know when you're ready."

She tossed the tissues into the trash. "I'm fine. Can we just get this over with?"

"Sure. Tell me about your social worker, when you last saw her, what you told Jason about her."

Rose answered his questions, appearing to do her best to be accurate with dates and places. The same was true when he moved on to her former foster mother. Her house had been the one place that had felt like a real home to Rose. She had screwed it up by acting out and finally stealing money from her foster mom's purse so she could impress some of her so-called friends at school. Yes, she had told Jason about living there. Now she confessed to Jack, amid more tears, that she had embellished some of the facts and completely altered others to make herself seem like the victim.

Jack studied Rose's face as Jason's motivation slowly dawned on her. She might not have wielded the knife. She might not be guilty of murder—certainly no jury would ever convict her—but her poor-me attitude, combined with her indiscretion and naïveté, had contributed to the senseless killing of three innocent people. Three people who had at various times cared for her and about her, whether or not they had done an adequate job of demonstrating it. Eventually, Rose would have to find a way to come to terms with the reality of what had happened to those women; otherwise she would stagger beneath the guilt for the rest of her life. There would always be doubt, self-recrimination, what-if questions. For Rose's sake, Jack hoped she didn't keep looking for answers in a bottle.

"I'm going to recommend that the Riverton police let you go, on one condition. No more disappearing acts. I want you to keep me informed of your whereabouts at all times, and we'll need you back in Chicago to testify at Jason's trial. Agreed?"

She nodded reluctantly. "Will I have to see him?"

"I'm afraid so. Just in the courtroom, though, and there'll be plenty of security." At the beginning of the interview, he had toyed with the idea of putting her and Jason together before the trial to see if she could get him to admit he'd acted alone. Now that Jack had met Rose, he could see that wouldn't be a good idea. Jason Caruthers was as intelligent as he was evil. He could easily manipulate Rose, and the whole plan could backfire. Better to let the forensics and Rose's testimony do the talking.

CHAPTER EIGHT

EMILY LOVED WORKING for the local newspaper. Being a journalist had been her dream for as long as she could remember, and most of the time it didn't feel like work. However, her on-line blog was the most fun she had ever had with her writing. The banner at the top of the page was a wide-angle shot she had taken of Main Street from inside the clock tower of the old town hall. Superimposed over the banner was the title of her blog—*Small Town, Big Hearts by Emily Finnegan*.

All these years later, she still remembered Miss Garth's advice on a sixth-grade English assignment she had proudly handed in. Emily had written a story about a scuba-diving pirate and a mermaid who teamed up to search for sunken treasure and were attacked by sea monsters. Her teacher had commented on her flare for colorful descriptions and praised her imagination, but she had given the paper a C-minus and suggested, "Try writing what you know, Emily." Her next piece had been about her dad who had fought in Desert Storm and returned home in a wheelchair, and what that had been like for her family. She had known it was a good story before she handed it in, but she had still been over the moon to see an A-plus at the bottom of the page.

As much as she loved writing for he *Riverton Gazette*, the subject matter was limited, and her boss's conservative ideas didn't allow much room for self-expression. To make up for the lack of creativity, Emily had started blogging not long after moving back home. Following through with Miss Garth's advice, Emily wrote about what she knew best—her hometown of Riverton, WI, and the humble and sometimes quirky people who made it her favorite place in the whole world. Some might think the blog a silly waste of time, but she had fun writing it. These days, she looked forward to the next report of a missing item, although she would never admit it to anyone. None of the items were valuable, so the police might be right to think the whole thing was a prank perpetrated by a handful of schoolkids or just plain carelessness on the part of the owners. Her boss told her things would probably stop disappearing if she stopped writing about them. That wasn't going to happen, though. The number of followers of her blog had increased after she'd posted the first theft article—"The Mysterious Case of the Disappearing Garden Gnome." The post had received more comments than earlier ones, and that trend had continued with subsequent articles, such as "Another Local Garden Gnome Gone Missing," "The Welcome Mat's Worrisome Whereabouts" and "The Window-Washing Squeegee from Gabe's Gas 'n' Go that Got Up and Went." Her silliest title yet was "The Wellingtons that Went for a Walk."

She clicked the new post button and typed in a title—"Digging Up Dirt on the Garden Gnome Burglar." Kind of corny, but she could always change it.

Dear Hearts,

The Garden Gnome Burglar has struck again, this time at the home of Walter and Norma Evans on Second Avenue. Norma, who we all know is an avid gardener, was ready to plant marigolds in her prize-winning front flower beds this afternoon. Imagine her dismay when she discovered her favorite garden trowel has vanished into thin air.

The Riverton PD has yet to nab the perpetrator. They have no suspects at this time, no ransom notes have been received and no pic-

tures of gnomes posing in Paris or Rome have come to light, either.
Love,
Emily

She searched the files on her hard drive for a related photo. She found a picture she had taken of the Evans's home after Norma had won first place in Riverton's "House Proud" competition held on the Fourth of July last summer. Marigolds, pansies, geraniums and numerous other flowers Emily couldn't identify bloomed everywhere. A pair of American flags fluttered patriotically on either side of the wide steps leading to the wreath-adorned front door and a covered veranda furnished with a wooden love seat swing and an inviting pair of Adirondacks. Emily closed her eyes and pictured herself sitting in one of those chairs, sipping sweet iced tea while Norma rocked on the swing with a baby in her arms.

Oh, my! Her eyes flew open, and she quickly clicked Publish and then logged out of her blog. She took another look at Sig's obituary, and again decided to leave it until tomorrow. Right now, she should get ready for… whatever it was she and Jack were doing tonight. He had called it a date, but she wasn't convinced. He could have already had a change of heart. Yes, the baby changed everything, but she needed to be realistic. Becoming parents didn't mean they were meant to be together or were right for one another. And it sure didn't mean they should rush to the altar. The biggest issue of all was he didn't love her. Emily wasn't a hopeless romantic, but marriage was love or nothing. She would never marry for the sake of convenience.

Fred had been absolutely right about her feelings. She had fallen crazy in love—or at least puppy love—with Jack Evans when she was fourteen. Back then, Jack and his perfect girlfriend, Belinda Bellows, had seemed inseparable. However, their relationship had ended after high school when Jack had gone away to college and Belinda hadn't.

Ancient history, she reminded herself. She sighed. She should really start getting ready for dinner, but instead she scrolled though older posts on her blog and perused the comments. More people read her articles in the *Gazette*, but they were all Riverton residents. With her blog, she could reach people worldwide. Not that the entire world read her stories, but the posts frequently had fifty or sixty hits, and some had garnered quite a few comments from readers, especially the garden-gnome posts. Many comments were made by people who disguised their identities with names like *Catwoman37*, *DragonSlayer* and *Miss_Piggy*. Some augmented their online personas with a corresponding avatar. Others, like *AnnieF*, were clearly her sister, while others still, like CJ's *Horsefeathers* and her father's *Wheelman* were slightly more subtle but still identifiable. Emily had been able to figure out the real identities of some of her local readers by the comments they posted, but quite a few remained a mystery. Who were they? Where were they? And was the garden-gnome thief himself—or herself—reading her posts? Pushing away from her desk, she scooped Tadpole out of her little red box and nuzzled her with her nose.

"Okay, stop stalling," she said to herself as she gazed into the tiny creature's shiny black eyes. "I need to get ready. I don't need to think of it as a date. It just is what it is, that's all."

She secured the hamster in her cage, picked up her mug, and made a face after taking a sip of tepid tea.

"Gross." She carried it into the kitchen, dumped the contents down the drain and set the empty mug in the sink along with her breakfast dishes.

"I would love a cup of coffee." She gazed longingly at the coffeemaker, desperately wishing for a cup of steaming hot caffeine. Instead, she settled for a glass of filtered water from the fridge.

Emily looked through the window in the kitchen door that led to a narrow wooden deck with a railing that would never pass a safety inspection and a flight of stairs that served as a fire escape. Emily stared at the backs of the buildings across the lane, thinking as she often did, that back lanes told a city or town's real story better than the facades that faced the street. Compared to most, Riverton's lanes were surprisingly hospitable, but they still told a tale of their own. Hmm. This would make a good series of photo essays for her blog. As soon as she solved the garden-gnome mystery.

Her stomach growled, bringing her back to reality.

And before she solved that, she needed to get ready for dinner.

She walked into her bedroom. It had been a crazy roller-coaster kind of day. She was having a baby, a reality she was still having an impossible time wrapping her mind around. On the one hand, she didn't feel any different, although she knew that would change as her body changed. On the other, she was an emotional wreck with serious doubts about her ability to raise a child compounded by a concern she might be doing it alone. Still, after years of fantasizing about dating Jack, it was actually happening. Tonight.

And now she was running a little late. She'd need to hurry if she was going to be ready when he arrived to pick her up. She shed her flowy top, peeled off her jeans and undies, and tossed everything into the hamper. In the bathroom, she turned on the shower, twisted her hair into a loose bun to keep it dry and stepped into the spray, lathering her loofah with vanilla-coconut-scented shower gel.

She had blindsided Jack with her pregnancy news. His suggestion of marriage had not only been a knee-jerk reaction; it was something they would quickly come to regret if she said yes. Besides, he was going back to Chicago tomorrow. That was where he lived and worked, but it was not the right place for her. He worked long hours every day, which meant she would be on her own with the baby. And right now, the only thing she knew for sure about raising a child was she couldn't do it alone. She needed her family.

Emily didn't know Jack well, but she knew he was used to getting what he wanted. The problem was he didn't so much want her—he hardly knew her, so how could he?—as much as he wanted to do the right thing. She liked that his gut reaction had taken him in that direction, but rushing into marriage with a virtual stranger was wrong on every level.

She rinsed away the tropical-scented foam from her body, stepped out of the shower, toweled herself dry and quickly slipped into her dressing gown.

So in spite of her turning down his offer of marriage, they were going out. A get-to-know-you dinner with the promise of a good-night kiss.

The memory of his mouth on hers turned her insides to molten lava, the thought of his hands…

No. No hands, not tonight. Throwing caution to the wind had landed them in this situation. Continuing to be impulsive would only complicate things further. They needed to be cautious, take this one step at a time. They were going to be parents, and nothing could change that. Now they needed to figure out if they could be parents *together*. That would take some time.

Enough with the ruminations. Emily swiped at the steamy, full-length mirror on the inside of the bathroom door. She had been obsessing over these thoughts and questions all day. It was time to get ready and face the music, and she still needed to figure out what to wear.

Under normal circumstances, she would call her sisters with a fashion 911, but not today. They would pepper her with questions she wasn't ready to answer. She would see how things went with Jack this evening, then tomorrow she would sit down for a heart-to-heart with Annie and CJ. Tonight, she and her wardrobe were on their own.

She flung open her closet. Over the years, she had learned to disguise her lack of fashion sense by adopting what she liked to think of as a classic wardrobe—slacks and pencil skirts in grays, browns and blacks that could be mixed and matched with shirts and sweaters in white, cream and tan. She also owned several pairs of jeans like the pair she'd squeezed herself into this morning, the new gold-colored top she'd worn with them, and one soft pink cashmere sweater she had purchased on a whim and from which she had yet to remove the tags.

She pulled open a dresser drawer. Even her underwear was boring. Plain white bras designed to get the job done. White cotton panties that covered everything that was supposed to be covered and didn't argue with the clothes she wore over top. Granny panties, CJ called them. Her little sister, by comparison, wouldn't dream of wearing anything so serviceable. CJ was tall and willowy with the muscle tone of a young woman who led an active life. Her underwear drawer displayed a rainbow of thongs, bikinis and boy-cut briefs, as well as matching bras designed to make a woman's natural endowments into something just a little bit more.

Emily withdrew a bag she'd tucked into the back of the drawer, held her breath, opened it. She stared at the luscious, lacy, cotton-candy-colored lingerie she had shopped for—again, on impulse—not long after that night with Jack. Back when she had believed there would be other nights. Carefully, she removed the garments from the bag, enjoying the memory of how vibrant and attractive she had felt when she'd tried them on in the fitting room at Victoria's Secret in St. Paul.

Emily's secret, she'd thought at the time, as she had fantasized about the next time she and Jack would be together. Maybe he would have driven in from Chicago on Friday and surprised her. Or maybe he would have called and invited her to come to the city for the weekend. Either way, she would have been ready.

Of course, neither had happened. Her secret had stayed in the vault, and her new undergarments hidden in the back of a dresser drawer.

She fingered the soft lace. Should she wear them tonight? Her self-esteem could use a boost, and it wasn't as though Jack was going to see them. She ran a hand over her belly. And it wouldn't be long before they didn't fit... No way. She stuffed them into the bag and returned them to the back of her drawer. She would wear the pink sweater, though, and a pair of black pants with her new black pumps. Maybe the extra height would elevate her self-confidence.

After she was dressed, she swiped mascara onto her lashes, applied a layer of shimmery lip gloss and studied her reflection as she picked up her hairbrush. Her hair was a boring shade of brown, and her bra size was still the same as it had been when she was a high school freshman. When Annie was expecting Isaac, she'd gone up two cup sizes. Emily turned sideways, studied her profile, and tried to picture how her body would look a few months from now, or in seven months before the baby was born.

"Oh, my." Her hands trembled, and then the tremors rolled through her like a wave, leaving her breathless and a little light-headed. *Oh, my. Oh, my-oh-my-oh-my.* She had another human being growing inside of her, a tiny little person whose father was a virtual stranger. She managed to slow her ragged breathing a mere moment before she heard the knock on her door.

CHAPTER NINE

JACK ANGLED INTO a parking space in front of the newspaper office, checked his reflection in the rearview mirror, ran his knuckles along his stubbled jaw. He hoped Emily could live with a little scruff. The session with Rose Daniels had taken a lot longer than anticipated, but he had managed to wrap things up at the police station just before the time he had arranged to pick up Emily. He couldn't afford to be late. He already had plenty to atone for without having her add another no-show to her growing list of his faults.

This had been a day like no other. His spur-of-the-moment trip to Riverton had delivered a lot of unexpected results. A baby, a job offer, a cooperative witness. A baby. With an uncooperative mother.

Over dinner, he would share the epiphany he'd had during his interview with Rose. That poor kid, born to a drug addict who had managed to stay clean during her pregnancy but had relapsed by the time the child was a toddler. Rose's father had taken off as soon as he'd found out she was on the way. Somehow, in spite of the drugs and a series of failed relationships with unsuitable men, Scarlett Daniels had managed to keep her life and the baby's life together for nearly a year and a half before Rose had been taken into foster care. Who did these things when they were responsible for a defenseless child? To a baby too small to do anything for herself, too vulnerable to know how to ask for help?

A lot of people, he reminded himself. During his years with the Chicago PD, he'd seen more than his share of neglected, abused and discarded children. He'd wanted to believe that once those kids were in the hands of the authorities, social services would take care of them. Any kind of foster home had to be better than where they'd come from. For many, he supposed that was true, but not for Rose Daniels. Not for a lot of kids.

He needed Emily to know that when it came to this baby…*their* baby…he was in. One hundred percent all in. His instincts told him she was going to be an amazing parent, just like her sister and her father. He thought about his own family—growing up with both parents, the comfortable home, every opportunity possible, never wanting for anything. He had his own perfect role model for being a great dad, and a big pair of shoes to fill.

Growing up in Riverton, Jack hadn't encountered many families that weren't like his and his friends. But after he'd moved to the city, he'd seen the difference almost immediately. At the first domestic dispute he'd attended as a rookie, he'd been sickened by the sight of two runny-nosed kids in disheveled clothes and dirty diapers cowering in the back of a bedroom closet. Riverton was an ideal place to raise a family. That thought set off a quiet voice in the back of his head reminding him of Gord Fenwick's job offer, but as he'd pointed out to the chief, he wasn't cut out for that kind of work. Besides, plenty of people raised healthy, well-adjusted kids in Chicago.

Jack stepped out of his Jeep and reached into the back seat for a small package. He'd figured that flowers would seem as though he was trying too hard, so he'd made a quick stop at the hardware store after leaving the barbershop that afternoon. Before second-guessing the appropriateness of the gift, or whether any gift was appropriate at this stage of their relationship, he tucked the box under his arm and knocked on Emily's door. He heard footsteps on the stairs, and then there she was on the

other side of the glass. She unlatched the door
and pushed it open for him.

"Hi," she said.

"Hi."

"You're right on time."

"I didn't want to give you a reason to cancel our dinner plans."

"I wouldn't have done that."

"Good to know."

"Do you want to come up? I need to get my
purse and a jacket."

"Sure." He followed her up the stairs, eye
level with some enticingly feminine curves.
He shook his head. Tonight was about building
trust. However, that wouldn't stop him from
looking. He stepped into the living room behind her and immediately his attention was
drawn to the cage on the bookshelf and the
squeak, squeak, squeak of the wire wheel
where a small rodent doggedly ran a race to
nowhere.

Emily faced him with a smile that was both
tentative and guarded.

"I have something for you," he said, offering
the package. It was personal, but not too personal, and he hoped she'd see the humor in it.

"Oh. You didn't need to get me anything."

"Well, I did."

He shoved his hands into his pockets, held

his breath while she quickly tore off the gift wrap, then felt himself relax when she laughed. "A new hamster wheel. Thanks."

"No problem. I remembered this one squeaks."

"It does, as you can hear, so thank you. From me and Tadpole." She picked up a gray jacket draped over the back of her desk chair.

"Let me help with that." He held the jacket so she could slip her arms into the sleeves, settled the garment onto her shoulders and resisted the urge to touch the soft earlobe she exposed by tucking her hair behind it.

"Did you say Tadpole?" he asked.

"Yes, that's my hamster's name."

"Interesting."

"My nephew came up with it. My sister let him get one for a pet, and about two weeks later his new pet gave birth to five pups. He named them after his favorite things—Firefly, Caterpillar, Ladybug, Tadpole and—" She paused as she tried to remember the fifth name. "And Pumpkin. They were born right before Halloween."

Jack laughed. "Sounds like he has a good imagination."

Emily's sudden smile was filled with fondness. "He does. Dinosaurs are his new favorite thing, so if she'd been born more recently, her name might have ended up being *Gigantosaurus*. Not exactly hamsterish."

"Not exactly," he said, glancing at the tiny honey-colored creature on the squeaky wheel. Neither was Tadpole, but it was oddly fitting at the same time.

Emily picked up her keys and a small black handbag off her desk. "I'm ready."

She didn't sound ready.

"After you." He followed her down the stairs, waited while she locked the street-level door, and held open the passenger door of his Jeep. The gift had served as a momentary ice-breaker, but now that they had covered her nephew's pet-naming conventions, neither of them seemed to know what to say. Emily was keeping her head down and eyes averted.

He slid behind the wheel, keyed the ignition, started the engine. He couldn't think of the last time a situation had made him feel this awkward, and now he felt he needed a knife to slice through the tension. Whether she liked it or not, he was in her life now, and if she needed time to get used to the idea, he was fine with that. He was a patient man and willing to give her time. Within reason.

"I thought we'd drive across the river to the Minnesota side, have dinner in Wabasha. Is that okay with you?"

"Oh, yes." Her relief was audible. "I hoped you'd suggest something like that. It would be weird to have dinner here in town."

He would have said uncomfortable, but weird? The conversation they were about to have would be awkward in a public place where everyone knew them, but he decided it best not to remind her they'd had dinner at the Riverton Bar & Grill not that long ago, and there'd been no weirdness. Now the only awkwardness stemmed from the silence filling the Jeep.

"Do you mind if I turn on the radio?" she asked.

"Not at all."

"What would you like to listen to?" She pushed the start button, and the voice that poured from the speakers made her turn to him. Saturday evening. Garrison Keillor. *A Prairie Home Companion.* "You listen to NPR?"

"Most of the time, yes."

She leaned back in her seat, and he could tell she was watching him. "Me, too."

"You sound surprised."

"No. Well, maybe. I thought…"

But she didn't say what she thought, and he found himself very much wanting to know. Still, they both relaxed a little and the tension eased as they crossed the Mississippi to the Minnesota side and drove onto a main street that resembled Riverton's in a lot of ways, with one exception. Few people here would know them, no one would be surprised to see them together and no one would be nosily straining to overhear their conversation.

He steered into a lot next to a pizzeria on the outskirts of town. He and Emily hadn't had time to talk about the kind of meal they were in the mood for, but based on experience, Italian was a safe bet. Emily climbed out of the Jeep before he made it around to her side. He understood why a woman would want to be independent, but this was a date. He was supposed to open doors and hold chairs and help with coats. If Emily thought he was old-fashioned, then fine. Guilty as charged.

EMILY CAREFULLY STUDIED the menu, hoping the time she spent reading each item's description, including the veal parmesan, which she had no intention of ordering, didn't seem to be the obvious pretense it was. She couldn't remember ever feeling this uncomfortable, and that included coming face-to-face with Jack in the barbershop that afternoon. She was on a first date with her baby's father, which felt even more ridiculous than it sounded. She'd been intimate with this man, and now she couldn't make eye contact. Dinner had been a bad idea. They should have started with coffee.

A young man in a white shirt and black pants with a white waiter's apron set two glasses of ice water on the table and the wine list in front of Jack. "Can I get you something else?" he asked. "A bottle of wine? A cocktail?"

"I'll have coffee," Emily said without looking up. "Decaf, please."

"Coffee for me, too," Jack said, setting the drink menu aside. "Not decaf."

She finally braved an upward glance. "Just because I'm not having anything stronger doesn't mean you can't."

"I'm driving."

"Right." She turned her attention back to the menu. She was ravenously hungry, and the scents of simmering tomato sauce and melting cheese wafting from the kitchen were making her light-headed. Those and Jack's commanding presence across the table. His proximity had her heart racing.

The waiter returned, set down two cups of coffee and a small pitcher of cream, tucked the tray under his arm and flicked a lighter to the candle in the center of the table.

"Are you ready to order?" the young man asked.

Emily nodded. "A garden salad to start. I'd like the spaghetti with marinara sauce, and a couple of meatballs on the side. Does that come with garlic bread?"

"I'll bring a bread basket for you. And for you, sir?"

"I'll have the same." Jack was smiling, she could tell. It was the same meal they'd had two months ago.

The waiter took their menus and returned a moment later, as promised, with a bread basket and a small plate of olive oil and balsamic vinegar. Emily pounced on a slice of warm focaccia, swirled it through the oil and savored the crunch of rosemary and coarsely ground salt as she bit into it.

"I'm so hungry, I could eat a house," she said.

Jack laughed. "I thought the saying was, 'I'm so hungry, I could eat a horse.'"

"My sister CJ always flipped out when anyone said that, so my dad changed it to house. I know it doesn't make sense. Eating a whole house is just silly, but we were all little, and we never really gave it much thought."

"When you think about it, it's not a lot sillier than eating a horse."

"That's true."

"So," Jack said, helping himself to a slice of bread. "Blue. Martin. April seventh."

Bewildered, Emily set her bread on her side plate and stared at him. "Excuse me?"

"In the spirit of getting to know one another… my favorite color, my middle name, my birthday."

His directness startled a laugh out of her. "Hmm. I didn't expect getting to know one another to work like a game show. And blue is every guy's favorite color."

"I guess that makes me predictable."

"Oh, I doubt it." But she decided to play along. "So it's Jack Martin Evans. Is that a family name?"

"Jack is short for Jackson, but don't even think about calling me that. Unless you want to sound like my mother after I've done something to annoy her."

She smiled. "Noted."

"Martin was my maternal grandfather's name."

"And your birthday was—" She narrowed her eyes as the memory of that day flooded back. "That was the day of Eric's funeral."

"It was."

"But you didn't say anything."

"That day wasn't about me, although…" He

reached across the table and briefly touched her hand. "When we were together, I was definitely thinking, *happy birthday to me*."

Of course you were. Emily lowered her gaze and fumbled with the slice of bread she'd been eating, knowing she was blushing every shade of pink imaginable and not wanting him to know her thoughts had taken the same path. Not to mention it had turned out to be the gift that would keep on giving.

"Your turn," he said.

"For what?"

"Three things about you."

"Well, I guess I have more than one favorite color. I love green. I never wear it, but I like to be surrounded by it, if that makes sense. I didn't used to like yellow until Annie renovated the kitchen at the farm. Now I love it, too. And red, because it reminds me of my mother." She had blurted that out without thinking and immediately wished she hadn't. She didn't want to talk about her mother, ever, and especially not tonight. Not with Jack.

"Red was your mom's favorite color?"

"No. I mean, I don't know what her favorite color was…is…but her name is Scarlett."

A look of surprise flashed across Jack's face, and then it was gone.

"Is something wrong?" she asked.

"What? No. Of course not. I—" He seemed to be trying to unscramble his thoughts. "I'm sorry. When you mentioned your sister's kitchen, I flashbacked to Eric. He was never that handy around the house, but I remember him telling me about the kitchen reno. He'd finally figured one end of the hammer from the other. It's hard to believe he's gone."

He watched her closely. She felt a sharp tug of emotion as she always did when she was unexpectedly reminded of her family's loss.

"I know. Some days it's impossible to believe. When I go out to the farm, I still expect to see him with Isaac, showing him how to shoot hoops, or playing a game of cribbage with my dad, or going on about some amazing meal Annie was making. I don't know how my sister does it, how she gets through each day."

"One day at a time, I guess. And she has Isaac."

Emily nodded. "She does. He's a great kid. And she's an amazing mother. I don't know how she learned to be that way, since we grew up without one."

Jack's scrutiny was intense, but he didn't respond. Instead, he flipped the conversation back to what they'd been talking about. "So now I know you have more than one favorite color. What about the other two things?"

"Very few people know my middle name."

"And now I'll be one of them."

She sighed. "This goes in the vault, okay?"
He nodded.

"You have to agree, or I'm not telling you."

"In the vault," he said. "I swear. But seriously, how bad can it be?"

"It's—" she lowered her voice "—Esmeralda."

The corners of Jack's mouth twitched, and she could tell it was a struggle for him to smile.

"Seriously," she said. "Who does that to a child?"

"I…I don't know."

"It's a good name for a witch. Or a flamenco dancer. But it's not a normal person's name. I would never do that to a child."

Jack reached across the table again, covered her hand with his and held it there this time. "Agreed. Especially not this one."

Emily swallowed hard against the lump forming in her throat. He was still being so okay with this, but what would happen when the shock wore off and reality finally hit him? Which would most likely happen the instant he returned to Chicago to his life and his job and his friends. It had happened the last time he'd left, and she had no reason to believe this time would be any different.

He gave her hand a gentle squeeze before he withdrew his. "You still need to give me one more piece of information."

"Right. My birthday's on August first." She selected another slice of bread from the basket, dipped it and bit into it.

Jack took his phone out of his pocket and tapped the screen. "It's in my calendar. What about the baby?"

"December thirtieth. Annie looked it up this morning."

Jack tapped that information into his phone and tucked it away as the waiter arrived with their salads. Emily drizzled a citrus vinaigrette over hers, and Jack spooned ranch dressing onto his.

They took their first bites in silence. As Jack stabbed a cherry tomato with his fork, his next question caught her off guard. "You've never mentioned your mother before now. She's not in Riverton, is she?"

"No. To be honest, I have no idea where she is. She left when I was four, and I don't remember much about what happened. Our dad was in the military in those days and he'd been deployed to Iraq during Desert Storm.

He left the three of us girls and our mom at the farm with his parents, my grandparents."

"I've heard about your dad's military service. He's always been something of a legend around Riverton."

Emily smiled at that. "To us, he's always just been Dad, but as I got older, I realized he is pretty amazing. He came back from that tour of duty in a wheelchair, raised a family, ran the farm. That wheelchair has never stopped him from doing anything he wanted to do. I don't have any memories of him without it, so for me, that chair is as much a part of him as his big heart and quirky sense of humor."

Jack nodded thoughtfully. "I remember him at Annie and Eric's wedding, accompanying her down the aisle, making the toast to the bride."

"There wasn't a dry eye in the room." She remembered sitting next to Jack at the reception—the maid of honor and the best man—and fantasizing about her wedding someday. An adult woman having silly, schoolgirl thoughts.

"After he came back from Iraq, did all of you stay on at the farm?"

"We did. Grandpa Finn had a stroke just before my dad returned and our grandma needed help running the place."

"And your mom?"

"She stuck around for a couple of months. Annie's two years older than I am, so she remembers more about what happened. She says our mom didn't like being in a small town and hated living on the farm even more. Plus, she didn't get along with my grandparents."

"Rural living isn't for everyone."

Emily shrugged. "I guess not. I can't imagine growing up anywhere else, though. I didn't mind being away when I went to college, but after I graduated and worked as a copy editor for the *Star Tribune*, I realized I wasn't cut out for life in the city. I need to be close to my family."

Jack either didn't pick up on that or chose to ignore it. "So, you and your sisters don't talk to your mother? See her?"

"No, we don't. And we've never seen her, not even once." No one had ever asked her so many questions about her mother. At first, she hadn't minded answering them. Now they made her wary. "Like I said, she left a few months after my dad came home. I don't know if he heard from her, either."

Emily and Jack sat back as the waiter arrived with their main courses. "Oh, my. This sauce smells so good." She picked up her knife and fork. "Anyway, no one ever specifically told me and my sisters not to ask about our mom, but somehow we knew we shouldn't."

"So you don't know where she went?" he asked. "Where she is now?" She could see him watching with amusement as she cut into a meatball and ate half of it, then swirled spaghetti onto her fork.

"I have no idea." She gave him a direct look, searching for clues to where this conversation was going. Instead, she got his poker face. She slid the pasta into her mouth and licked the excess sauce off her lips.

For a few seconds, he seemed to forget what they were talking about, then shook his head and picked up his own fork. "Have you tried looking for her? There's a wealth of information on the internet."

She laughed. "I'd be a lousy reporter if I hadn't thought of that, so, yeah, I've looked."

"And?"

"Nothing besides a couple of dead ends, but maybe I didn't look hard enough. I know it sounds crazy, but I've always had this dream she would come home someday, that we'd be a family again." *Sounds crazy?* she asked herself. What was completely crazy was the fact she had never shared this secret with anyone but Fred, not even her family, although she knew they suspected it. Why had she blurted it out to Jack?

"Nothing crazy about that," he said. "Wanting your family to be together has to be the most natural thing in the world."

His understanding was touching, but his questions were stirring up emotions she rarely allowed herself to explore.

"Tell me about your family," she said, and for the rest of the meal he did. He talked about his older sister, Faith, who lived in a refurbished loft in San Francisco and worked as a travel agent. He told her tales about growing up in his family's home on Second Avenue and how he and his sister had both known from an early age they had wanted to get out of Riverton. And with a sinking heart, Emily realized that baby or no baby, she and Jack didn't just want different things, they *needed* different things.

BY THE TIME dinner was over and they were back in Riverton, Emily experienced something akin to relief.

When Jack parked in front of her building, he put a hand on her arm. "Let me get the door for you."

She knew Jack would honor her date-night

request and not expect to be invited up, but there was no need for him to walk her to her door. It was right there across the sidewalk. But he would anyway. He was that kind of man.

They had lingered over coffee and dessert— one serving of tiramisu, two forks—just like a real date. And it was going to end like a real date, she thought with trepidation. He was going to walk her to her door and kiss her good-night.

So, she waited as he walked around to her side of the Jeep. The way he looked—the thick, dark hair swept away from his forehead, the stubble on his jaw—literally took her breath away. He opened the door, offered his hand, which she accepted. It took them four steps to reach her apartment door.

"Someone might see us," she reminded him.

"I'm not worried about that."

Anticipation heated her belly, setting every nerve ending alight. "I thought that's why we went across to Wabasha to have dinner, so no one would see us together."

He shook his head. "We went there, so no one would listen in on our conversation. This…"

He lowered his head and brought his mouth to hers, softly and with purpose, gently but with passion. Light-headed, Emily closed her eyes, swayed, secure in knowing the strong arms around her wouldn't let her fall. She lifted one hand and indulged her desire to touch his face.

A few moments passed, and then Jack lifted his head. "I'm okay with the whole world seeing this."

She let her hand fall away, wishing she felt as easy with this as Jack did, but how could she? He was going back to Chicago tomorrow, and she was staying here. This was her world. They hadn't talked about when he would be back again or if he would be back. They had spent the evening talking about family, friends, the past. There had been no talk about the future.

For anyone who might be watching, she and Jack probably looked like two people who were falling in love, or who were already in love. A real couple who potentially had a future together instead of two impulsive adults who had let their grief over losing a loved one override their common sense. The truth was they lived very separate lives in two very different places. Tomorrow, he would return to a life that, by his own admission, fully consumed him to the point he had no time for anything or anyone.

"What about you?" he asked.

"What about me?"

"Are you okay with us being seen together?"

His hands still rested on her shoulders. As much as the kiss had set her nerves humming, she wished he would let her go. If anyone saw them like this, if word of this found its way to her sisters before she talked to them…

His hands fell away. "You had to think about that."

"It's just…my family… They don't know about us yet, and I'd like to be the one to tell them."

"Of course. I could have gone inside with you, kissed you there, but there would have been a problem with that, too." He smiled.

"What kind of problem?"

"I wouldn't want to leave." He touched his lips to her forehead. "Good night, Emily. I'll stop by in the morning before I head back to Chicago."

He waited until she was inside with the door locked before he climbed into his Jeep and drove away. With the memory of his kiss still tingling on her lips, her skin warm from his touch, she climbed the stairs, dreamily reflecting on what he had said. *I wouldn't want to leave.*

She might not have let him.

CHAPTER TEN

AFTER THE BRIEF drive to his parents' house, Jack spent an hour in the kitchen with them over coffee and his mother's homemade banana bread. He didn't visit as often as he should, so he owed them that much.

His mother had done most of the talking, bringing him up to date on the local happenings around town, including Sig Sorrenson's upcoming funeral, as well as a rumor that had been circulating about Mayor Bartlett. Supposedly, he was to make a big announcement at the town council meeting on Monday. Jack knew exactly what that was about and kept quiet. His mother could hear about Chief Fenwick's retirement the same time everyone else did.

Jack answered her questions to the best of his ability while hoping she wouldn't think he was being evasive, though he definitely was. Yes, his interview with the witness had gone well that afternoon. No, he hadn't been working undercover; he hadn't found time to get a haircut. No, he hadn't heard about the mysterious disappearances of local garden gnomes. In his opinion, Riverton had far too many of them—garden gnomes, not mysterious disappearances—although he kept that to himself. Yes, the loss of her garden trowel was distressing. On that note, he faked a yawn and explained he'd had a long day, which was true, and excused himself.

She accepted a kiss on the cheek, tutted and waved him out of the kitchen when he tried to load his dishes into the dishwasher. He and his father exchanged a wink, and he finally climbed the stairs to his old room.

His mother hadn't changed a thing, so stepping through the doorway was usually akin to passing through a portal to his past. Tonight was different, though. The posters on the walls, the denim bedspread and the bedside lamp with the wobbly shade had lost the power to pull him back in time. Right now he was completely focused on the future.

He tossed his duffel bag onto the bed, unzipped it and removed his shaving kit. A future that made him feel like the driver of a tractor tailor careening downhill with no brakes. He was going to be a father. A father! The enormity of the situation hadn't really sunk in yet. Maybe that explained why he wasn't in full-blown panic mode. This morning, sitting at his desk in Chicago, he had dallied over the notion he might be halfway in love with Emily Finnegan. Was there even such a thing as halfway in love? It had felt a little more than halfway when he'd seen her at Morris's that afternoon.

He crossed the hall to the bathroom. Unfortunately, according to every woman he'd ever had a relationship with, he was lousy at them. And now Emily had added herself to that list. But Emily wasn't like the others. And while it seemed to him that turning down his proposal was unreasonable, he admired her for having a mind of her own.

He took out his electric razor, faced the mirror and went to work. Emily would come around, though. She would have to. Maybe her sisters could talk some sense into her, make her see that moving to Chicago would be the best and simplest thing for everyone. It wasn't like he was asking her to go to the ends of the earth. Chicago was less than a day's drive from Riverton. She could visit her family as often as she liked.

He hadn't mentioned the job offer to her. Not because he was trying to hide anything, but because he wasn't going to take it. Him, chief of police? Did he have what it would take to head up a police department, even a small one like Riverton's? Gord believed he did. And then there was the matter of returning to Riverton. Could he make this his home? No way.

Then again, what if Emily refused to go to Chicago? He didn't see himself being a satellite parent, only dropping by when it was convenient. Would Emily even tolerate that? Doubtful. She challenged him to look at things in a way he hadn't considered before, the way she talked about her family being a case in point. Maybe it was the journalist in her. Her independence intrigued him. She downplayed her total gorgeousness. Her emotions were carefully controlled, and he suspected if she were to fall in love with someone like him—and baby or no baby, that could be a very big if—she would never wear her heart on her sleeve. She might not take it out of its concrete casing, either, he thought wryly. There was no question she dearly loved her family, but from listening to her tonight, he'd come away with the sense she had never fully recovered from being abandoned by her mother.

A mother named Scarlett. The name had hit him like a bolt out of the blue, and for a few seconds, he had replayed his interview with Rose Daniels. Was Emily's mother…? Was

Rose's mother…'? No. No way. But how weird would that be?

He had nearly given himself away when Emily had said her mother's name. Now he congratulated himself on making the save, letting her think he'd been reacting to memories of Eric.

Jack had no trouble believing in coincidences. He'd experienced one today, coming to town on the very day Emily discovered she was having his baby. But for Rose Daniels, who also had a mother named Scarlett, to appear in Riverton, a town she apparently had no previous ties to, with a plan to stay at a B & B that was the former home of Scarlett Finnegan and now run by the woman's oldest daughter? Coincidences like that were harder to swallow. Make that impossible.

First thing in the morning, he intended to see Emily before he returned to the city, and nothing was going to derail that plan. He needed to reassure her he wouldn't disappear, not this time. Maybe he would take her out for breakfast. Or, better idea, he could take breakfast to her.

He had also agreed to swing by the station and have coffee with Chief Fenwick, who had probably invited him so he could keep urging him to accept the job offer. Then, on his way out of town, he would stop at the Finnegan farm. Dropping in to see his best friend's widow and her son was a perfectly natural thing to do, and the impromptu visit would give him a chance to check up on Rose, remind her he was keeping an eye on her. And if she did have ulterior motives for hanging around the Finnegan family home, well, she would know he'd be keeping tabs on that, too.

Jack angled his head and ran a hand over his face while he checked his reflection in the mirror. Emily didn't seem to mind the scruff, but this should satisfy his mother.

As soon as he was back in Chicago, he'd dig into Scarlett Daniels's past. If Emily's mother and Rose's mother turned out to be the same woman…

He squeezed toothpaste onto his toothbrush.

If it turned out that Emily and Rose had the same mother—and although that was a big if, it was entirely possible—then someone would need to break the news to Emily and the rest of her family. After everything she'd told him today—how she doubted her ability to be a good mother in the absence of a role model, how she secretly dreamed about the day when her mother would come home, that she'd been keeping journals most of her life so she could share them with her mom when that day finally arrived—he worried about her reaction.

Oh, man. He'd sure hate to be the one to burst that bubble. Emily clearly didn't trust him, and he could hardly blame her for that. So far, he hadn't done much to earn that trust. With her here in Riverton and him in Chicago, closing the gap between them would be tough enough. Telling her about her mother—if indeed Scarlett Daniels was her mother—would not endear him to her. It could even widen the rift between them.

He rinsed his toothbrush and then gargled a mouthful of some nasty-tasting mouthwash he found in the medicine cabinet.

"You're getting ahead of yourself."

For as long as he'd been friends with Annie and Eric, he had known that the Finnegan sisters' mother had left when the girls were young, but that was all he knew. Tomorrow, he could ask his mother about Scarlett Finnegan, find out if she remembered anything about the woman. That would seem kind of random, though. He had promised Emily to keep quiet about the two of them and the baby until she had talked to her sisters. Until she did, it was best not to arouse his mother's suspicion. She would insist on an explanation, and she had a knack for knowing when he was being evasive.

Safer to put those questions on hold till he was back in Chicago and could take a closer look at Scarlett Daniels's file, maybe call social services to see if they could shed more light on her background. Someone would have the answers he was looking for. He just hoped he was going to like what he heard.

ALONE IN HER APARTMENT, Emily slipped off her jacket and tossed it onto the back of a chair, set her purse on her desk next to the box with the new hamster wheel. It was an unusual gift, and yet strangely intimate at the same time. The morning after their one night together, he had commented that for a small animal, the hamster made a lot of racket. She wondered if the new wheel meant to say that if he did spend the night again, he didn't want Tad to keep him awake. Thinking about it meant tonight would be a sleepless night for her.

She prowled around the apartment, unable to settle her nerves. Finally, she decided on a cup of the tea her sister had given her. Chamomile was supposed to have a soporific effect, wasn't it? As she waited for the kettle to boil, her phone buzzed with an incoming text message.

How was your date? FM

Emily rolled her eyes and replied to Fred.

It wasn't a date. Em

He walked you to your door & kissed you g'night.

How on earth did he know that?

Are you spying on me?

Nope. Grabbing a bite to eat at the café.

For heaven's sake. She poured boiling water over the tea bag in her cup. *This* was why she shouldn't have let Jack kiss her in public. What if someone else had seen them?

Who else is there?

No one. Slow night. I'm the only one sitting by the window. :)

She pulled the tea bag out of her mug, dropped it into the sink by its string and stirred in a little sugar. She carried her phone and the steaming mug of disgustingly yellow liquid into the living room and looked out the front window. Fred waved from the window of the Riverton Bar & Grill. She set the mug on the sill.

Good night Fred.

Sweet dreams Em. ;)

The winky face bugged her more than it should have, and she was tempted to try having the last word. Then again, considering the lie she'd told her sisters, she owed it to him to back down gracefully. Besides, he was having far too much fun with this, and he would gleefully persist with this cyber-banter for as long as she let him. So she gave him a casual wave, then used the same hand to give her hair a dramatic flip as she grabbed her mug and twirled away from the window. Fred's wide grin, which she caught out of the corner of her eye, took some of the fun out of her flounce.

She busied herself by replacing the squeaky wheel in the hamster cage with the new one from Jack, laughing at the sleepy-eyed glare she received from Tadpole. The animal didn't enjoy being woken up even though she had no compunction about disturbing the slumbers of others.

Emily eyed her laptop, debated turning it on to check her blog and her email, and decided against it, finding herself drawn to the ancient oak filing cabinet she'd salvaged from the newspaper office after her boss had decided to spruce up the place.

She opened the bottom drawer and surveyed the notebooks filling it. Some were hardbound with pretty pictures on the covers—a field of wildflowers, a cluster of unbearably cute kittens, majestic snow-capped mountains—impractical, but cherished gifts from friends and family. Most, though, were spiral-bound notebooks, which she preferred because they would lie flat when open. Much easier to write in.

She pulled out several books at random and thumbed through them. She had first started keeping a diary when she was eleven. She had graduated to journaling story ideas while in college. She still recorded her private thoughts in a diary and had scribblers filled with rough notes and outlines for her *Gazette* articles. When she'd started keeping diaries, she had played around with the idea of addressing the entries to her mother, only Emily had never been able to figure out what to call her. She was pretty sure that before her mother left she had called her Mommy, although she couldn't be absolutely certain. *Dear Mommy* had sounded hopelessly juvenile to her pre-teen sensibilities. But *Dear Mom* didn't sound right, either. *Dear Mother* was too formal, and *Dear Scarlett* was too impersonal. In the end, Emily had elected to address the entries to herself. When her mother came back—and in those days, it had still been when and not if—Emily could share the journals with her because, of course, her mother would want to get to know her, to read all the hopes and dreams and secrets Emily would have shared with her mother if she had stayed.

Digging a little deeper into the drawer, she selected one of the fancier notebooks, one that had been a gift for her fourteenth birthday from Annie. That summer, Emily had saved the book and started writing it on the first day of high school. The sepia-tone cover featured a vintage typewriter superimposed over a background of canceled postage stamps from exotic locales. At the time, the image was meant to represent Emily's lofty dream of some-day being a foreign correspondent. Now, she flipped it open and was transported back to her first day of high school.

Dear Heart,
High school freaks me out. There's so

much stuff going on, so many kids I don't know—and that doesn't really make sense because Riverton's not that big and I thought I knew everyone. But as Fred pointed out (Fred's my best friend, BTW, not my boyfriend), Riverton has two elementary schools, but only one high school. So all those kids from the school on the other side of town who we never got to know are now our classmates.

My sister Annie is a junior this year, and it turns out she's pretty cool and popular at school. I had no idea. She's always just been Annie, the sister who's always looked out for me. Even though she's only two years older, she's been kind of like a surrogate mom, making sure my little sister, CJ, and I brush our teeth before we go to bed and stuff like that. Last year, she took me bra shopping when I finally started to grow what some might say pass for boobs. And she made sure I knew where she kept the pads and tampons when I started my first period.

But I digress. Today's journal entry isn't about that stuff. It's about me and high school and the cutest boy in Riverton. Probably the world. He's a friend of Annie's, but not *that* kind of friend. Annie has a thing for this boy named Eric, and the boy I like is Eric's best friend. After school today, I sneaked into Annie's bedroom and found his picture in last year's yearbook. His name is Jack Evans.

If Jack and I get married, do you know what that means? My name will be Emily Evans.

Emily closed her eyes and let the memories of that afternoon roll through her mind like a movie. It had been a typical late summer day in the Midwest. Her bedroom window had been open, a cool breeze fluttering the curtains. But she'd felt all warm and tingly. She'd been awash with hormonally fueled emotions, and hadn't known why, not understanding that puberty and a first crush had lit a fire in her.

She had studied herself in the mirror that afternoon, all those years ago, wishing for long blond hair, a bigger bra size and the kind of easygoing personality that let a girl giggle at anything a guy said.

"Face it, Emily. You wanted to be an airhead," she chided herself now, standing in front of a different mirror. Instead, reality had persisted. According to Fred, she still had the annoying tendency to tell a guy exactly what she thought, which was usually the polar opposite of how cool he considered himself to be.

She continued reading the sappy words she'd poured onto the pages all those years ago. She hadn't had a clue what love was, but she had certainly perfected infatuation. She paged ahead, smiled when she found the heart she'd drawn with red pen. Inside, "E. F. luvs J. E." At that point, they'd yet to have a conversation, and if he had known she even existed, it was only as his friend Eric's girlfriend's dorky little sister.

She flipped through more pages and was relieved to see her journal included other details about school and home. Fred had tried to talk her into joining the chess club, but she had joined the school newspaper and yearbook club instead. She had written about CJ, already a budding equestrian, and the blue ribbon she'd won for show jumping at the fall fair. Annie had been on student council and busily organizing bake sales and car washes to raise money for the year's activities at school.

Emily turned a few more pages. Ah, yes. Her first-ever school dance. Fred had gone, too, but not with her. He had all but ignored her and hung out with the boys from the chess club instead. Emily hadn't had a clue what to wear or how to do her hair, so Annie had helped. Taped to the page was the photograph their father had taken of them before he'd driven them to the school that night. Annie looked totally preppy and all grown up in a slim black skirt and a robin's-egg-blue sweater that set off her natural blond hair and vibrant blue eyes. Emily had worn a coral-colored baby-doll dress, white slouch socks and...she squinted at the picture...white sneakers? Her hair had been crimped and pulled into a side ponytail.

"Oh, Emily. Seriously, *what* were you thinking?" She stared a moment longer, transfixed by her utter lack of fashion sense. She had to have been at least three or four years out of style. If that train wreck of an outfit had ever been *in* style.

Pressing on, she read the entry she scrawled into her journal after the dance. A few of the words were blurred by watermarks—tears, she remembered—but she had no trouble reading them.

Dear Heart,
The dance was a complete, total, unmitigated disaster, and I am a dismal failure of a human being.

Not one boy asked me to dance. Not one, not even Fred. He didn't ask anyone else, either, which is lucky for him, otherwise our friendship would be o-v-e-r. Done. Finished.

Jack was there, of course, and he still doesn't know I exist. His girlfriend, Belinda, was there, too, of course. I think I hate her more than anything on the planet. Seriously, I like the leeches in our pond here at the farm better than her. Jack danced with her all night and they totally broke the school rule about slow dancing and how much space there's supposed to be between the guy and the girl. I thought the rule was completely gross until I saw them together, but now I know why there has to be a rule. What I'd like to know is why no one was enforcing it.

As always, Annie was amazing. How come she got all the cool genes in the family and I'm stuck with the nerdy ones? It's totally not fair. She's so pretty and popular and her boyfriend, Eric, is completely and madly in love with her. She told me that he's even said the L-word. Can you imagine? And she said she said it back.

On the bright side—and according to my dad there is always a bright side—nothing that happens in my life after this horrible night could possibly come close to being this desperately humiliating.

She had been so naive. Just as well that her sweet and innocent—not to mention overly verbose—fourteen-year-old self had no idea what the future had in store for her.

Not only did no one ask me to dance, but I overheard Belinda say to Jack how lame all the niners were, especially the girl geeks who have zero fashion sense. And she was looking right at me when she said it!!!!!

The exclamation points had been blurred by tears, but Emily could still count all five of them. And she still remembered Jack's lack of response to the insult.

Seriously, I wanted to shrivel up and die right then and there. Jack laughed, but he didn't notice me since he was too busy noticing Belinda. And believe me, there was a lot to notice! Her dress didn't cover up much. If you ask me, if the school can have a rule about slow dancing, then there should be a rule about what people are allowed to wear while slow dancing. Let's get real. There's a dress code for school. There should be one for school dances, too.

Emily groaned and shook her head, thinking back to the English essay she had written on that very topic. "You were so lame," she said to herself. Lame, lame, lame.

Fred had agreed, and then he had been annoyed she'd earned an A-plus on the paper. Apparently, their teacher had agreed with her. Fred's essay had been about the chess club, and how more students would discover how cool it was if they were only willing to give it a chance. Like that wasn't lame. He hadn't understood why their teacher had given him a B-minus. He had been equally annoyed when Emily had pointed out that while he might be a whiz at chess, his spelling and grammar needed work.

Emily smiled, thinking about fourteen-year-old Fred. He had also been a math genius, at least by her standards, and they had gradually fallen into a pattern of hanging out in the back room of his dad's barbershop after school. In exchange for her help with outlining and proofreading his English and history assignments, he had patiently explained algebraic formulas to her.

She continued reading the last paragraph of the school dance diary entry.

A few girls from my class and I hung out. We danced together a few times, but none of the boys noticed us. Even Fred ignored me, so why would a guy like Jack Evans pay attention to me? I might as well have been invisible. And as long as there are girls like Belinda Bellows around, then girls like me always will be. And so, dear Heart, that's it for me and school dances. I'm totally swearing off them. Good night.
Love, Emily

The entry was rife with teenage melodrama, but Emily found herself awash with the same emotions she'd experienced that night. If she'd had a mother, she would have curled up in her arms and cried her eyes out. Instead, she had crawled under the covers with her diary and her flashlight, and written her heart out.

There had been other dances, though, and she had gone to them, mostly because there was a chance Jack might notice her. But by the end of her sophomore year, she was still invisible. None of the boys at school, not even the ones in her class, paid any attention to her, and no one ever asked her to dance, let alone go on a date. By the time Annie was preparing for her senior prom, Emily had been in a complete funk, and she had been shocked by her sister's response when she finally confessed how she felt.

"You're always with Fred," Annie said.

"So? We're friends."

"Sure you are, but that's not how it looks to other boys. To them, the two of you look like a couple. If you want boys to notice you, you need to put yourself out there."

Thinking back on it now made Emily cringe. She had made up every excuse in the book to avoid hanging around with Fred and to "put herself out there." It hadn't worked, and after a week, she had decided to go back to being invisible because she missed her best friend.

Emily closed the diary and put it back in the cabinet. She ran a hand over her belly. "I never want you to feel this way, okay? Even if no one asks you to dance, I'll always be here to dry your tears and to tell you that things will get better."

They had for Emily, and she definitely hadn't been invisible tonight. Jack's full attention had been on her. He had even turned off his cell phone. He'd been thoughtful, attentive, involved, and he'd kissed her in public, saying he didn't care who saw them. So why wasn't she convinced he was one hundred percent committed? Because tomorrow he was going back to Chicago, and he would once again be caught up in some murder case, and Emily would once again be out of sight. Last time, she had also been out of mind. Would that happen again? Only time would tell.

CHAPTER ELEVEN

THE NEXT MORNING Emily blinked groggily and stretched her arms over her head. Something felt strange, and it took a moment to figure out what it was. The familiar squeak of Tadpole's old wheel had been replaced by the barely audible whisper of the new one. That should make Jack happy.

Thinking about him brought a rush of memories of last night's date, which were quickly swamped when she recalled the tender touch of his lips to hers. The kiss that almost wasn't.

She blinked, realizing she had dreamt about him last night, too. It had been one of those weirdly vivid dreams that seemed real and completely unreal all at the same time.

She was fourteen and sitting in homeroom with her crimped hair and wearing the ridiculous baby-doll dress. Everyone, even Fred, was pointing at her and laughing. Then Jack walked in, though it wasn't his homeroom. He completely ignored her and asked her homeroom teacher to dance, but old Mrs. Potter asked to see his hall pass and then gave him a detention when he couldn't produce one. Unfazed, Jack grabbed the teacher and spun her across the front of the classroom in a series of pirouettes. Emily's classmates leaped to their feet and broke into a chorus of "Girls Just Want To Have Fun." Mrs. Potter was surprisingly graceful in spite of her serviceable lace-up oxfords and arthritic hip. And then, as only happens in dreams and schmaltzy TV shows, Mrs. Potter turned into Belinda Bellows wearing a tiara. Her Miss Riverboat Queen sash didn't quite conceal her cleavage. Emily was left to watch from the sidelines.

She groaned and rubbed her eyes. Her dream had turned into an episode of *Glee*, and she was a total loser.

"I need coffee," she said out loud to herself, flinging back the covers and swinging her feet onto the floor. She ran her hands over her belly. "But I can't have coffee." Someday, this little person had better appreciate her giving up her favorite thing in the whole world. Emily wandered into the kitchen, still wearing the T-shirt and pajama pants she'd pulled on last night, not bothering with a robe. The morning sunshine streaming through the windows was already warming her apartment.

In all fairness to Jack, he had not left her sitting on the sidelines yesterday. As first dates went, it had been pretty wonderful. She loved that quaint little restaurant, and the only person she knew there was a woman whose son was in CJ's therapeutic riding program, but the woman didn't know who Jack was and wasn't at all surprised that Emily was having dinner with him.

She put on a pot of decaf, and while it brewed, she sliced a bagel in half and popped it into the toaster.

Last night, Jack had been, well, amazing. He had asked about her family, about how Annie and Isaac were managing since Eric's funeral, about her work on the newspaper. He had even asked about Tadpole, although she sensed he wasn't a fan of rodents. He hadn't seemed to want to talk about the case he was currently working on, a case that had coincidentally brought him back to Riverton, yesterday of all days, to interview a witness. He had talked about police work in general, though. She could tell he was proud of his work. He should be, and she knew he loved living in a big city. To him, the obvious solution to their situation was to get married and for her to move to Chicago with him. After having feelings for him for all these years—and she could privately acknowledge she still had them—

LEE McKENZIE   177

those feelings weren't enough to make her leave Riverton. He wasn't in love with her. She would be miserable in the city, and before long, he would miserable, too. That was the impasse, and she saw no way to bridge the gap between their two very different lives.

Then a knock at the door downstairs had her scurrying back to the bedroom and hastily pulling on her bathrobe.

EMILY ANSWERED THE door looking as though she had just rolled out of bed, a robe haphazardly cinched at the waist, hair adorably mussed, an empty coffee cup clutched in one hand.

"Good morning," Jack said.

"Good morning. You're early."

He glanced at his watch. "It's ten after nine. Did I wake you?"

"No, I've been up for a while. Just waiting for my coffee to finish brewing."

"I see."

"It's decaf," she said, sounding a little defensive. "Pregnant women aren't supposed to have caffeine."

"Ah, well, then, that explains a lot."

"What exactly?"

"Why you're so grumpy. Why you still haven't invited me in." He smiled as he said it, hoping to lighten her mood, and she returned the smile.

"Sorry," she said, stepping aside.

He joined her in the narrow vestibule. "No apology necessary."

"I'm not a morning person, and I really like to start my day with a good, strong cup of coffee," she said. "And then follow that up with at least four more throughout the day."

He locked the door behind him and followed her up the stairs, noting the pink-pigs-with-wings print on her yellow pajama pants and her bright green fuzzy frog slippers. Unpretentious, quirky, cute as all get-out.

"Coffee's ready," she said when they reached her apartment. "Would you like some?"

"Sure."

"It's decaf."

"So you said."

"Sorry, I'm not—"

"A morning person. I think we've established that." He set a bakery box on the tiny table for two in the small dining area next to the kitchen. "But here's the more important question. Are you a doughnut person?"

She gave him a narrow-eyed smirk. "Doughnuts? Isn't that kind of a cliché?"

"There's a cliché about pregnant women and doughnuts?" he asked, feigning innocence.

"Very clever, Mr. Police Officer stopping at the doughnut shop." She filled the mug she'd been clutching with eager anticipation, pulled another from a cupboard and filled it for him. Then she sat, lifted the lid of the box and sighed. "Mmm, jelly-filled. My favorite. How did you know?"

"Is there anyone who doesn't like them?" He waited till she chose one, then picked up another.

They sat and bumped doughnuts across the table, fell silent as they both bit and chewed and savored. He must have been grinning when she made eye contact again.

"What?" she asked.

He plucked a paper napkin from the holder on the table and swiped at her powdered sugar–dusted nose, a task that could have been accomplished with a kiss under different circumstances.

She laughed. "Not my best look."

"Distractingly cute, actually."

"I don't think anyone's ever called me cute. I've always been more of a plain Jane." Her eyes widened, and she hurried on. "Sorry, that was a dumb thing to say. I'm not fishing for compliments."

"No need to fish for them." Could a woman who looked knock-your-socks-off gorgeous in a natty bathrobe and fuzzy slippers really be insecure about her looks? Apparently. He made a mental note to say something nice to her more often.

"Did you have a good visit with your parents?" she asked. She was blushing now.

"I did, mostly over breakfast this morning. My mother made pancakes, bacon and eggs, and some kind of fruit-and-yogurt parfait thing that was surprisingly good."

Emily stared at him. "You had all that for breakfast, and now you're eating doughnuts?"

He grinned. He couldn't help himself. "Every good meal deserves dessert."

"I'd be as big as a house in no time," Emily said, laughing and then blushing again. "I will be anyway. I'm already getting too big for my jeans."

Knowing it was never wise to talk to a woman about her weight under any circumstances, he redirected the conversation back to his family. "My mother's biggest worry these days is the suspicious disappearance of her garden trowel." She had mentioned it again over breakfast that morning, and for the second time he had changed the subject.

"It's all very strange. I'm glad she told you."

It was a misplaced garden trowel. What was strange about that? "You know about this?"

Emily nodded. "She sent me an email yesterday."

Panic grabbed Jack by the throat. "I see."

But he didn't. Did Emily have regular email contact with his mother? And if so, why?

"It was for my blog," she explained. "I've written a series of posts on all the mysterious disappearances around town."

"So you don't have regular email contact with my mother?"

"Not at all. Why would I?"

Good question. He relaxed a little, knowing that his mother and his...the mother of his child...weren't in regular contact. "My mother didn't mention you had a blog." Or maybe he hadn't been paying attention. "She mentioned something about garden gnomes, though. What else has gone missing?"

"Stuff from people's yards, mostly. Garden ornaments, several gnomes, those sorts of things. And now your mom's trowel. The police think it's probably kids playing a prank, and Ken won't let me print the stories in the *Gazette*. He says they're not newsworthy enough, but the truth is, he doesn't want 'his town,' as he calls it, to look like a haven for petty thieves. So I've been blogging about it instead."

"Are you sure people haven't just misplaced them?"

She shrugged. "I've been marking the locations on the town map on my bulletin board, and there's definitely a pattern. All the thefts—" she must've seen his raised eyebrows because she amended that statement "—all the missing items are from the same part of town, and they always seem to disappear after dark."

He decided to play along. "So, no gnome-nappings in broad daylight. Interesting."

She frowned. "Now you're making fun of me."

"Guilty as charged. What's the name of your blog? I'll check it out, maybe put in a good word for you with Chief Fenwick."

"Very funny." She devoured the rest of the doughnut and chose another—a double-chocolate glazed this time. "My blog is called *Small Town, Big Hearts*. It should come up if you do a search for it."

"And my mother reads your blog?"

"I guess so. I'll be honest. I was completely shocked to get an email from her yesterday afternoon. Initially, I thought she was writing to me because you told her about…us. You have no idea how relieved I was to know she doesn't know yet."

*And you have no idea how relieved I am
that you and my mother aren't email buddies.*
"When are you going to tell your family?" he
asked.

"My sisters already know. They just don't
know about you."

"And Fred?"

"He's the best secret-keeper there is."

Jack wished he could believe that.

"I always go for Annie's Sunday dinner,
so I'll tell them tonight. I'm not ready to tell
my dad, though, and my sisters will keep this
under their hats."

"So, your sisters know about the baby and
they didn't ask about the father?"

Emily turned six shades of red. "Oh, um,
they did. I sort of…lied."

"Sort of? What exactly does that mean?"

She hung her head. "I wasn't going to tell
you this… It's so embarrassing… But I hadn't
heard from you, so I thought you thought it
had been a one-night stand. Since we weren't
together, I thought you might not want anyone
to know, so I lied. Sort of."

"And that lie was…?"

He watched her close her eyes and take a
deep breath, then let it out.

"I told them it was Fred's." She opened her
eyes and looked at him.

Momentarily speechless and not liking the direction his thoughts were headed in, he stared back.

"It was stupid and irresponsible and I'm sorry, but I'll fix it tonight."

Right now, her sisters were the least of his worries. "Is there a chance that Fred could be—"

Her eyes turned into saucers. "No! Good grief, no way! Fred and I are friends, always have been *just* friends." Her visceral response was a typical reaction for someone who was telling the truth and genuinely shocked by someone else's misconception. "You have to believe me. Fred and I were never... Oh, I can't even say it."

"Does he know your sisters think it's his?"

She nodded. "Trust me, he was as freaked out as you are. That's why he texted me to come to the shop yesterday afternoon."

And which further explained the man's nervous behavior when Jack had walked in for a haircut.

"Do you believe me?"

He did believe her. He briefly considered leaving her on the hook for a few minutes, but she seemed to be having difficulty catching her breath.

"I believe you. Just promise me you'll straighten this out today."

"I will," she said, still a little breathless. "If it's any consolation, they didn't believe me."

No consolation whatsoever. Add to that the fact that three people already knew Emily was pregnant. One of those people knew Jack was the father, and by tonight, the other two would be in the know. Emily trusted them to keep her secret until she was ready to tell her father and then announce the big news to the world.

Jack didn't trust anyone that much. He had woken up early, surprisingly refreshed and clearheaded from a sound sleep in his old maple captain's bed—a bed he'd slept in for half his life. He hadn't changed his mind about convincing Emily to marry him and move to Chicago. It was the only logical thing to do. Emily might think she could postpone the inevitable with a handful of get-to-know-you dates, but not for long. Once their families knew the truth, the pressure would be on. But what if Emily still refused to move to Chicago?

He planned to meet with Gord Fenwick later that morning. There would be more pressure to seriously consider if not outright accept the job offer. Jack had never contemplated a move back to Riverton, but one of them would have to compromise. He hoped that person didn't have to be him, but it couldn't hurt to listen to whatever Gordon had to say.

Jack watched Emily lick chocolate off her fingers. She had known he was going to drop by this morning, but she hadn't tried to get all dolled up for him. Quite the opposite, in fact. And he loved that. She didn't worry about putting away a huge plate of pasta for dinner or eating doughnuts for breakfast—she didn't need to—and he loved that about her, too.

"Why are you looking at me weird?" Emily asked. "Do I have chocolate on my face?" She swiped her mouth with a napkin. "I do, don't I?"

Back in the moment, Jack shook his head. "No chocolate. Like I said, you look kind of cute, that's all."

She rolled her eyes. "I doubt that."

"You shouldn't." He wanted to pull her into his arms and kiss her senseless. He wanted to tell her she was beautiful, assure her he would take care of her and the baby. She wasn't ready to hear it, though, and he didn't want her to feel pressured. Easier to wait until their families knew he was the baby's father and let them apply the pressure. That way, he could be the buffer.

He swallowed the rest of his coffee and

stood. "I'd like to stay, but there's something I need to wrap up at the station before I head back to Chicago."

She stood, too, and the tiny apartment seemed to shrink. "I'll walk you out."

"I'll call you when I get back to the city tonight."

"Sure." She sounded as though she didn't believe him, and he couldn't blame her.

"I'll call." He would also send a text message when he stopped at Madison to grab some lunch. He pulled his business card out of his jacket pocket. "And I want you to call me if you need anything, okay?"

She slipped the card into the pocket of her bathrobe and nodded.

At the top of the stairs, he put his arms around her, touched his lips to her forehead. He wanted to ask her to give more thought to coming to the city, but he already knew what her answer would be. Best not to give her any more opportunities to say no.

"I'll be back next weekend. I promise."

"What about the big case you're working on?"

"It's wrapping up."

"Then won't you have another one? According to the statistics, there's more than one homicide a day in Chicago."

Don't remind me. "I don't investigate all of them. Besides, they owe me some time off." They owed him a life. "So I'll be back next weekend. And you're going to talk to your sisters, right?"

"I'll talk to them while I'm there for dinner tonight. I promise."

He took her face in his hands and brushed his mouth over hers, thinking that if he deepened the kiss, she'd taste like coffee and chocolate. Better to stick with his plan, he reminded himself. And so he backed away, for now.

FROM HER LIVING room window, Emily watched Jack drive away. Again. How was this going to work? She sighed. It wasn't. Jack didn't simply have a job in Chicago—he had a life there, too. A career he loved and was extremely good at, by all reports. He said he would be back next weekend, and she believed him. But every weekend? That would be impossible. Something would come up, and he would call to let her know he couldn't make it. Eventually, he would be embroiled in another horrible case, and he would forget to call altogether. And if he did come to town several weekends in a row, people were going to get suspicious. She could go to Chicago instead. She hated the city, but she could handle the occasional weekend. Could she live there, though? Her breath caught in her throat, and her heart started to race. She struggled to inflate her lungs.

"Stop it, just stop." Inhale, slow and steady. Exhale, long and slow. She planted her palms on the wide windowsill, closed her eyes and calmed her breathing before the panic set in.

She had planned to finish a couple of articles for the newspaper, check her email, draft another story for her blog. Not today. She rushed into her bedroom and flung open her closet doors. Half an hour later, she was showered, dressed in dark jeans, a white tank top and a slouchy, oversize beige sweater. She pulled on her glossy green Hunter boots in case CJ talked her into spending some time in the stable, popped her sunglasses on top of her head, grabbed her keys and handbag and let herself out the back door. Work could wait. Talking to her sisters could not. Today, she needed to go home.

CHAPTER TWELVE

JACK HAD ALWAYS liked the drive along River Road, from town to farm country. It brought back a host of memories, all of them good. As a kid, he'd come out here with his dad to watch the bald eagles soar over the river and swoop down to snag their prey. On one of those excursions, they'd found an eagle with a broken wing. Jack would never forget the way his father had carefully covered the bird with an old blanket and kept it calm until a conservation officer arrived and took the animal to a rehabilitation center.

In his preteen years, Jack and his friends had cycled here in the summer, their bike tires skidding off the loose gravel on the shoulders of the road, kicking up little swirls of dust. As soon as he obtained a driver's license—and somehow convinced his mother he was responsible enough to be trusted with her Astro van—he and Eric and Paul would load up the cargo space with blankets, bags of chips and contraband from Bootlegger Barney, whose primary source of income was disguised as a scrap yard. They would pick up their girl-friends, and, with the CD player blasting Bon Jovi, they'd drive out here to Finnegan Farm to pick up Annie, then run up to Lake Pepin, which was really just a widening of the Mis-sissippi River, for the day. Lucky for him, his mother never found out about their outings, or his driving days would have been over. Luck-ier still, his complete absence of responsibil-ity in those days hadn't turned him and his friends into car-crash statistics.

The pitfalls of parenting, he thought. Was he ready for this? Some of Emily's doubts crept into his consciousness. Thankfully, babies weren't born with a driver's license in one hand and their parents' car keys in the other. He thought about his own father, and decided yes, he could do this. *They* could do this. He and Emily.

Up ahead, the white gazebo on the river-bank came into view. Emily's grandfather had built it on the narrow strip of public land that ran between the road and the river. He had also made a pull-in off the main road so pass-ersby could stop and spend time there, but the landmark had always been known to locals as Finnegan's gazebo.

Jack swung the Jeep off the main road, up the sloping, fence-lined gravel drive, and

parked in the roundabout next to a beater with
Illinois plates—Rose Daniels's car—in front
of the freshly painted wooden sign that read
Finnegan Farm Bed & Breakfast. Behind
that stood a century-old two-and-a-half-story
farmhouse. It had been one of Jack's favorite
places ever since Eric had married Annie and
moved out here.

The white clapboard siding and barn-red
trim, the comfortably furnished wraparound
screened porch, the front windows with their
white lace curtains and the big old yellow dog
sleeping on the mat by the front door were like
a throwback to another time. The only addition was the wheelchair ramp made necessary
by Thomas Finnegan's acts of heroism during
Desert Storm. The man had saved three lives
by nearly making the ultimate sacrifice himself, then he'd come home to his family in a
wheelchair, only to be abandoned by his wife
and left on his own to raise three little girls.

A wife and mother whose name was Scarlett. He couldn't very well ask Annie or
Thomas about her, but maybe there'd be a
photograph of her somewhere in the house. It
wouldn't be a recent one, but he would have
no trouble recognizing a younger version of
Scarlett Daniels.

Jack took the front steps two at time, pushed

through the screen door and onto the veranda. The golden retriever lifted his head.

"Hey, Chester. You standing guard, old fella? Keeping an eye on the family?"

The dog winked sleepily.

"Good boy," he said, rapping lightly on the wood frame of another screen door. The main door was open to the warm spring air, and he caught the scent of coffee and something else. He inhaled deeply and with anticipation.

Was that...? Yes, it was. Annie's apple strudel. Eric had loved his wife's cooking almost as much as he'd loved her, and he had never stopped talking about it.

A miniature version of Eric flew across the foyer toward the front door. "Uncle Jack! Mom, it's Uncle Jack! He's here!"

"Stop shouting, Isaac, and tell him to come on in."

"Come in, Uncle Jack! What're you doing here?"

Jack let himself in, caught the young boy in midleap and swung him onto his shoulders.

"Jack, is that really you?" Annie called from the back of the house. "Coffee's on. Come join us in the kitchen."

"Be right there," he replied. "Duck your head, Isaac. Your mom won't be happy with me if you crack your noggin on the transom."

The boy was giggling by the time they made their way to the kitchen. Jack lifted him off his shoulders, settled him on a stool and ruffled his hair. Jack then turned to Annie.

"You're looking good."

She accepted his compliment and a hug. "This is a surprise. How long will you be in town?"

"I was just here overnight, thought I'd stop by on my way back to the city."

"I'm glad you did. Sit, sit. I'll get you some coffee."

He studied her closely. "How are you?"

She faced him squarely, as though determined to put on a brave face, then looked away and dabbed the corners of her eyes with the sleeve of her light blue, hooded pullover. "Sorry. I'm being... I don't know. Silly, I guess. It's good to see you, nice to know you're thinking about us."

She'd always been slender, but she looked thinner. It could just be her slim gray jeans, but knowing Annie, she was taking care of everyone but herself.

"I've thought about you and Isaac a lot, wondered how you're doing. I'm sorry I haven't picked up the phone."

"No need to apologize, I know you're busy. How's work?"

"Are you carrying your gun?" Isaac asked.

"No weapons, sport. I'm off-duty."

"How 'bout your badge?"

Jack smiled and pulled his badge from his pocket, handed it to the boy. "You bet. I always carry that."

"Cool." Isaac flipped it open. "I'm gonna be a police officer when I grow up."

Annie was smiling again as she poured coffee into a mug, handed it to Jack. "I thought you were going to be a paleontologist."

"I'll be a police officer who digs up bones," Isaac said, looking smug about having dreamed up a new profession.

"In police work, we call that forensics." Jack sat on a stool next to Isaac, sipping his coffee.

"Foren…what kind of sick?"

"Not sick. Forensics. The people who do forensics help cops like me solve crimes."

"Do they have guns and badges, too?"

He caught Annie's warning look, gave her a nod, and directed the conversation away from guns. "They have cooler stuff," he told Isaac. "Microscopes, lasers, and they get those awesome white suits so they don't contaminate the crime scene."

Annie smiled her appreciation. "Would you like a slice of strudel?"

"I was hoping you'd ask. I could smell it from the porch."

Annie took plates from a cupboard and forks from a drawer. "Isaac, be a sweetie and tell your granddad that Jack is here."

The boy slid off his stool, clutching Jack's badge in one hand. "Gramps!"

"Isaac! Run down to his room and tell him," Annie said. "I could have yelled at him myself."

"Whoa." Jack held out his hand to indicate he needed the badge back. "Better hand that over, buddy. It's against the law to impersonate a police officer."

Isaac slapped it into his palm and dashed out of the room, giggling. "Gramps!" he hollered again from the hallway.

Annie chuckled. "Sorry about that. Never a dull moment around here. And thank you for humoring him with all the talk about police work."

"No problem." Jack watched her slice a freshly baked strudel into slabs and slide them onto plates. "So, are you really doing okay? Getting enough rest?"

"Oh, sure, but, you know…it's good to keep busy."

He figured she had been born busy. Given the recent loss of her husband, he imagined she was using it as a coping mechanism. She looked tired, though, and a little too gaunt.

"Have you heard from Paul?" he asked. Jack had been best friends with Eric and Paul Woodward since they'd started high school. The three of them had gone off to college right after graduation. Eric had come home, landed a job as the physical education teacher at Riverton High. Jack and Paul had gone to Chicago where Jack joined the police department. Paul had gone to the college of medicine at UIC, just as his father had expected him to, but he hadn't returned home to join his dad's practice at the clinic. Instead, he practiced general medicine, with a particular interest in pediatrics, at Mercy Medical Center. After Eric's funeral, Jack and Paul had sworn they'd do better at keeping in touch, get together to grab a bite, maybe catch a White Sox game, but that hadn't happened. They were both caught up with work, and Paul came home to Riverton even less frequently than Jack did.

"No, I haven't heard from him," Annie said. "You?"

Jack shook his head. "The guy works longer hours than I do. Any word on how his dad is doing?"

"Still running the clinic in town," she said. "He took such good care of Eric. Dr. Woodward hasn't been the same, though, since his wife passed away."

Dr. Paul Woodward, Sr. had a gentle bedside manner that infused his patients with confidence and belied the iron-fisted way he'd ruled his family. "It's been a couple of years since Audrey's been gone. I'd've thought he'd be over that by now."

"Some people think he might be losing it." Annie gave her temple a two-fingered tap. "It'll be a real shame if that's true. It would be good if Paul could come home once in a while. I know they haven't always seen eye to eye, but old Doc Woodward could probably use some family from time to time."

If that was truly the case, then the old man should have done a better job of creating family ties, but Jack knew his friend had other reasons for not wanting to come home. Paul had been in love with Annie since high school. Eric and Annie had never known, of course, and Paul had used his dysfunctional relationship with his father as an excuse to stay away all this time. Jack was the only one who knew the real reason. Maybe now…

No. It was none of his business. He had plenty on his own plate. Plenty. Still, it couldn't hurt to give Paul a shout when he got back to the city, get together like they'd planned. Catch up on old times, and a few current ones.

Thomas rolled into the kitchen with Isaac sitting on his lap, making engine noises. "Vroom, vroom. Faster, Gramps!"

"We have to stick to the speed limit," Thomas said. "The Chicago PD is here. Jack, good to see you, son. What brings you to town?"

"A police matter that needed to be dealt with." And he was still hoping to encounter Rose at the farm, although there'd been no sign of her so far. "And I also had a...a family thing to take care of."

"Your folks doing okay?"

Jack nodded. "Thanks for asking. They're great, although my mother would tell you her son doesn't visit often enough. My sister shows me up by visiting from San Francisco more often than I make the trek from Chicago."

The older man chuckled. "Tell them they should've had another daughter. Or maybe they just need a daughter-in-law."

Coming from Emily's father, the implication that Jack should think about getting married hit a little too close for comfort. "You won't get any argument from them on that score," Jack said, keeping his tone light.

Thomas rolled his chair to the end of the bi-level kitchen island, which had obviously been specially designed with a counter-height work space at one end and a lower level at the other to accommodate lower stools and the wheelchair. Isaac stayed put on the man's lap and reached for the glass of milk his mother poured for him. Thomas picked up his coffee mug and they clinked them together.

Jack watched with equal parts envy and admiration. This was what family was all about, and Emily was right to want to keep on being part of this, for their child to be part of this.

Thomas Finnegan had the patience of a saint, the smile of an angel and the blue-eyed sparkle of a prankster. He was a survivor and a war hero, a good friend to many and a devoted family man to everyone in his life who mattered. To Jack, it seemed a lot of men who had two working legs didn't stand as tall and as proud as Thomas somehow managed to project from that chair.

Annie doled out plates of her legendary strudel as two people stomped across the back deck, kicked off boots and flung open the French doors. Emily's younger sister, CJ, burst into the kitchen, followed by a slender brunette he almost didn't recognize. Rose Daniels had toned down her appearance since yesterday. Big-time. For one thing, she wore a lot less makeup, and the dark bangs that had all but obscured her face yesterday were now clipped off her face. She still looked out of place, though, in jeans with too many rips to be considered fashionably distressed, and an off-the-shoulder charcoal-gray pullover that was more Friday-night bar scene than Sunday-morning farmhouse kitchen.

"Jack!" CJ rushed across the kitchen and flung her arms around him. "How's my other big brother? And what are you doing here?" She'd still been a teenager when Annie and Eric had married, and she had decided back then she wasn't getting just one big brother aka brother-in-law—she was getting three: Eric, Jack and Paul. Annie and Emily's youngest sister had a way of making almost everything about her and still be adorable while doing it.

Laughing, he hugged her back. "I'm here to beat off the boys with a stick."

That earned him a nod from Thomas and an eye roll from CJ.

"I can take care of myself, I'll have you know."

As if anyone had ever doubted that. Jack turned his attention to her companion. "Who's your friend?"

"Oh, this is Rose. She's booked into the B & B for the week. I've been giving her a tour of the stable."

Jack trained his gaze on her. "Nice to meet you, Rose."

He watched her roll through all the emotions he would have expected—shock, panic and then fear he was going to out her.

"Um, yeah. You, too."

"Where are you from, Rose?" Had she been honest with her hosts? This would be the test.

"Chicago." She said it with a hint of challenge that only he would notice.

"Interesting. Me, too. What brings you to Riverton?"

"Sort of a vacation."

Right.

"Rose says she's looking for a change," Annie said. "She'll be with us for a week, long enough to find out if small-town living is really for her."

CJ helped herself to a cup of coffee. "Towns don't get much smaller or sleepier than Riverton. Would you like some?" she asked Rose.

"Oh, sure, thanks."

"I'll get it for you," Annie said, filling another mug and passing it across the island to her guest.

Jack noted the tremor in Rose's hand as she took the mug, the way the cream sloshed as she poured it, and how a few drops splattered onto the counter.

"Rose didn't like the horses," CJ said.

The girl nodded. "I've never been close to one before. They're huge. Scary huge."

CJ rolled her eyes. What was it with these sisters and their eye rolls? "Molly is the gentlest mare you'll ever find. She's great with the kids in my therapeutic riding program."

"Therapeutic riding? What's that?" Rose asked.

While CJ gave an animated description of the kids she worked with and their various disabilities, Jack studied Rose's reaction. She was feigning interest and doing a lousy job of it. In spite of being twenty years old, which in Jack's opinion was adulthood, she gave the impression of a much younger person, too caught up with her own issues to think or care about anyone else's. And given the way her hands trembled, before long she would be heading up to the privacy of her room where she had no doubt stashed a bottle of vodka and possibly a vial of unprescribed meds. Unlike her mother, she didn't exhibit any of the signs she was using street drugs. Maybe there was some hope for the poor kid, after all. If she really was looking to make a change, a place to turn her life around, Riverton was a pretty soft spot to land. But the big question for him was her motive for being here. Did these women have the same mother? If so, what did she plan to do about it? As soon as he was back at the office, he would do some digging and find out what she was up to and why.

Jack drained his mug and set it on the counter next to his empty plate. He was starting to feel like an intruder, or at the very least, an outsider in this hub of domesticity, and he had a long drive ahead of him. On his way through the house to the kitchen, he hadn't spotted any photographs of anyone resembling a young Scarlett Daniels. The next time he was in town, he would casually ask Emily if she had any pictures of her mother.

"It's been good to see you, Thomas. Isaac."

"Good to see you, son. Stop by again," Thomas said.

"Thanks, I will."

Isaac waved the arm of a transformer robot at him, making him smile.

"And thank you for coffee and strudel, Annie. Delicious as always."

"I'm glad you dropped by." She gave him a quick hug. "It's comforting to know Eric's friends haven't forgotten about us," she said quietly.

"Never going to happen. You need anything, anything at all, you call me, okay?"

"I will. Thanks."

He waved at CJ, who was still talking excitedly to Rose about her work. The youngest Finnegan sister was a live wire. And a knockout. It was both hard to believe and no surprise at all that some lucky guy hadn't put a ring on her finger.

Rose kept her head averted, but he knew she was watching him from the corner of her eye. Good, he thought. *I'm keeping an eye on you, too.*

"It's too bad you didn't get to see Emily while you were here," Annie said. "She has… um…some stuff going on right now."

Annie's out-of-the-blue comment startled him, and it took him a second to recover. Poker face, he told himself. He knew Annie knew about the baby, and he also knew she didn't know it was his. "Maybe next time."

"Come on." Annie linked her arm with his. "I'll walk you out. Maybe next time you can stay long enough to join us for Sunday dinner."

They hadn't left the kitchen when he heard the front door open and bang shut again.

"Hello! It's me!"

Emily.

Busted.

CHAPTER THIRTEEN

ASTONISHMENT AND DISBELIEF didn't come close to describing the emotions Emily had experienced when she'd pulled into the driveway and spotted Jack's Jeep. Then to go inside and find him and Annie engaged in what was obviously a conspiratorial conversation. What was he up to? What were they up to? She looked from one to the other, several times, telling herself not to panic and knowing full well she looked as though she had something to hide.

Annie cocked her head, puzzled. "Look who's here. It was such a nice surprise to have Jack stop by for coffee this morning, and I was just saying it's too bad he hadn't had a chance to see you. Now here you are."

Jack stared hard at Emily and she returned the scrutiny, each wondering what the other was doing here. Annie glanced from one to the other, and then she grinned.

Her sister's smug cat-that-got-the-cream expression implied she knew more than she should. Had she talked to Fred? Had Jack told her the baby was his? Did anyone mind their own business anymore? Well, technically this was Fred's business because she had dragged him into it, and of course it was Jack's business, too, but they had both agreed to let her handle this on her terms. They had promised.

Annie pulled her into a hug, whispering in her ear as she did. "It's okay. I just figured it out. No one else knows."

Emily met Jack's cool blue gaze over her sister's shoulder. He narrowed his eyes questioningly, which darkened them to navy. Mesmerizing. But she gave her head a tiny shake. *Don't ask*, she mouthed. His nod was almost imperceptible. And those thick, dark, wickedly long eyelashes...

Honestly, no man had the right to be this gorgeous.

Annie let her go and hugged Jack, then stepped away and looked from one to the other. "I'll head back to the kitchen and leave the two of you to..." She had the most foolish-looking grin.

Emily waved her off, pushed the screen door open and pulled Jack onto the veranda. "What are you doing here?"

"I dropped by to see Annie and Isaac on my way out of town. Eric was one of my best friends. There's no crime in wanting to make sure his family is doing okay."

Emily studied him closely. "I don't believe you."

"Why not?" he asked. "Why else would I come here?"

"I don't know, but you don't look like you're telling the truth."

"Emily, be reasonable. Why would I lie about this?"

"Maybe because you wanted Annie to find out about…" She glanced sideways and over her shoulder, lowered her voice to a stage whisper. "About the baby, and to get her to try to convince me to go along with your plan for a shotgun wedding."

Jack's laugh was unexpectedly annoying.

"What's so funny?" she asked.

"I never said I felt pressured. I said we should get married. No shotguns needed."

"Maybe I'm the one who feels pressured."

Jack gave her a long, thoughtful look, then smiled. He pulled her into his arms, not roughly, but not exactly gently, either, and kissed her. Not passionately, but not exactly chastely, either.

"No pressure." He kissed her again. "I really do have to get going, though. Long drive. I'll see you next weekend. Annie invited me to Sunday dinner."

Of course she did, Emily thought, watching the screen door swing shut behind him. He slid behind the steering wheel of his Jeep, started the engine and flashed the high beams at her before he turned around and drove down the driveway to the main road.

She stood there even after he was out of sight, gazing at the wide expanse of paddock, the two grazing horses, then turned her attention to the gazebo by the river. Growing up, she'd spent many happy hours there, reading library books and scribbling in her journals, and now she felt the pull of solitude. She had a notebook and her laptop in her bag. She never went anywhere without them. She could sit in the gazebo, pour her heart onto the page, lose herself in a story for the blog or the paper.

Not today, though. She turned away from the view and realized Jack had kissed her right in front of one of the living room windows.

"Seriously?" What if someone had seen them together? She peered through the glass but the lace curtain prevented her from getting a good look inside. "I just can't catch a break." Some alone time in the gazebo had more appeal than ever. She cast one last longing glance over her shoulder but instead of yielding to temptation, she walked to the front door and went inside, prepared to face the music.

JACK SAT AT his desk that evening and swiped a hand over tired eyes. In spite of sleeping well the night before, it had been a long day. And he had a lot on his mind. Discovering he was going to become a father, having Emily turn down his offer to marry her, the unexpected job offer with the Riverton police—it all made his head spin. Add to that the interview with Rose Daniels, and not getting to the bottom of why the young woman was in Riverton and staying at Annie's B & B. On top of everything, the long drive back to Chicago.

He was beat, and he'd like nothing more than to head across town to his apartment, microwave a frozen dinner and grab a shower and some shut-eye. But he also knew he wouldn't get any rest until he solved the puzzle of why Rose was in Riverton and whether he was dealing with two women named Scarlett…or one.

He crossed the office to the coffeemaker, popped in a pod and brewed himself a cup while his computer booted up. Then he sat at his desk, gulped the dark, strong brew and slowly scrolled through Scarlett Daniels's lengthy police record. There'd been numerous arrests for drug possession. Two counts of theft under five hundred—shoplifting, no doubt. One assault charge. Four complaints filed against others at various times—three of them men, one a woman—for assaulting her. On all four occasions, charges had been dropped.

Please, don't let this be Emily's mother, he thought. She obviously idolized a woman she had never known, and she had lived her whole life believing her mother would come home some day.

There was still a lot he didn't know about Scarlett Daniels. Was Daniels her maiden name? An ex-husband's name? He rifled through Rose's file and found the documents from social services, which included a copy of her birth certificate. Born in Chicago. Mother was listed as Scarlett Daniels. Father unknown. That may or may not have been the truth, but that was one secret Rose's mother had taken to her grave. Now Jack wondered how many others she had taken with her.

Using his computer, he pulled up the autopsy report on Scarlett Daniels. Female, fifty-one years old. He skimmed the introductory stuff. Hair color: brown. Eye color: brown. Like Emily. Like millions of other people, he reminded himself.

He skipped the detailed descriptions and photos of the lacerations and knife wounds. Those he'd already committed to memory.

Overall condition: emaciated.

A series of black-and-white photographs showed track marks up and down both arms. The tox report indicated she'd been high on heroin, Vicodin and Adderall, with a blood-alcohol reading of point-one-nine—a toxic slurry that could have easily finished her off if Jason Caruthers hadn't shown up with a chip on his shoulder and a butcher knife in hand.

None of this revealed anything about Scarlett's past, though, so he kept reading.

The black tar in her lungs indicated she was a smoker. According to her stomach contents, she'd eaten McDonald's earlier that night. Reproductive organs had been removed. Medical records stated she had undergone a hysterectomy ten years earlier.

Jack had been looking for anything that might indicate Scarlett had given birth to more than one child, but there was no mention of it. The medical records from the hysterectomy would likely reveal how many children she'd had, but that had no relevance to this case. Unless…

What if the police had reason to believe there were more next of kin? He turned that option over in his mind, then ruled it out. If there were other children, then their names would become part of the permanent police record, maybe even the court proceedings when Caruthers went to trial. If this was Emily's mother, Emily would be shattered. And there were also her sisters and father to think about. Not to mention the small-town gossip that would be stirred up when this went public, as it surely would.

No, there had to be another way to dig into Scarlett Daniels's past. He simply had to find it, and he worried he wouldn't like what he found.

DRESSED FOR BED in comfy pajama bottoms and an oversize T-shirt, Emily studied her reflection in the mirror as she brushed her teeth. It had been an interesting day and, especially for a Sunday, an eventful one. She gargled, rinsed her toothbrush and tossed it into the holder.

In her bedroom, she pulled her journal and a pen from the drawer in her bedside table, fluffed her pillows and slid beneath the celadon-green duvet cover. Some people couldn't wait to roll out of bed in the morning and find out what the new day had in store for them, but just before bed was her favorite time. Emily had long ago learned she had very little control over how the day unfolded, but reflecting on it after the fact usually helped her to make sense of it.

Dear Heart,
I ate doughnuts for breakfast. Jack brought them. I, Emily Finnegan, ate doughnuts for breakfast that Jack Evans brought especially for me. Doughnuts. For breakfast.

Maybe if she said it, wrote it, often enough, she would believe it instead of feeling as though it had been a dream.

And then he kissed me. Kissing Jack is so much better than anything I could ever imagine or dream on my own. Kissing Jack is pure magic.

That sounded lame, but that was the beauty of her journal. No one else read the contents, so she could be as over the top as she liked. She indulged herself by rambling on about running into Jack at the farm, her sisters' wildly enthusiastic reaction to finding out he was the baby's father, and the strange girl who was staying at the B & B. Rose Daniels looked like a teenager, though she was probably older, maybe early twenties. She had a Goth vibe going on with hair dyed black and streaked purple, a black-on-black wardrobe and an attitude of disinterest bordering on disdain. Most of Annie's guests were young families wanting their kids to experience country living, middle-aged couples celebrating a milestone birthday or anniversary, and the occasional traveler from abroad.

Emily set her pen down and stared at the four framed prints on her bedroom wall. The Golden Gate Bridge, the Statue of Liberty, London Bridge, the Eiffel Tower. She had always had such big dreams about the things she wanted to do, the places she wanted to go, the sights she wanted to see. She had never visited any of them.

She shifted her gaze to the photo of her and her sisters with their father, all four of them on horseback. It had been taken not long after Emily graduated high school. CJ had started the therapeutic riding program at the farm during the summer, and the lift they'd installed in the stable had allowed their father to get back on a horse for the first time in years. It had taken him several weeks and a couple of falls before he had learned to maintain his balance and to train the horse to respond to commands that didn't require the use of the rider's legs. This photograph had been taken on their first trail ride together. To Emily, it represented family and home, and home had always been where her heart was.

After Annie had started the B & B, Emily hadn't minded having strangers in their home. She was seldom there, and when she was, the guests mostly kept to themselves except when Annie was serving breakfast in the dining room or CJ was taking them on a trail ride.

Maybe that was why it bothered her to see this strange girl named Rose sitting in the kitchen with her family. She had only checked in the day before—Emily remembered her sister saying yesterday that she was expecting a woman from Chicago that afternoon. Rose had barely picked at Annie's strudel. Instead, she had fidgeted with her paper napkin, nervously shredding the edges of it while gazing guardedly at everyone sitting around the table.

Emily was used to dropping by and seeing guests lounging on the screened-in veranda reading books and newspapers, doing crossword puzzles and drinking cups of tea and coffee. She was comfortable encountering them over breakfast in the dining room, eating off the china Annie used for guests. For reasons she didn't fully understand, finding Rose sitting in the kitchen with her family and eat-

ing off the everyday dishes had bothered her.
A lot.

She picked up her pen.

Rose is weird. Very weird. I wanted her
to stop staring at my family. I've been
told I have an overactive imagination, and
it's true, I do, but I wanted to tell Annie
to lock up the silverware and the butcher
knives.

An icy shiver slid down Emily's spine. She
tossed aside her pen and journal, grabbed her
phone off the bedside table and called Annie.

"Emily, hi. Is everything okay?" her sister
asked.

"Everything's fine. Why?"

"No reason, but you don't usually call this
late. I was worried when I saw it was you."

"I'm fine," she repeated. "Actually, I was
kind of worried about you."

"I'm okay. Losing Eric is devastating, but I
shouldn't need to have a nervous breakdown
to prove to everyone I'm grieving."

"Whoa!" Her sister was almost never on
the defensive. "Where is this coming from?"

"Isn't that why you're calling?"

"No."

"Oh. I thought maybe Jack had said something to you."

"No, he didn't, and that's kind of an over-the-top reaction for someone who claims to be okay."

Annie sighed. She sounded tired. "I'm sorry. Seeing Jack today was great, but he used to drop by to see Eric. This time, it was a special visit to check up on me and Isaac, and having him do that really hit home."

Like everyone in her family, Emily had been heartbroken when Eric died. "I'm so sorry, Annie. I'm here for whatever you need, whenever you need me. You know that."

"I know, honey. I'm sorry to be such a downer, and you said this isn't why you called. What's up?"

Typical Annie. Change the subject rather than meet the subject head-on.

"I was thinking about your B & B guest."

A moment of silence. Then, "Really? Why?"

"How many kids like her have stayed there on their own?"

"I know she's not your typical—"

"How many?" Emily asked again.

"Until now, none."

"It's weird. *She's* weird."

"Emily, she's a kid, and she's on her own. She's from Chicago, and she told me she was working in a diner till her mother passed away. Now she has no family and she's looking for a change. She thought a small town might be a better fit for her."

Emily couldn't imagine having no family, but she was concerned about Annie's desire to help this person. She didn't like to think of anyone taking advantage of her sister, and she hated to think Annie was filling the void in her life by taking in strays.

"Fair enough," she said. "I have no doubt she could use a little mothering, and because of that she's tugging on your heartstrings. I'm only saying you should be careful."

"Why are you so concerned?" Annie asked.

"I can't put my finger on it, exactly." But she needed to be honest. "Like I said, she's not your typical guest. I also thought it was odd you invited her to join us for family dinner. I mean, she's not family, and apparently she doesn't eat, either. She mostly pushed her food around on her plate."

"I feel sorry for her."

Emily sighed. Annie had enough people to take care of. Their father, Isaac, CJ. Not that CJ needed to be taken care of, but she was always more than happy to go along with Annie's need to do it.

"Did she say how long she's planning to stay?"

"She paid for a week when she checked in, gave me the cash because she doesn't have a credit card."

A whole week? Paid for by cash? Again, weird. Who in this day and age didn't have a credit card? Who carried that much money around with them? Better question: *Why* would anyone carry around that much money?

"And you don't find that…odd?" Emily asked.

"No, I don't."

"What did you say her last name is?"

"Danvers. Rose Danvers."

"Did you ask to see her ID?" Emily asked, reaching for her laptop and typing into Google: *Rose Danvers Chicago*.

"Of course not. Why would I do that?"

"To make sure she is who she says she is."

"Don't you think you're overreacting?"

Not even a little bit, she thought, studying the few hits that came up. A young person like Rose Danvers would almost certainly have an online presence. Unless she had something to hide.

"Maybe I am. All I'm asking is that you be careful and not take everything at face value. People aren't always who they seem to be."

She wondered if Jack could find out something about Rose. Could the police do that? Check into someone's background, even though they weren't under investigation? It couldn't hurt to ask, and if he could, he would do it for her, she was sure.

"I'm always careful, and everything's going to be fine. Rose is only here for a week, and then we'll probably never hear from her again."

"I hope so." She truly did, although she still intended to talk to Jack about her.

"It's getting late, Em. You should get some sleep. You're going to need more rest now that you're expecting."

Emily sighed. "Good night, Annie."

"Good night, Em. Stop worrying and go to bed."

Emily set her phone on the table next to the bed and yawned. She couldn't tell if she was more tired than usual, or if she was simply feeling the effects of the whirlwind weekend. She would definitely get some sleep, right after Jack called. He said he would, and she believed him, so she picked up her pen and her journal and snuggled beneath the covers to wait for her phone to ring.

BY THE TIME Jack shut down his computer and straightened the paperwork he had strewn across his desk, his eyelids felt as though they were made of sandpaper. It had been a long, tiring day, and he was ready to head home for some shut-eye. Maybe a bite to eat, too. He checked the time. It was late, and he hadn't eaten since… Oh, no. He smacked his forehead. It was really late, and he had forgotten to call Emily.

What was wrong with him? On the long drive back to the city, he'd thought about little else other than her and the baby. She had been on his mind the whole time he'd been digging through the Scarlett Daniels murder files.

He was a moron. Emily would be furious, and she had every right to be. He grabbed his phone and tapped out a text message.

Too late to call. Hope you sleep well. Talk to you in the morning.

Within seconds, his phone buzzed and her reply flashed on the screen.

I'm still awake.

Which was doublespeak for call now.

Give me five.

He dashed down the stairs to the main entrance and pushed through the doors to State Street where he'd parked his Jeep between two cruisers. As soon as he was behind the wheel, he made the call.

"Hello." She sounded sleepy.

"Hey. Sorry to call so late."

"I thought you'd forgotten about me."

"Not a chance. I had to stop at the station to tie up a few loose ends, and I lost track of the time."

"That happens a lot."

Too often. "It does, but I'm working on making some changes. And you can always call me or send a text."

"I know, but tonight was a test." He liked her honesty. And how in spite of her serious tone of voice, he knew she was smiling.

"How did I do?"

"You get a passing grade. Another twenty minutes, though, and you would have been calling me tomorrow."

"The text message should count for something."

"I might have given you half marks for effort."

"Ouch."

She laughed. "I have high expectations."

And he hoped to live up to them. "How was the day with your family?"

"Good. I usually don't spend the whole day out there, but it was nice for a change. CJ and I took Isaac for a trail ride this afternoon. That was fun."

Horseback riding? Really? "Are you sure that's okay? I mean in your—"

"In my *condition*?" she cut in. "Yes, even Annie agreed it's fine, but I'll check with the doctor when I see him this week."

"How did your sisters take the news?"

"Annie figured it out when the two of you met me at the front door. If she hadn't, she would have caught on when you kissed me. She was watching us from the living room."

Jack found himself grinning. "And?"

"And what?"

"How did she take it? What did she say?"

"She hadn't believed me when I told her it was Fred's, and neither had CJ. Annie says she's delighted to have you become part of the family, and CJ..." Emily paused, cleared her throat.

"What did CJ say?" He could only imagine.

"She says I need to make an honest man out of you."

He thought the world of Annie, but CJ was well on her way to becoming his favorite sister-in-law-to-be. "Does that mean you've changed your mind?"

"No."

He reminded himself that he found her honesty refreshing. He knew it would take more than a few phone calls to change her opinion of him, but having her sisters on his side was definitely promising. "And your father?"

"My dad is completely in the dark about the pregnancy, and he's going to stay there until I'm ready to enlighten him." There was a pause, and he didn't speak because he knew she wasn't finished. "And heaven help my sisters…*or anyone*…who tells him before I'm ready."

Jack leaned back in the driver's seat and listened with amusement to Emily's version of trash talk.

"Our secret is safe with me," he told her. This was the wrong time to remind her in a few months they wouldn't be keeping this a secret from anyone. "I wish I could have stayed for dinner. What did you have?"

"Annie made pork roast with blackberry gastrique and these little oven-roasted potatoes."

"Sounds amazing. She should open a restaurant."

"There were buttered peas, too. It doesn't

matter what she serves for Sunday dinner, buttered peas are my dad's idea of fancy."

"Hey, who doesn't like peas? What about dessert? And spare no details."

Emily laughed. It was a sound he liked to hear because it meant the tension he'd heard in her voice moments ago had dissipated. "Living vicariously, Detective Evans?"

"Completely on the edge. Just, please, tell me she didn't serve doughnuts."

More laughter. "No. She made another of my dad's favorites—pecan pie with whipped cream. He says her pastry is like shortbread."

Jack groaned out loud. He hadn't eaten since Madison and that had been hours ago. "You're killing me here. You know that, right?"

"You're invited to dinner next Sunday. If you're in town, of course."

"I told you I would be, and I'm not backing out."

"What about the case you're working on?"

"Winding down. I'll be there."

"That'll be…nice."

Nice? "Glad you think so."

"I'm already looking forward to next Sunday. I just hope my sister's houseguest has cleared out by then."

He knew she was talking about Rose, and he fought back a clawing sense of unease. Play it cool, he warned himself. "What's up with the guest?"

"I don't know, exactly. There's something strange about her, and I can't help thinking how weird it is that a kid her age would want to spend a week at a country B & B."

He had been thinking the same thing.

"Did you meet her?" Emily asked.

"I did. She and CJ came in from the stable while Annie and I were having coffee."

"And she's weird, right? Am I right?"

He agreed with Emily, of course, but he needed to choose his words carefully. "You could be."

"I think she might be hiding something. She paid cash for the week instead of using a credit card, and get this. When I did an internet search for her, nothing came up. Nothing at all. How many young people do you know who aren't online?"

Huh. For more than a month now, Rose Daniels's name had been splashed all over the news. If Emily couldn't find her...

"Her name is Rose, isn't it?" Playing dumb could easily come back to bite him, but he didn't know any other way to fish for information.

"That's right. Rose Danvers."

So, the kid was using a phony surname. In-

LEE McKENZIE

teresting. She might be doing it for the very reason Emily suggested—to avoid being discovered on the internet. He'd like to believe that, and he hoped it wasn't something more insidious.

"So, I was wondering... Since she's from Chicago, is there any chance you could check up on her? Find out if she is who she says she is?"

"I'm sorry, Emily. I could get into a lot of trouble. It's one thing if information happens to be part of the public record, but I can't use my connections as a police officer to dig into anyone's private business and then share that information with someone else. That would be a complete breach of privacy."

"Of course, I get that. I do." But her voice was thick with disappointment.

"I'm sorry."

"Don't be. I shouldn't have asked."

"Emily, you can ask me for anything." He thought of Rose being pulled over on a suspected DUI early yesterday morning. The kid definitely had her share of problems. "I know you have good instincts, but being weird isn't against the law. If you notice anything specific, though, you can always call the Riverton PD. I keep in touch with Gord Fenwick. I'll let him know about your concerns." Jack had already briefed the chief with the details of this case, and especially about Rose since she was staying in Riverton. "If you think Rose is up to something, give him a call. He'll listen to you."

"Good idea. I'll keep that in mind. Oh, and that reminds me, Ken Bartlett is making a big announcement at the town council meeting tomorrow afternoon. Rumor has it he's going to announce Chief Fenwick's retirement. Do you know anything about that?"

"Interesting," he said, hoping she wouldn't notice that he avoided answering the question. "What time is the meeting?"

"Two o'clock."

"Will you let me know how it goes?"

"Sure. I'll text you when it's over."

Of course, Jack already knew what the meeting was about. Gord Fenwick had also encouraged Jack to meet with him and the mayor before Jack left Riverton that afternoon, but he had declined. Figuring out whether or not to accept this job was a big decision. Huge. Could he give up his job here, everything he had worked for? These were not spur-of-the-moment decisions.

"I'll call you tomorrow night, but at a decent hour."

"Better late than never." She stifled a yawn. "Good night, Jack."

"Good night, Emily." He pictured her as she'd looked that morning in her flannel pajama pants and fuzzy slippers, her hair tousled. She was adorable. She was carrying his child. And he was feeling fiercely overprotective. Decisions would have to be made because the sooner they were together, the better.

CHAPTER FOURTEEN

WITH JACK BACK in Chicago, Emily's days more or less returned to their familiar old pattern. Grudgingly roll out of bed when the alarm sounded, make coffee—decaf—check her blog, start the day's notes in her journal, feed Tadpole, hop in the shower and get dressed. Downstairs, she spent the mornings in the newspaper office, checking the wire service, running a few of the lead stories past her boss, and following up on the emails and telephone messages forwarded to her by the office administrator, Hilde Emerson.

Hilde was a fifty-something-year-old empty nester who had already given up on ever becoming a grandmother. Hilde and Ken Bartlett's wife, Marthe, were twin sisters.

She had worked from ten to two every weekday since her kids were all in school, making sure the *Gazette*'s filing was caught up and the bills were paid. In a pinch, she was also an excellent proofreader.

From Emily's perspective, the only drawback to working with Hilde was the woman's tendency to want to be a stand-in mother. Every morning when she arrived promptly at ten, she asked Emily how she'd slept the night before and what she had eaten for breakfast. "A young woman needs to start her day with something more substantial than two cups of coffee."

Emily seldom ate breakfast, but she had learned to tell Hilde she had eaten a bowl of yogurt and a banana, or granola with blueberries, or a poached egg on toast. Truthfully, Emily had never poached an egg in her life. Lately, food had a lot of appeal, though, and her voracious appetite was a constant reminder she was having a baby and was nowhere near ready to be a mother. Emily didn't want to think about the kind of advice her coworker would dole out once she knew.

Before Hilde left at two o'clock every afternoon, she would impart another piece of matronly wisdom. "You've been at that computer for three hours now. Be sure to take a break." Or, "Don't forget the interview you have scheduled at three-thirty."

Emily had never missed an appointment or an interview. The calendars on her computer and her cell phone were synced to give her reminders, but Hilde didn't believe in relying on technology. Mostly, Emily thought, because she didn't have a clue how it worked. So, in spite of the recent turmoil in her life, Emily's daily routines marched along with a certain sameness that was comforting, with the exception of a few new developments.

Fred had started dropping by the office to check on her every morning before he opened the barbershop across the street. "Are you feeling okay?"

Yes.

"Have you given any thought to naming the baby Fred if it's a boy?"

No.

"Have you finally come to your senses and accepted Jack's spur-of-the-moment marriage proposal?"

Absolutely not.

Then there were the emails from Annie.

Have you made an appointment to see Dr. Woodward?

Yes.

Have you started to think about where you're going to live? Your apartment doesn't have room for a nursery.

No.

Have you given any more thought to Jack's proposal?

Absolutely not.
She heard from CJ, too, but her text messages were sporadic, and in typical little sister fashion, she managed to make them about her.

When people find out about you and Jack and the baby, do you think they'll wonder if I'm next?

Yes.

Is having a bunch of nieces and nephews going to make me seem like an old-maid aunt?

No.

When you come to your senses and finally marry Jack, can I be your maid of honor?

Absolutely not. Okay, maybe.
But Emily wasn't thinking that far ahead.
This morning, she was hunkered down at her desk in the newspaper office, after having told Hilde she'd eaten a bowl of instant

apple-cinnamon oatmeal—and this time it was the truth because she'd woken up famished and couldn't wait till midmorning to grab a bite—and pretending to focus on her computer monitor. Instead she was looking at her phone and scrolling through the text messages Jack had sent early that morning.

Sleep well last night?

I did. You?

Like a baby. Busy day lined up?

She ignored the baby reference, although it made her smile.

The usual. Any new cases?

Not so far. I'll call you tonight.

And she knew he would. It was often late by the time he called, but so far he hadn't missed a night. They'd had similar text-message exchanges every morning this week, even before her alarm went off, and those had definitely contributed to her reluctance to crawl out of bed and start her day. He had asked about her work, her family and her hamster, even though she knew he wasn't crazy about Tadpole. It had been nice. Nicer than nice. She had never talked to him on the phone before this week, and it was a whole new experience. She'd been able to lie back against her pillow and listen to his voice without being distracted by his cool blue eyes and the temptation to trace his stubbled jawline with her fingertip.

Now it was Wednesday morning, and the week was almost half over. Jack had promised he'd be back for the weekend. She wanted to believe him, but could he get away? Would he?

He had accepted Annie's invitation to Sunday dinner. That was a huge step. He planned to be in town for the whole weekend, and this meant he wasn't planning to rush back to Chicago on Sunday, which in itself was an interesting development. Her sister had also made a suggestion for a Sunday afternoon get-to-know-each-other date and Emily liked the idea—a horseback ride and picnic—a lot. She was reluctant to suggest it to Jack, though, in case he said no. Annie was certain he'd never ridden before, so Emily decided to go ahead with the plan and let him in on it at the last minute. He might be reluctant to get on a horse, but no one in their right mind ever said no to one of Annie's picnic lunches.

Wednesdays were usually slow at the office.

The new issue of the *Gazette* had come out that morning, with the announcement at Monday's council meeting in the headline: "Chief Fenwick Retires after 39 Years with the Riverton PD." Emily often spent her time working on an outline for the next edition. As she sipped decaf from her travel mug and listened to the clack, clack, clacking of Hilde's oddly contoured ergonomic keyboard, she was finding it impossible to focus on anything other than impending motherhood, her date with Jack and food. She needed a break. She would go for a walk, maybe wander by the barbershop to see if Fred was free. Anything but this, she thought.

She shut down her laptop, stood and pulled on her jacket. "I have to run an errand this morning," she told Hilde. "Is there anything you need me to look at before I go?"

"I'm good. I'm working on the classifieds that came in after last edition's cutoff."

"Thanks. If anyone needs me, could you have them call my cell phone?"

"Will do."

Emily slung her messenger bag over her shoulder and left the office, nearly colliding with Mable Potter and her dog. Déjà vu.

"Good morning, Mrs. Potter. We have to stop meeting this way."

The elderly woman laughed. "I had to go to the bank and pay my phone bill," she said. "I brought Banjo along because he can always use the exercise. He's a rambunctious little rascal."

Emily stroked the mutt's scruffy fur and smiled when he gazed up at her with a playful look in his eyes. His tongue dangled out of the corner of his mouth.

"It's nice to see you both," she said. "Did you have a good visit with your daughter on Sunday?"

"We had a lovely time. She helped me plant my window boxes and then we had lunch with red velvet cake for dessert."

"That sounds very nice."

"I took some of the leftover cake out of the freezer this morning. Would you like to join me for a slice and a cup of tea?" Mable asked. "Last time I bumped into you, you said you would."

At the mention of cake, Emily realized she was hungry again. "You know what? I'd love to." If she wasn't careful, she was going to turn into a whale, but she would worry about that later.

The dog's antics amused Emily as they walked the several blocks to Mable's house, particularly his fondness for sniffing out abandoned objects. He discovered a crushed pop can beneath the hedge in front of the Fenwicks' house, which he carried for half a block, and then dropped it when he encountered a child's blue bouncy ball on the boulevard.

"Oh, no, you don't, Banjo," Mable admonished, tugging on his leash. "Your ball is at home. This one belongs to the Hubert children."

Emily picked it up and tossed it over the gate and into their front yard. She picked up the pop can, too, and tucked it into one of the outer pockets of her bag. "I'll carry this to your place, and we can put it in your recycling bin."

"That's a good idea, dear."

At the Potter home, Emily opened the gate for the elderly woman and her dog and followed them up the front steps. Once again, the front door was unlocked. In the kitchen, the dog lapped water from the bowl next to his bed, then curled up, chin on his back feet, and closed his eyes.

Mrs. Potter put the kettle on for tea, told Emily where to find the cups and saucers and dessert plates, and rattled on about the weather, her daughter, the neighbors and the news that Chief Fenwick was retiring from the Riverton PD.

Emily watched with amusement and mild concern as Mrs. Potter took a quart of milk out of the refrigerator, filled an old-fashioned, floral-patterned creamer, and then put the milk—and the sugar bowl—away in the fridge. The woman had seemed distracted last Saturday morning when Emily had helped her carry her groceries home, but Emily had attributed that to her being excited about the long-overdue visit from her daughter.

"Why don't you take a seat, Mrs. Potter, and let me finish setting the table for tea?"

"Are you sure you don't mind, dear? You are my guest, after all."

"I don't mind one bit." She held a chair for the woman, and then discreetly retrieved the sugar bowl and placed it next to the creamer on the white lace-covered table.

"Well, I don't mind sitting for a spell. My hip has been acting up again. I keep saying I need one of those hip replacements, but Doc Woodward says it's just arthritis."

Emily wondered if Dr. Woodward had noticed that Mrs. Potter was also getting a bit absentminded. Surely her daughter would have noticed, since she'd spent the whole day with her mother on Sunday.

None of your business, Emily reminded herself. She had plenty of her own family issues to deal with and worry about without taking on someone else's. So she poured the tea and served the red velvet cake. Her hostess had insisted on a thin slice, but Emily served herself a generous portion and savored every mouthful.

Half an hour and another cup of tea later, she excused herself. "Thank you for inviting me, Mrs. Potter. This has been lovely, but I have to get back to thc office. I'll give you a hand with the dishes, though."

"You will do no such thing. I'll take care of these myself."

"Are you sure? What about your hip?"

"I'll manage just fine. Will you come again?"

"Of course I will." Emily looped the strap of her bag over her shoulder and noticed the crumpled pop can in the side pocket. "Where's your recycling bin?"

"I keep it out on the back porch, dear."

"I'll let myself out the back door, then."

Banjo sprang to his feet the instant the door creaked open.

"You can let him out, too," Mable said. "He goes out there to do his business."

The delicate reference made Emily smile. "I'll be sure to close the gate, then, so he doesn't get out."

The dog raced in a wide arc around the

backyard while Emily eyed the garden shed again. To satisfy what was probably an unnatural curiosity, she checked the door and found it locked as before. She still found it curious that Mable would lock the shed but leave her home unsecured when she went out, unless she had misplaced her keys. Perhaps they were in the fridge. Ha!

With that thought, Emily let herself through the front gate, carefully latching it, so Banjo couldn't get out. Having tea with Mrs. Potter had been a pleasant diversion, she thought, as she ambled back to Main Street. It was almost lunchtime, and she was hungry, again, so she decided to stop by the barbershop to see if Fred could get away a little early. She usually settled for a light lunch—a salad or maybe a grilled cheese sandwich—but today she was going all out. She could almost taste the Riverton Bar & Grill's cheddar-bacon burger with a chocolate malt and a side of fries. Fred would patiently listen to her self-doubts, and then he would dismiss them and remind her that no matter how things played out, she had a whole village to help her raise her child. She needed to hear that right now. That, and eat a cheeseburger.

CHAPTER FIFTEEN

JACK ARRIVED AT his favorite pizza joint in Little Italy to find his longtime friend Paul Woodward already seated, stirring cream into a cup of coffee. He stood as Jack approached the table, grinning. They greeted one another with a handshake that quickly morphed into a one-armed hug and shoulder slap.

"Good to see you," Paul said.

"Likewise. It's been too long."

"Since Eric's funeral. Has it been two months already?"

"Yeah, it has been." Because that was exactly how pregnant Emily was.

The server stopped at their table. "Something to drink for you?"

"Coffee, please."

"Sure thing. You fellows ready to order?" he asked.

Jack and his friend exchanged glances. Paul raised an eyebrow. "What do you say? The usual?"

Jack laughed. "Works for me. An extra-large pepperoni, ham and salami."

"With extra cheese," Paul added.

"You got it," the waiter said. "I'll be right back with the coffee."

"Thanks. So, what have you been up to?" Jack asked after the server walked away.

"The clinic's been busy. One of our doctors retired, and we haven't found a replacement yet, so we're all working extra hours until we do."

It was true Paul had gone to medical school because his father had practically demanded it. However, the guy had turned out to be a top-notch family doctor. Instead of joining his father's practice in Riverton, Paul had opted for a busy practice in Chicago. He wasn't the type of person to toot his own horn, but he'd been instrumental in setting up a community program for single mothers who lived below the poverty line and struggled to raise healthy kids.

"How's your dad these days?" Jack asked.

"I talk to him every Sunday morning. My father is as dedicated to his patients as always, and as high-handed with me as he's ever been."

"Sorry to hear that."

Paul shrugged. "I'm starting to worry about

him. I called him on Sunday morning, and he told me the same story twice, practically word for word, with only a minute or two in between. Something about the chief of police resigning because his wife is having health problems."

"Could be a normal part of aging, couldn't it?" Jack asked, avoiding the subject of Gord Fenwick's retirement. He wasn't surprised that word was out, but he didn't want to let on he had all but been offered the job. No point, since he wasn't going to take it. Or was he? And why did he keep asking himself that when he had no intention of accepting the offer?

"Forgetfulness is normal," Paul agreed. "Up to a point. I'm getting concerned, though, so I guess it means I'll need to schedule another trip to Riverton so I can see firsthand how he's doing. In your text message you mentioned you were just there yourself."

"I was." Jack waited, knowing what his friend's next question would be.

Paul hesitated before he asked it. "Did you get out to the farm to see Annie?"

"I did. She asked about you."

"Hmm. Did she?"

Jack knew it had practically gutted Paul to watch Annie fall in love with Eric, marry him, have his child. Jack had always thought she and Paul were better suited. Annie had constantly taken a backseat to Eric's love of the limelight. Paul would have placed her on a pedestal. But as Jack's sister, Faith, was fond of saying, "The heart wants what the heart wants." Jack was lousy at figuring out what his heart wanted. Did he really want Emily Finnegan or did he simply want to do the right thing? She had accused him of the latter, but couldn't it be both?

"Annie always asks about you," he told Paul. "You should call her. Better yet, go out to see her when you're in town."

Paul stared into his coffee mug. "I will. I figured I'd give her some time. So," he said, glancing up and looking more composed. "What took you back so soon?"

"A case I'm working on."

Paul nodded. "Is that still the South Side Slayer I've been reading about in the papers?"

"That's the one."

"Thought you already had that guy behind bars."

"We do, but we'd been trying to track down a witness."

"And there's a Riverton connection?"

Jack shrugged, keeping it vague. "Could be. The person we've been trying to track down is the daughter of one of the murder victims—

the homeless woman—and that's where she turned up."

"Strange."

"And it gets stranger."

"How so?"

"The girl is staying at Annie's B & B."

"Huh. You're right, that is strange."

"And that's not the strangest part. This girl's mother's name was Scarlett Daniels. When I had dinner with Emily the other night, she mentioned her mother—the one who ran out on them all those years ago—is also named Scarlett."

Paul let out a long, low whistle. "And you think this dead woman, Scarlett Daniels, might be the Finnegan sisters' mother?"

The waitress returned with Jack's coffee. "Thanks. I haven't connected all the dots yet, but, yeah, I'd say there's a pretty good chance."

"Did you tell Annie about it?"

"No. I figured I'd hold off until I see what I can dig up on these two Scarletts, then take it from there."

"Interesting. What about Emily?"

"Didn't mention it to her, either."

"But you took her out to dinner."

"I did." It was Jack's turn to stare into his mug as though it might be a crystal ball. He sure could use one.

"I didn't know you knew her that well. Interesting."

Jack shot him a look. "You have no idea."

Paul leaned forward, his elbows on the table. "The doctor is in."

Jack gulped some coffee. So far he hadn't breathed a word about any of this to anyone, but he needed some perspective. Who better to help him get there than a lifelong friend? "I stuck around the church for a bit after Eric's funeral, but it was all too much, you know?"

Paul nodded. "It was a shock, for sure."

"He was our age. His kid is still just a little kid. It didn't make any sense, still doesn't. Anyway, I'd had enough and decided I needed to get out of there. I ran into Emily leaving the church—she was feeling pretty blindsided, too—so we both left."

"Together?"

"Yeah, we decided to go for coffee, and then that turned into dinner, and then I took her home. She has an apartment in town."

"I know where she lives. When you say you took her home..."

Jack stabbed the fingers of one hand through his hair. "I spent the night."

"Ah, got it." Paul smiled. "And now the two of you had 'dinner' again this week," he said, using air quotes to turn the word *dinner* into a double entendre. "I had no idea the two of you had a thing going on."

"For the record, it really was just dinner this week. And until last time happened, there was nothing going on."

Paul raised his eyebrows.

"It was one of those things," Jack said. "With the funeral and everything, we were both in a bad way that night, and it sort of just…"

"Happened?"

"I've always liked her. She's supersmart and she's—"

"Hot."

Jack smiled at that. "Smokin'. Those sisters are really something, as you know yourself," he said. "And to be honest, I've had a thing for her since Eric and Annie's wedding, but I never acted on it. We're totally different people. I live here, and she lives there."

"And now that your relationship has changed?" Paul asked.

"I was planning to keep in touch, see her when I could, but now there's a little more to it."

Paul narrowed his eyes. "And that would be…?"

Jack lowered his head, rubbed the fingers

of one hand hand back and forth across his forehead, glanced up again. "She's pregnant."

"Dude." Paul reverted to the lingo they had used as fifteen-year-old dorks who thought they were too cool for school. "I... Wow...I don't know what to say."

"I experienced a loss of words myself." He might feel like less of an idiot right now if Paul wasn't sporting an ear-to-ear grin. "And when I found them again, I apparently said the wrong thing."

The waiter's untimely appearance interrupted them, and they put their conversation on pause while the guy dealt out plates and set a huge pizza in the center of the table. "Anything else for you gentlemen?" he asked.

"Looks good," Jack said. They each took a thick wedge of the pie, snapping off the long, stretchy bands of cheese, savoring the first bites.

"So, let me guess," Paul said after swallowing several large mouthfuls. "When she told you, you asked, 'Are you sure?' Or did you go with the old tried and true 'How did this happen?'"

"Sounds as though you have some experience with this sort of thing."

"Not personally, but doctors hear freaked-out guys ask their girlfriends and wives those questions all the time."

Jack sighed. "For the record, I didn't ask either of those things. All I said was we would get married right away."

"Whoa. So it's *that* serious."

"No, it's not. At least, it wasn't. Not yet, anyway. But a baby's a game-changer."

"Without a doubt," Paul said. "But a wedding? That's kind of a game-changer, too."

Tell me about it, Jack thought. "Lately, especially since Eric's funeral, I've been feeling like something's missing, that I'm ready for a change."

"I know what you mean. I've been thinking along those lines myself."

"Annie."

Paul gave a single nod, his mouth forming a grim line. "Always Annie."

In spite of having his own life suddenly turned upside down, Jack acknowledged his friend's turmoil. "Give her some time, man. You never know."

"Did you set a date for the wedding?"

"No. She turned me down."

Paul leaned back in his seat. "Okay, now *that*, my friend, is the game-changer."

"No kidding."

"But are you sure getting married right away is the best option?"

As far as Jack was concerned, it was the only option. "Can you imagine the buzz around town when people hear about this?"

"Apparently, Emily's not too concerned. Otherwise, she'd have said yes."

"She's as freaked out as I am, so she's not being rational."

Paul chuckled. "I sure hope you didn't tell her that."

"Even I'm not that dense. I simply told her we'd get married, she could move here and I'd take care of everything."

"Very romantic. Sounds like you really pulled out all the stops."

Jack ran his hand through his hair. "The situation calls for action, not romance."

Paul was outright laughing now. "Way to sweep a woman off her feet, Evans."

"You sound like Emily. She's refusing to leave Riverton, and she won't even consider getting married until we—" his turn to employ the air quotes "—get to know each other better."

"What now?" Paul asked.

"So now I go to Riverton every chance I get and take her out to dinner, maybe a movie."

"The hardship."

This was getting him nowhere. "I thought you'd be more sympathetic. It doesn't make sense to do this long-distance, and it doesn't make sense for her to stay in Riverton."

Paul picked up his coffee cup, touched it to Jack's. "You're in a relationship with one of the Finnegan sisters, she's going to have your baby and she wants to spend time with you. Do you have any idea how many times I've wished I were in that situation?"

Countless times, no doubt. "Sorry, man. I didn't mean to sound like a jerk."

"Hey, no need to apologize. You're having a completely normal reaction to being blind-sided by impending fatherhood. Can I offer you one piece of advice?"

"I've been hoping you would."

"Next time you decide to play the marriage card, make her an offer she can't refuse."

"Meaning?"

His friend's head shake hinted he was being clueless. Fair enough. Jack would be the first to agree.

"Do you remember Emily's maid-of-honor speech at Eric and Annie's wedding?"

"Vaguely." To be honest, at that point, he'd been paying more attention to her physical attributes than her elocution.

"She described the way Eric proposed to her

sister, how he staged the Finnegans' gazebo on the riverbank with candles, rose petals and her favorite song playing on his iPod speaker. She talked about how surprised and happy her sister was, how that marriage proposal was every woman's dream, and of course Annie had said yes."

The gazebo. Of course. He remembered Eric planning that night, picking out the ring, and now he remembered Emily's speech, as well. He also knew it wasn't easy for Paul to talk about Eric and Annie. "Thanks. I needed to hear that."

Paul nodded. "Happy to help. One more thing, and you probably won't want to hear this."

"What's that?"

"If you really expect her to marry you, you might have to be the one to make the biggest compromise."

"Such as?"

"Those sisters are not going to leave their home, and they're never going to leave their father. If you really want to be with Emily, it'll have to be in Riverton."

Somewhere deep in his subconscious, Jack already knew this, but Paul was right. He just wasn't ready or willing to accept it. Still, he decided against mentioning the possibility of the chief of police position with the Riverton PD. For the life of him, he had a hard time seeing himself giving up the career he'd worked so hard to achieve here in Chicago. And he did not feel ready to take on the responsibility of running an entire police department, even a small one. He knew what Paul would say, though. Paul would tell him that if he had a chance with one of the Finnegan sisters, he'd be a fool not to go for it. He also knew that Paul would give up his lucrative Chicago practice and return to Riverton in a heartbeat if it meant having Annie Finnegan in his life.

After they polished off the pizza and the server had refilled their cups a second time, they each tossed several bills on the table and walked out to the parking lot.

"We need to do this again," Jack said. His mind felt clearer than it had in weeks. "Soon."

Paul pulled out his phone, swiped the screen to bring up his calendar. "Two weeks from now?"

"Sounds good." Jack plugged the date into his calendar, too.

Minutes later, Jack sat behind the wheel of his Jeep and reflected on the evening's conversation. Until tonight, he hadn't understood why he wasn't freaking out about the baby. Now he knew. The baby was changing everything for the better. Two months ago, the death of a longtime friend had forced him to examine who he was, what he was doing with his life, why he felt as though something was missing. What was missing was a life. Now, in fewer than twenty-four hours, everything looked crystal clear. He was in love with Emily. It was that simple.

He couldn't pinpoint the precise moment it had happened but, looking back, it had started at Annie and Eric's wedding. She'd had a glass of champagne, possibly two, and had seemed a little light-headed when he'd walked her onto the dance floor. With her cheek resting against his shoulder and her eyes closed, she had swayed in his arms to "You Send Me." And at the time, like Sam Cooke, he'd been sure it was an infatuation. Now he needed to prove to her it was more than that. He'd never been good at compromise, but Paul was right about that, too. He knew precisely what form that compromise would take. First thing tomorrow morning, he would put his plan in motion.

CHAPTER SIXTEEN

ANNIE HAD BEEN RIGHT. Sunday dawned clear and bright, and the warm afternoon sunshine made it a perfect day for a horseback ride and a picnic by the pond. She had filled a pair of saddlebags with food, and Emily knew that the meal would be delicious. Now, helping CJ saddle up Honey and Heathcliffe while surreptitiously watching Jack watch them with uncertainty, she was more grateful than ever her big sister had suggested this date. He had been less than enthusiastic, but for whatever reason he had agreed to go along with her plan.

Since the moment Emily had laid eyes on Jack, back on that fateful first day of high school, she had been love-struck. He was taller than the other boys and ten times better looking, but there'd been more to it. Even as a teenager, when most of the other guys had been awkward or insecure, or both, Jack had exuded a quiet confidence. Right now, though, he looked nervous. He had never ridden a horse before, and it showed.

"Are you sure this is a good idea?" he asked as she led her mare, Honey, into the cross ties and slid the saddle pad across her back. "What if you fall?"

"We're going for a trail ride. I'm not going to fall." Emily laid the saddle over the pad and snugged the cinch around Honey's girth.

"What if I fall?"

She smiled at him. "Nobody falls off a horse on a trail ride." Which wasn't exactly true, as CJ could attest. Hardly anyone ever did, but he didn't need to know that.

Emily unclipped the cross ties, patted Honey's shoulder and led her out of the stable and into the yard. Without looking back at Jack, she stuck her foot into a stirrup and swung herself up and onto the saddle. Before long, her expanding belly wouldn't allow her to perform a move like that. She held the reins in one hand and rubbed her horse's shoulder with the other while she waited.

"Would you like to use the mounting block?" CJ asked Jack, indicating the wooden platform that beginners accessed by a short set of steps.

Jack frowned, looking insulted.

CJ laughed. "All right, then. Up you go. I'll adjust the length of your stirrups after you're in the saddle."

From her vantage point on Honey's back,

Emily watched with amusement as Jack made two attempts to get his left foot in the stirrup, stumbling both times. Heathcliffe angled his head, trying to get a look at what was going on, rolling his eyes sideways so the whites showed.

Emily allowed herself a secret little smile. One hundred percent of Jack's attention was focused on the horse, so he wasn't paying attention to her anyway.

"Not as easy as it looks." CJ waved him aside and set a plastic mounting stool on the ground next to Heathcliffe. "Better to use this than spook your horse."

Jack acquiesced. A moment later, he sat in the saddle while CJ adjusted the stirrups. By the time he looked over to Emily, she had composed herself and dialed back her grin to a smile.

CJ patiently demonstrated how to hold the reins and made Jack walk Heathcliffe around the ring until she was satisfied he could guide the horse without confusing the poor animal, gently rein him in, and nudge him into action again.

"Okay. That was good," CJ said. She led Heathcliffe next to Honey, patted both horses' hindquarters. "Off you go, you crazy kids. Be sure to stay out of trouble." And then with a saucy toss of her long blond ponytail, she disappeared into the stable, chuckling at her inappropriateness.

Emily wished she could blame her flushed face on the warmth of the afternoon sun. "I am *so* sorry. I can't believe she said that. Ugh, I *can't* believe it."

"Emily, it's fine." Jack wasn't looking at her because he was fixated on a point on the ground just ahead of Heathcliffe's head, but he was grinning. "And you have to admit, it was kind of funny."

Funny. Right. Because being pregnant, single and completely skeptical that the father of your baby was in this for the long haul never mind be willing to honor his totally clichéd reaction to finding out about the baby—was hilarious. *We'll get married.* Right. Because that was always the best solution.

"So…" Jack said, with a hint of accusation.

"What?" It came out shriller than she would have liked. Not that any amount of shrill was ever a good thing.

"When I told you to decide what you'd like to do on our next date, I sure didn't expect this."

"Believe it or not, it was Annie's idea. She said it's hard to truly get to know someone over dinner at a restaurant, that it's better to do things we love to do." So this afternoon was meant to be part test—to see if he was willing to be part of her world—and part retribution. Based on their conversations throughout the week, she had a hunch he was withholding something important, although she couldn't imagine what it might be. She would not tolerate being sheltered from whatever he thought she might not need to know. Not for a minute. He could think again.

He had agreed to the date, though. He was here, and he was on horseback. She needed to lighten up.

"So that means you'll go to a White Sox game with me?" And just like that, he turned the table on her.

"Will you buy me a hot dog and popcorn and one of those giant foam fingers?"

"Yes to the food, no to the finger."

She laughed at that.

"I can see why you enjoy this," he said. "It's quiet out here. Peaceful."

"It is, and it's a beautiful afternoon. This is one of my favorite places in the world. Probably my second most favorite place after the gazebo on the riverbank. And this is my first trail ride of the season and…"

"And?"

"I'm glad you're here." She was. She had

dreamed of this moment…this…exact…
moment…so many times over the years. "I
love it here. This is my favorite season, and
green is my favorite color and this…the trees
starting to leaf out and the fields coming to
life and… I love it here."

"You sound like a writer."

Emily decided that might be the nicest thing
anyone had ever said to her.

"And I can see why you love it," Jack said.
"I lived here for the first half of my life, but I
never saw the countryside from this perspective."

"That's because you didn't see it from the
back of a horse."

"You could be right. Or maybe I wasn't seeing it from the right perspective, with the right
person."

"And your perspective has changed?" she
asked, ignoring, for now, his implication there
was a chance she might be the right person.

"I'd say it has."

They rode in silence for a while, guiding
the horses along a narrow gravel access road
that sliced between a cornfield and a hay field.
It was one of those perfect early summer af-
ternoons. The warmth from the sun mingled
with the breeze and stirred up the scents of the

dusty road, the freshly tilled soil and the wild-flowers that were starting to put on a show.

Emily was beginning to feel more at ease with Jack. The silence was companionable, and it was a relief to not have to fill every second with nervous prattle. It gave her a chance to take in the soothing sounds around her—the crunch of gravel beneath hooves, the chitter of black-capped chickadees, the soft snuffles and whinnying of the horses.

"It sounds like they're talking to one another," Jack said.

"They are. Honey and Heathcliffe have been stable buddies for years. Their stalls are side by side, and they always graze together in the same paddock."

"So you've always had horses?"

"For as long as I can remember. The three of us—Annie, CJ and I—grew up with them, but CJ's the one who turned into a real horse-woman. She started winning blue ribbons when she was ten or eleven. We've always boarded horses out here, and she started training them, then offering riding lessons. Then she got the idea to get my dad back on a horse—"

"I used to think it was amazing that your father could ride a horse. Now that I'm on one myself, it's nothing short of miraculous."

Jack sounded no less surprised than anyone else when they discovered Thomas Finnegan was as comfortable in the saddle as he was in his wheelchair.

Emily nodded. "He is amazing. CJ spent a lot of time researching the kind of lift we'd need. By the time she was sixteen, she had started a therapeutic riding program for a couple of kids in town. One child with cerebral palsy and the other has Down syndrome. Word spread quickly, and now CJ's program is known throughout the county and beyond."

"Wow, that's impressive."

"She's pretty amazing, too, although sometimes she's still my annoying little sister." Her sensibilities still stung from CJ's tongue-in-cheek warning about not getting into trouble.

"What about Annie?"

"She tends to be less annoying."

Jack laughed. "I meant, how is she with the horses?"

"Oh, right." Emily steered her thoughts away from CJ's tendency to have her nose in everyone's business and back to their initial conversation. "Annie is Annie, as I'm sure you know. She excels at everything, including take care of the family. I can't remember a time when she wasn't looking after me and

CJ, and our dad, of course, and then Eric and Isaac. That's who she is."

"She was that way at school, too. If anything needed to be done, it was always, 'Ask Annie.'"

Ask Annie. Emily liked that. She could use that as a title for a blog post, or maybe even a series of weekly posts.

"That's my big sister, all right. And now, on top of taking care of the family and the house, she has guests to look after, as well. When she opened the B & B, she hired a part-time housekeeper to come in for a few hours every morning. Otherwise, she manages everything pretty much single-handedly. To get back to your question, she's a very accomplished rider, as she is with everything else, but she doesn't have much time for it."

They were approaching the end of the road where a bank led from the gravel easement to a well-traveled trail through the woods.

"We'll stop here for a bit. Whoa, girl," Emily said, reining in her horse.

Jack did the same. Emily leaned forward and stroked Honey's shoulder as she came to a stop.

"We'll go single file down the bank," she said to Jack. "I'll go down first. You can wait up here, then follow me. Keep the reins slack and lean back a little in the saddle. Heathcliffe knows what to do, so let him do all the work."

She squeezed Honey's sides with her legs, felt the familiar sway as the horse picked her way down the incline. At the base of the slope, she swung Honey around so she could watch Jack and Heathcliffe make their descent. With his killer good looks and broad-shouldered strength, Jack looked as if he was born to ride, but his lack of ease in the saddle gave him away. For a change, it felt good to be the confident one, and she liked that this was something she could teach him. Silly thoughts, but she was having them nonetheless.

"Well done. You look like a pro already," she said, adopting CJ's approach to teaching riding lessons.

He hiked up one eyebrow, making her smile.

She turned Honey toward the trail as Jack rode up alongside, then they entered the woods together. Sunlight filtered through the canopy of birch and cottonwood, but the air was a few degrees cooler than when they'd been out in the open.

"Not much farther," she said. "Maybe half a mile to the pond."

Here, the horses' hooves were quieter on the soft ground. The twitter and chirp of songbirds were abundant, and at one point, a squirrel scolded them from a branch overhead. However, it still felt quiet and calm here.

"So, what about you?" Jack said after they were underway and had resumed their earlier rhythm.

"What about me?"

"One sister's a horsewoman, the other is a homemaker. What's Emily's strong suit?"

Head in the clouds? Hopeless romantic? "I guess I'm the bookworm. And I always wanted to be a writer—"

"You are a writer."

"Not just a writer for the local paper. For as long as I can remember, I've had this dream I would write something…I don't know…more important."

"News is pretty important."

"It it, for sure, but it's fleeting. Yesterday's paper is already in the bottom of the birdcage, so to speak, and last week's is long forgotten."

"What about your blog? My mother was raving about it this morning." Was he serious or poking fun at her? She couldn't tell from his tone.

"Did you read it?" She loved her blog and was thrilled that more and more people were checking out her posts, but the thought of Jack perusing them gave her heart palpitations.

"I did. It's good. Really good."

"Thanks. It's mostly stories about small-town life, but they're fun to write."

"Like the missing garden gnomes."

Emily laughed. "Correct. When I first heard about the missing items, I knew it would be fun to write about them." The stories were meant to be lighthearted, and it still surprised her that many people took them so seriously.

"They're charming stories, Emily. Well written, too. Actually, they remind me a little of Garrison Keillor's work."

"Oh." *Charming. Well written. Garrison Keillor?* High praise from a man who most likely didn't have time to read much more than police reports and witness statements. "Wow. Well, thank you. As I said before, Ken Bartlett wouldn't let me put those stories in the *Gazette* so I found a work-around."

"And a good one, considering no actual crimes have been committed."

Emily shot him a sideways look. "You sound pretty sure about that. Or are you saying it's not okay to steal a car or rob a bank, but it's quite all right to make off with a gnome, a welcome mat or your mother's garden trowel."

"Never, but based on my experience—"

"You have experience with missing garden gnomes?"

Jack smiled. "Mysterious disappearances

don't always equate to theft, and a good detective always looks for the motive."

She shrugged. "I don't know about the thief's motive, but mine is to entertain my readers."

"Then I'd say mission accomplished. I enjoyed reading your stories—all of them—and I can see why everyone in Riverton and beyond is following along."

"Thank you." His praise meant a lot. "I'm trying to capture small-town life, you know? Really get to the heart of it. Not because it's old-fashioned or silly, but because it's real and special, and because even though the things that happen aren't always earthshaking or newsworthy, they're real for the people experiencing them."

Jack was full-out grinning now.

"What?" she asked.

"I'm wondering if you're going to write about teaching a city slicker how to ride a horse."

"You know, I just might do that."

The woods thinned out as they approached a grassy meadow surrounding the pond.

"Nice spot," Jack said as they rode out of the trees. "Is this still part of your family's farm?"

"It is, and the fields we rode past are ours, too. We lease them to Arnie Jacobson, and he gives us hay for the horses as partial payment." Emily let him ride ahead, then quickly pulled out her phone and snapped a photo as he and the horse gazed over the pond. By the time he glanced back at her, she had stowed the phone in her pocket and was drafting a story in her head.

"The lease sounds like an ideal arrangement."

"It is." She slid off Honey's back and stepped up to hold Heathcliffe's bridle while Jack dismounted. "A lot of people thought my dad should sell the place after he was injured and my mother left."

Jack gave her a sharp, almost startled look, but he didn't say anything.

"There was no way my dad would have sold the farm, and we're all grateful for that. It still provides livelihoods for my sisters, and Isaac is the fifth generation to live here." She led the horses to the pond's edge, and both animals lowered their heads to drink.

"I know I keep saying this, but your father's a pretty amazing guy."

"We think so."

Honey lifted her head first, then Heathcliffe, and together they backed away from the water. Emily pulled a carrot out of her pocket, snapped it in half and offered a piece to each of them. "Good girl, Honey. Gently, Heathcliffe. No need to take my fingers with it. Good ride, you two."

She handed Heathcliffe's reins to Jack. "We'll tether them to the rail over here," she said, indicating the birch log on a pair of fence posts, which CJ had put up for this very purpose. After the horses were secured with leads long enough to let them graze, Emily unbuckled the saddlebags and handed one to Jack.

They strolled to a grassy spot near the pond. Emily pulled out the old picnic blanket and spread it on the grass. They both sat down, Jack somewhat gingerly.

"How are you feeling?" she asked. "Riding usually tests a few muscles most people don't even know they have."

"I'm pretty sure I'll know about them tomorrow. How about you?" he asked pointedly. "Are you feeling okay?"

Emily met his concerned gaze with a direct one of her own. "I'm fine. I saw Doc Woodward this week, and he says riding is okay."

Emily opened one of the leather saddlebags. "Let's see what Annie packed for us."

As usual, her sister had outdone herself. She'd made two of her famous meatloaf sandwiches— one of Emily's all-time favorites—with little containers of coleslaw to go with them and chocolate brownies for dessert. In addition, she had packed napkins, plastic forks and two bottles of water.

"Wow," Jack said. "I'm impressed."

"Wait'll you try one of these sandwiches. You'll be completely blown away."

They both bit into a sandwich, and Emily smiled at the ecstatic roll of Jack's eyes. "What did I tell you?"

He simply nodded and took another bite.

"So, what were we talking about before we got here?"

Jack swallowed and took a swig of water. "You were telling me about your father."

"Right. A lot of people see my dad in that wheelchair and immediately think of him as disabled. But other than not being able to walk, there's nothing he can't do."

"I believe you," he said. "Especially knowing he rides a horse. And I don't think there was a dry eye in the house when he danced with Annie at her wedding."

"Oh, my gosh, wasn't that incredible? I'll *never* forget that. None of us will. We still have my grandmother's record collection, and that Maurice Chevalier song "Thank Heaven for Little Girls" has always been special to us because our dad played it at every one of our birthday parties. He and CJ came up with the idea of using it for the father-daughter dance and they practiced when no one was around. It was a complete surprise to everyone, even Annie."

"Maybe it'll become a family tradition."

Emily, about to take another bite of her sandwich, paused and stared at him. "You said you wouldn't ask again until I was sure I was ready, remember? You promised."

"And I haven't asked. That wasn't even a question." His eyes held a subtle glint of defiance, but she wasn't backing down.

"Now you're nitpicking."

"I'd say you're the one who's nitpicking. I'm a patient man, Emily, and I haven't asked you anything. I was making an observation that your father's choice of songs for a father-daughter dance would be a nice touch at *your* wedding, too. The fact that I expect to be there is, of course, a given."

She knew she was blushing like crazy and wished she could make it stop. She didn't know what to say. She wasn't ready to talk about marriage. Jack had made his presence known every single day since she'd told him about the baby, texting her in the morning before he left for work, calling every evening, sending emails with interesting tidbits about his day. He was holding something back, though, and it was the most important thing of all. He had never said he loved her.

They finished their lunch in awkward silence. While Emily stuffed the sandwich wrappers and empty containers back into the saddlebags, Jack stretched out his long jean-clad legs, crossed them at the ankles and leaned back on one elbow.

"There is something I'd like to tell you," he said, finally breaking the silence that was now beyond uncomfortable. "And I promise not to turn it into a question, okay?"

"Okay." The word felt thick in her throat.

He picked a daisy from a clump blooming next to where they had spread the blanket. "Last Saturday, when I had to make the unexpected trip back here, I was kicking myself for being such an idiot. Not calling you for all those weeks was easily one of the dumbest things I've ever done."

At this point, she decided it was best not to agree or disagree.

He studied the daisy thoughtfully, as though looking for an answer to a question. "I'd thought about you a lot since our night together, but something always came up, and I put off calling. Once I knew I would be in town, I didn't call because it would be too easy for you to tell me to get lost."

She couldn't help smiling at that.

"And you probably would have." He tugged a petal from the daisy.

"Well, not likely, given the current… situation." Startled, Emily watched the petal fall onto the blanket. *He loves me.*

"Right. Still, I decided the element of surprise would be to my advantage." Another petal fell.

"And instead it was just…surprise!" *He loves me not.*

"It was." He dropped a third petal.

He loves me. "And you seem sort of okay with it, which surprises me."

He let the daisy fall to the blanket along with the few scattered petals. She wondered where he was going with this, if he would try to soften her up and suggest she move to Chicago, and if he would pick up the daisy and finish what he'd started.

"After we were best man and maid of honor at Eric and Annie's wedding, you were on my mind. A lot."

Okay, that was a surprise. She wasn't completely sure she should believe him. He must have sensed her thoughts, because he kept talking.

"And after we became Isaac's godparents."

"Why didn't you ever say anything?"

"Honestly, I assumed I didn't have a shot. I thought you and Fred Morris had something going on."

"Fred and I are friends."

"I know, but even back in high school the two of you were joined at the hip. And then when you came back to Riverton after college, you were always together."

"How do you know that? You were living in Chicago."

"Eric and Annie mentioned you from time to time. From the way they described you and Fred, I figured you were at least friends with benefits."

Emily's face flamed. "Friends with benefits? *Benefits?* Is that what Eric told you? That's just…ugh… That's disgusting." She picked up the daisy and threw it at him.

He laughed and ducked, and the flower sailed over his shoulder. "And yet his was the first name that came to mind when your sisters asked who the baby's father was."

Blurting out Fred's name—dumbest thing ever. Emily knew that. What she hadn't known was that she had been on Jack's mind, just as he had been on hers. She wished she hadn't thrown the daisy at him because she was dying to know how the game ended.

CHAPTER SEVENTEEN

A WEEK AFTER the picnic with Jack, life had taken on an easy rhythm. Relatively speaking. Emily talked to him on the phone every night and for the most part, he was the one who initiated the call. He had come to Riverton two weekends in a row to see her, three if she counted their fateful encounter in the barbershop. Her sisters' nagging to accept Jack's offer of marriage—she refused to consider it a proposal because it hadn't been—had tapered off from incessant to periodic. And she and Fred had resumed their easygoing friendship, including meeting daily for lunch as they were doing today.

Emily pushed her empty plate aside and picked up her coffee cup.

"I have to stop eating like this," she said to Fred, who sat across from her in their usual booth at the Riverton Bar & Grill. The lunch special—corned beef on rye with salad or fries—was far more food than she usually ate. She didn't even like corned beef, and she should have ordered the salad.

Fred grinned. "Isn't this normal? You're eating for two now."

"Unless the second person is a seven-hundred-pound sumo wrestler, I need to stop eating like this."

That morning, she had been hard-pressed to find business attire in her closet that still fit. She had settled on a sleeveless beige dress for two reasons. One, she was able to put it on *and* zip it up, and two, the gathering on one side of the dress produced a series of asymmetrical folds across her tummy that had been designed to hide a multitude of sins. To wear with it, she had debated over a black blazer and a dark beige one. The weather promised to be too warm to wear black, so she'd opted for the beige on beige, and accessorized with small onyx hoop earrings and matching bangle, a pair of black pumps and her black briefcase.

Last night, while she and her sisters were clearing up after dinner, Annie had taken her and CJ aside and suggested they take a day off and drive into St. Paul to shop for maternity clothes. Out of necessity, Emily had agreed. CJ, who hated the city, passed, saying she would stay home and take care of Isaac.

Fred leaned against the back of the booth, giving her the once-over. "You do realize that with all the food you've been devouring, the reason for this gluttony is going to become very obvious, very soon."

"Gluttony. Gee, thanks. Just what every woman wants to hear."

He was undeterred. "Have you made a decision yet?"

"About what?"

"Jack's proposal."

"That wasn't a 'proposal.' It was an idea, a suggestion, an attempt to remedy a situation. And, no, I haven't accepted. Besides, he hasn't brought it up again." Not exactly.

"You haven't answered my question."

"You asked if I'd accepted, and I said no, I haven't."

"That's not what I asked."

"Yes, it is."

"No, it's not. I asked if you'd made a decision about how you will answer the next time he does bring it up."

Talk about splitting hairs. "Do you know what he told me when I took him riding? He said he's been interested in me since we were in Annie and Eric's wedding party, but he was afraid to do anything about it."

Fred blinked, fully taken aback. "Afraid of you?"

"No, he was afraid of you. He thought there was something going on between us."

Fred's coffee cup clattered against the saucer. "That's crazy. Everyone knows we're just friends."

"Yes, well, he thought we were friends with benefits."

Poor Fred. Now his ears were blushing. He opened his mouth and closed it again. "What?" he said, finally finding his voice. "You set him straight, right?"

She cast a glance at the ceiling, then back at Fred. "Of course I did."

Flustered now, he picked up his cup and set it back down. "Well, that's a relief. Do you think maybe he's waiting for you to make a move?"

"I am not making a move. And if I'm going to say yes to a—" she gave a quick glance around the café and lowered her voice to a stage whisper "—to a marriage proposal, it will have to be a proper one."

"I don't know, Em. Jack doesn't seem like the kind of guy who comes up with one of those over-the-top, sweep-a-girl-off-her-feet proposals that goes viral on YouTube."

"I don't need a grand gesture. I just need

to know…" She glanced around the restaurant and lowered her voice. "That he wants to marry me for the right reasons instead of just the obvious one."

"Fair enough. I'm only saying—"

"I know what you're saying. I've already heard it all from my sisters." She checked her watch and reached for her briefcase next to her on the bench seat. "I need to get over to the town hall. The council meeting starts in half an hour, and I'd like to be there a little early to see what I can find out about the new chief of police. Have you heard anything?"

"Not a word," he said. "The mayor has been playing this hand mighty close to his chest."

She nodded. "The consensus seems to be that no one who is currently with the Riverton PD is either interested or qualified, so he's had to look elsewhere."

"Interesting. Well, the wait is almost over." Fred stood and so did she. Emily fumbled for her wallet.

"My treat," he said, reaching into his pocket and tossing several bills onto the table with the check. "You can get it next time."

They left the café and walked to her car, which she had parked near the entrance so she could get underway right after lunch.

"Thank you." She hugged him.

"No problem." He hugged her back, but without his usual enthusiasm. "You'd better go before someone else starts thinking we're friends with benefits."

Emily gazed up at him. "Can we promise each other something?"

"What's that?"

"That we'll never say that friends thing out loud ever again."

"Works for me," he said. "Give me a call if there's any earthshaking news at the meeting. My customers like it when I have the inside scoop."

"This is Riverton. Nothing earthshaking ever happens."

"Oh, I don't know about that. I, for one, will be on tenterhooks till someone cracks the case of the missing garden gnomes."

Very funny. "Maybe the new chief of police will take this case seriously."

He opened her car door for her. "Or he may be even stodgier than Gord Fenwick. Either way, the new chief is going to be announced without you if you don't get over there."

"All right, fine, I'm on my way. I'll text you with the news, so you'll have something to gossip about with your customers this afternoon."

He waved and crossed the street to the barbershop. Emily slid behind the wheel of her car, made the short drive to the new town hall, and congratulated herself on arriving early when she easily found a parking space.

Inside the council chamber, she took a seat next to the reporter from the Wabasha, MN, newspaper. He was the only other person at the press table. If Ken Bartlett had been hoping for a reporter from the Minneapolis *Star Tribune* or even the Madison *Capital Times*, Emily had a hunch he was going to be disappointed.

"Hi, Jim."

"Hmmph." The single syllable sounded more like a sigh than a greeting, and the middle-aged man didn't even glance away from the screen of his cell phone, suggesting he'd rather be almost anywhere but here.

His disinterest was fine with her. Emily flipped open her laptop and turned it on. She had plenty on her mind. She had also already drafted an outline for this story, including a nice little send-off for Gordon Fenwick.

More than once she had to stifle a yawn. As soon as this was over, she would go back to the office and do a smattering of research on the newly appointed chief, draft the article for the *Gazette*, and then head upstairs to her apartment for a nap. In spite of having a good night's sleep, she was uncharacteristically tired. Maybe it was the huge lunch she'd devoured.

She dug her digital camera out of her bag, checked the settings and placed it on the table next to her laptop. She would take some candid photos during the introductions and the formal handover from the old chief to the new one, and then shoot several staged photographs afterward. Since the mayor was also the *Gazette*'s editor-in-chief, he would want final approval on which image would appear on the front page of the newspaper, but she could share some of the others on her blog. She already planned to do a post on the new chief and another on a tribute to Chief Fenwick. He had been with the Riverton police department for as long as Emily could remember. She knew his wife, and she had gone to school with their children, so it seemed fitting to make something of his retirement.

Over the next several minutes, the chamber gradually filled with town councilors, a handful of off-duty police officers and the Fenwick family. To Emily's surprise, and somewhat to her dismay, Walt and Norma Evans—Jack's parents!—walked in and joined Gordon Fenwick's wife in the front row. The two families lived across the street from one another, so she supposed it made sense they would be here.

Still, they were the last people Emily wanted to see right now, so she avoided eye contact by pretending to concentrate on the file open on her computer. She was beginning to wrap her head around the idea of having a baby, of having Jack in her life, one way or another, forever. The prospect of breaking the news to her father and his parents had her heart hammering.

Riverton was so small, and she was out and about so much that she saw a lot of people every day. Just last week she'd run into Norma at Henderson's Hardware when she'd popped in to buy a bag of wood shavings for the bottom of Tadpole's cage. Several days later, Walt had waved at her as she was pulling out of Gabe's Gas 'n' Go. Friendly encounters both times, the kind that indicated they suspected nothing about her and Jack.

Whatever she and Jack were, whatever they were going to become.

Her heart hammered harder. She lightly touched the tips of the fingers on her right hand to the pulse point on the inside of her left wrist.

Stay calm. This is not *the time or place for a panic attack.* Nor was it the time or place to be looking for answers about her future. She needed to stop posing the questions.

Right on schedule, the side door opened. Ken Bartlett stepped into the council chamber, followed by Chief Fenwick and…

Jack?

Every head in the place swiveled in her direction.

Oh, dear. Had she said his name out loud?

Her fingers fell away from her wrist, her pulse ratcheted up again, and her breath shuddered in and out of her lungs as she struggled for control. She steadied herself by white-knuckling the edge of the press table. Breathe…breathe…breathe. There. Better.

Jack's presence behind the podium could only mean one thing. He was the mayor's very well-kept secret. He was Riverton's new police chief.

She had been all too aware of Ken Bartlett's desire to conceal this information from his public. He loved nothing more than making the big reveal—her father called it grandstanding—but she didn't care about that. She cared about Jack. Why hadn't he told her? They had spent most of the past three weekends together. Last night he had joined her family for his second consecutive Sunday dinner and he hadn't breathed a word, not even a hint. This meant he would be living in Riverton, which she knew was a huge sacrifice for him and which also meant she didn't even have to consider a move to Chicago. Not that she had. Still, he should have told her rather than spring this on her.

Ken was at the podium now. She needed to focus, be professional, do her job, when the only thing she truly wanted to do was rush to the front of the council chambers and throw her arms around him.

Jack was Riverton's new chief of police. He had to be. That was the only explanation for his being here. Was he really giving up a job he loved so he could be here for her and the baby? For the baby, for sure, and for now that was good enough, and far more than she had anticipated. He was watching her, the way he did when he was trying to gauge her reaction, and his secret smile, the one that seemed just for her, made her bones melt.

The mayor leaned into the microphone. "Ladies and gentlemen, it is my great pleasure to offer my deepest gratitude to my longtime friend, Police Chief Gordon Fenwick, and to thank him on your behalf for his many years of service to our fair town." He paused, puffed up his chest and cast a slow, calculating glance around the room, ever the politician.

Ken was wearing one of the three decades-old suits—one navy, one brown, one gray—that he alternated for events like this one. By rotating the scant, outdated contents of his closet, he avoided being photographed in the same suit at successive events. Emily had always thought if he eventually followed through on his ambitious desire to run for state representative, someone would have to help the man update his wardrobe.

Chief Fenwick was all spit and polish in his official police uniform. Jack, who had yet to be sworn in and had therefore not been issued a Riverton PD uniform, was dressed in black dress pants and a blue crew neck that was a perfect match for his eyes. His leather jacket was a deep shade of espresso and had, she knew firsthand, the texture of butter. His hair had been trimmed to a respectable length, and no longer curled over his collar at the back, but there was a don't-mess-with-me quality to the day's growth of beard gracing his jawline. The intriguing dichotomy that was Jack Evans.

He was taller than the two men standing with him on the raised dais, and his shoulders were broader, making his presence more imposing than if he'd been up there alone. She could tell from the murmurs in the room that a person didn't have to be in love with him to recognize his importance.

If the mayor was aware of this, he wasn't letting on. "I also take great pleasure…great pleasure," he repeated, puffing up his chest, "in extending a warm Riverton welcome to our new chief of police, former Chicago PD Detective Jack Evans."

Former detective. This meant that not only had Jack been offered the position and accepted it, he had already resigned. The pieces were gradually falling into place. The chief of police appointment had been in the works for several weeks, at least since the last council meeting, and Jack hadn't breathed a word about it to her. She might have been miffed if it weren't for her sheer sense of giddiness over the sacrifice he was obviously making for her and the baby.

Somehow her fingers found the keyboard, and she transcribed what the men were saying, almost word for word, though none of it quite registered, not even as the words scrolled across the monitor in front of her.

After the mayor wrapped up the meeting, Emily was much more composed. It was photo time. She picked up her camera, glad she'd checked the light and exposures before being slammed with the unexpected news that Jack Evans was Riverton's new chief of police.

The three men posed in front of the flags that stood behind the podium. For each photo, Jack's smile softened his features and took the edge off the laser-sharp stare he'd been giving her since he had walked into the room. Click, click, click.

The former chief stepped aside so she could take a formal shot of Jack sharing a hearty handshake with the mayor. Click.

The mayor decided she should also take one of Jack by himself—which felt ridiculously awkward, as though he was looking right through the camera and into her soul. Finally, she snapped a few shots of Jack with his parents.

Click, click, click.

"Riverton will be the safest town in Wisconsin, and if anyone can solve the mystery of the missing garden gnomes, my son can," Norma Evans said to Emily. "Just you wait and see."

Jack gave Emily a look that asked her to tread cautiously, but Emily simply nodded and gave his mother a weak smile. After the photo shoot, everyone mingled, gravitating to the refreshment table set up at the back of the room. Emily hastily scrolled through the images she had captured and, satisfied she had what she needed, packed up her camera and laptop with trembling hands and slung the bag over her shoulder. More than anything she wanted to talk to Jack tell him how grateful she was—now that she was over the shock— that he would make this kind of committment for their child. But not here, not now. She walked quickly toward the door, head down so no one would see the tears of relief in her eyes. Luckily, as far as everyone else knew, she was merely the reporter, and no one expected her to stay.

JACK MOVED THROUGH the room, shaking hands, accepting congratulations and making small talk while keeping Emily in his field of view. She was in a hurry to leave, judging by the way she was cramming things into her bag. He wished he could have told her about this ahead of time, but a combination of factors had prevented that.

He'd had to make this decision on his own, although talking to his friend, Paul, and his bureau chief had helped. Especially after he'd told them about the Emily and the baby. He already knew he was gaining much more than he was giving up.

To complicate things even further, the

mayor, in his typical fashion, had wanted to make a big splash by keeping this top secret. If he had told Emily, he had a niggling suspicion she might let it slip to Fred, and then it would have spread through town like wildfire. That was not how he wanted to start his tenure as Riverton's new police chief. Now Emily was leaving, and all he wanted was to rush out the door after her.

"Jack, I'm sure you know Reverend Frank Hammond and his wife, Alice," the mayor said. "Frank's been the minister at Grace Memorial for what, thirty years?"

"Thirty-two." The reverend had a hearty handshake. "Welcome back to Riverton, son. Good to know we'll have one of our own looking out for us." The reverend had officiated at Eric's funeral.

"It's good to be home."

Mrs. Hammond beamed at him. "The church is hosting the Hospital Auxiliary's bazaar and rummage sale next Saturday," she said. "We'd love to have you officially open the event for us."

"I would be honored. I'll check my schedule and let you know." He did his best to be attentive while he watched Emily hoist her bag off the table and haul it onto her shoulder. She exchanged a few words with the reporter who'd sat next to her at the press table, then briskly walked toward the exit without so much as a backward glance.

"Very nice to see you both," Jack said. "Could you excuse me? There's someone I need to have a few words with."

He tried to make a beeline for the door but instead ended up dodging several more well-wishers, including his mother.

"We're so proud of you." Norma Evans was literally beaming, and her pleasure made his heart swell.

"Thanks, Mom. Look, I need to—"

"About dinner tonight. I thought we would—"

"Can I call you?" He kissed her cheek. "There's someone I need to speak to."

"We usually eat at six," she reminded him.

He acknowledged the time with a wave before he shoved through the exit door.

Usually? His mother had been serving dinner at six o'clock sharp since forever. He would have to stay with them until he found a place of his own or, better yet, a place with Emily. Which would have to be soon because checking in with his mother at mealtimes, letting her know if he had to work late… Yeah, that would get old real fast.

He stepped outside in time to see Emily pull out of the lot. He jumped in his Jeep and set

off after her. She was headed in the direction
of the *Gazette*, or possibly her apartment. Or
was she planning to stop at the barbershop?
He shoved back a tickle of annoyance that she
would go to Fred to talk about this before she
said anything to him. They were just friends,
he reminded himself.

She parked in front of the newspaper office,
and he pulled in beside her. She climbed out
of her car, cell phone in hand and looked surprised to see him. She smiled, though, and in
that instant, he knew everything was going
to work out.

"Emily."

She waved her phone at him. "I was just
about to text you, ask you to meet me here
when all the excitement died down."

He stopped beside her on the sidewalk. "I
thought maybe you were angry."

She furrowed her forehead. "Why would I
be angry? I was surprised, shocked. I didn't
understand why you didn't tell me, but now
that I'm getting used to the idea...I'm happy."

"You are?"

She beamed at him like the cat that stole
the cream. "I would never be happy in a place
like Chicago, but I'll always be happy here."

He took her keys and opened the door to
her apartment.

Inside, she let her bag slip to the floor, flung her arms around his neck and kissed him. "Congratulations, Chief Evans."

And with her sweet, full lips on his, he knew he'd made the right decision.

CHAPTER EIGHTEEN

"I STILL CAN'T BELIEVE you did this," Emily said, clinging to the lapels of his leather jacket, breathless from an impulsive kiss that had rapidly turned into several more very deliberate ones.

"It was the right thing to do," Jack said, one hand still on her back, the other gently brushing her hair from her face. "For me, for the baby, for us."

For us. She could stand here in his arms forever, but she had work to do. "We held up production of this week's paper so this story could be on the front page."

"How long will that take?"

"A few hours."

His face fell. "My mother wants me home for a celebratory dinner. I thought you could join us."

No way. "It's too soon for that."

"I guess you're right. Maybe I could stay here and watch you write?"

She loved he could make her laugh this way.

"Not a chance. Go, enjoy your evening with your family. I'll let you know when I'm finished."

He kissed her again, lightly. "Maybe we can get together for dessert."

She opened the door and playfully pushed him outside. "Go, before I change my mind."

Upstairs, she set her laptop on her desk, took out her camera and downloaded the photographs she'd shot at the press conference. She'd use one of the formal poses for her article in the *Gazette*. The one with Jack flanked by the mayor and the former police chief, she decided. She'd managed to get them positioned with the flags centered behind them, the Stars and Stripes and the blue state flag. The paper didn't often run color, but Ken had already said he would make an exception for the front page of this edition. No surprise, she had thought at the time, given he would be in the photograph.

When the article was finished to her satisfaction, she logged in to her blog. As soon as the paper came out on Wednesday, she knew people would be checking her blog for a story about the new police chief, and she wanted this one to be more personal. She would write it now, while she was on a roll, and schedule it to go live as soon as Wednesday's paper hit the stands.

No need for formality here, she decided. She scrolled through the photographs and stopped at a candid shot she had taken of Jack with his mother. The top of Norma's head barely reached her son's shoulder. She had stretched up to smooth his hair and ended up with her hands on his cheeks, her smile wide and her eyes lit with maternal pride. Emily opened the photograph in her editing program, cropped some of the distracting details from the edges and adjusted the color tones to counteract the effects of the council chamber's harsh fluorescent lighting. Satisfied with the results, she saved the photograph to a folder on her desktop and opened a new blog post.

This entry would not be about Jack, she decided. For the title, she typed, A Mother's Pride.

Dear Hearts,
It's not every day that a mother has the honor of witnessing the community celebrate her son's career achievement. For Norma Evans, Monday was one of those days. At an afternoon press conference, Mayor Bartlett announced that her son, Jack, who has spent the

past decade with the Chicago Police Department, will be Riverton's new chief of police.

Emily inserted the photograph and considered what else she should write. This was about Jack's mother, after all. She ran a hand over her belly. A soon-to-be grandmother. She quickly placed her hands back on the keyboard.

Norma's community spirit is well known to Rivertonians. Every year, she directs the Christmas pageant at Grace Memorial Church, and she recently headed up a successful campaign to raise funds for new playground equipment at Riverside Park.

Emily opened a folder on her hard drive, found a photograph of the newly constructed playground, and inserted it into her blog post. She had snapped the photo after the ribbon-cutting ceremony, capturing two colorfully dressed children testing the equipment. A little girl in jeans and a red jacket emerging from a bright blue tunnel slide, pigtails flying. A boy in a green hoodie swinging monkey-style from the overhead bars. The faces of both children were angled away from the camera, eliminating the need for her to ask their parents to sign a release form.

When asked what she hopes the future will hold for Riverton and its new homegrown police chief, Norma says, "Riverton will be the safest town in Wisconsin, and if anyone can solve the mystery of the missing garden gnomes, my son can."

There you have it, Dear Hearts. And speaking of the garden gnome mystery, be sure to check back tomorrow to see if there are any new developments.

Love, Emily

She quickly read over what she'd written and set her post to go live on Wednesday.

ON MONDAY MORNING, Jack stood behind his desk and surveyed his new office. The space was now devoid of the decades-worth of memorabilia his predecessor had accumulated. All that remained were the massive desk with its large leather chair, a pair of guest chairs, and a gray steel filing cabinet. Inside the cabinet, various folders and reports had been filed in a system that apparently only the former chief had understood. Karla Caldwell, the department's office administrator, had already offered to refile everything in a more logical way, and Jack had gratefully accepted her help.

Right now there were only three items on his desk. One was a gift from his parents—a gold pen in an oak holder, engraved with his name and his new rank on a brass plate. The second was a framed photograph of him and Emily on horseback the day of the picnic. CJ had snapped it as the two of them had ridden away, their backs to the camera. In the card she had attached to the package, she'd written, "Here's to the future and to riding off into the sunset. Together. Your future sister-in-law, CJ." The card was tucked safely in his top desk drawer, away from prying eyes.

Emily still hadn't agreed to provide him with any sisters-in-law, but she was close to changing her mind. He sensed it in the way she looked at him, in the way she would sometimes unconsciously reach out and touch his arm to get his attention. And this morning, after he had stopped by her place with take-out coffee, which they drank while sharing a couple of slices of his mother's banana bread, still warm from the oven, she hadn't just wished him good luck on his first day here.

Emily had given him a horseshoe, then had draped her arms around his neck and kissed him in a way that made him feel like the luckiest man alive. She had explained that he needed to hang it with the pointy parts up, but when he arrived at the office this morning, he figured it made a better paperweight. It now rested on a low stack of files next to his desk blotter. He liked having it within arm's reach.

Now that he was an official resident of Riverton, he needed to follow Paul's advice. He'd already done the compromise. Next was the proposal, and he was working on that. For now, all he knew was that it would take place in the gazebo. He was still working on the romantic part, but he needed to move quickly. Last night, on his way home from Emily's place, he had spotted Rose Daniels's car parked in front of the Riverton Bar & Grill. He'd gone in and spotted her alone in a booth with a half-eaten burger and a fresh pint of beer. She hadn't seen him come in, so he'd sat at the counter, ordered coffee and watched her in the mirrored backsplash behind the bar. In the time it took him to down a cup of coffee, she had polished off the pint and ordered another.

Back outside in his Jeep, he had called Brett Watters, his former colleague in Chicago. Sure enough, after Rose had returned to Chicago, she had checked in to say she had landed a job as a waitress in Riverton and was moving there for good.

From where Jack had sat out front, he'd seen her drain her glass and signal she'd like another. Looked as though she was about to become the restaurant's best new customer.

But the real bombshell had been Brett's report on the latest bit of information that had come in from vital statistics—Scarlett Daniels's birth certificate and Thomas Finnegan's marriage license. The name on both documents was Scarlett Franklin. Somehow Rose had found out about her long-lost stepfamily in Wisconsin and had come here to… Well, he had yet to figure out her motive. Right now, Emily was his only concern. She would be devastated to learn the truth about her mother—who wouldn't?—and he had no idea how to tell her. What he knew for sure was the ring in his pocket needed to be on her finger when he did.

There was a light tap on his office door, then it opened, and Karla appeared. "Everyone's waiting for you in the staff lounge. Coffee's ready, too."

"That's great. Tell them I'll be right there. Oh, and here." He picked up the extra-large Tupperware container from the top of the filing cabinet and handed it to her. "A friend of mine sent this for everyone." He had almost said my future sister-in-law, which is how he thought of Annie. She had presented him with the container after dinner last night. He'd become a permanent fixture at the Finnegan family's Sunday night dinner. He wondered if Emily's father questioned why that was, but Emily assured him her father accepted their explanation that, as Eric's best friend, he was there to provide moral support for Annie and her son.

"This friend of mine is some sort of pastry genius," he said.

Karla lifted a corner of the lid and peeked inside. "Is this Annie Finnegan's apple strudel?"

"It is."

"Oh, my," she said reverently. "If there's a direct line between her kitchen and your office, well, what can I say? Welcome to Riverton, sir."

Sir? "It's Jack. No need for formality."

"I'll let them know you're on your way. No rush, though. This will keep them happy," she said with a grin, scurrying off to the lounge, clutching the container in both hands.

Jack snagged his jacket off the back of his chair, slid his arms into the sleeves, straightened his tie. His mother had fussed over his newly issued uniform, pressing it until the shirt was wrinkle free and the creases in the pant legs could cut butter. Emily had never seen him in uniform and had seemed pleasantly surprised, although she hinted she preferred slightly the scruffy undercover Jack to spit-and-polish Chief of Police Jack. For everyday attire, he hoped to find his comfort zone someplace between the two, but for today, his first day on the job, he wanted to get off on the right foot.

And good first impressions started with punctuality, he reminded himself, as he left his office and made his way around Karla's desk, down the corridor, past the interview room where he had not long ago questioned Rose Daniels, and into the staff room.

The men and women assembled there moved to get up from their seats as he walked into the lounge, but he waved them down. Karla jumped up to pour him a cup of coffee, and he stilled her with the same motion. "Thanks, but I'll get my own."

He poured himself a cup and faced the group around the table, noting that several had already helped themselves to Annie's strudel.

"I want to thank each of you for making the effort to be here this morning," he said, glancing around at the members of the department who had all gathered to meet with him on his first day on the job. "I appreciate it, especially those of you who came in on your day off."

"No problem, Chief."

"Thanks." He acknowledged the title with a smile and a nod. "One thing, though. I'd like to keep the 'sirs' and the 'chiefs' to a minimum."

"Fenwick said he'd be back to give a serious whooping to anyone who gives you any grief," a young patrol officer said, grinning.

"Besides, we figure it never hurts to earn a few brownie points," another quipped.

"Noted," Jack said, laughing as he assessed the members of the Riverton Police Department. The department was made up of a lieutenant, seven patrol officers—five men and two women—and their full-time administrator, Karla. One of the officers was running a bicycle safety session at the elementary school that morning, and another was on regular patrol duty. The rest were here.

This was his first day on the job, and this was his team. He had known several of these men and women for most of his life, some of the others he had only just met. Their collective experience, commitment and dedication inspired him and filled him with doubt. They would be looking to him for leadership and direction. Could he deliver? Mayor Bartlett, former Chief Fenwick and his family certainly had faith in him. But it had been Emily's spontaneous kisses on the afternoon of the mayor's announcement that had made a believer out of him. Time would tell whether or not he was ready for this new challenge, but she had convinced him he had done the right thing. And once she agreed to marry him, he would need to find a way to share what he had discovered about her mother.

He smiled at his staff. "I know you all have more important things to do than listen to speeches, so I intend to keep this short," he told them. "I just want to say that I'd like you to consider me part of this team. My door will always be open if anyone of you ever needs anything, although I don't plan on spending a lot of time keeping the chair in my office warm. I'll be taking my turn on the front desk from time to time, and taking a few shifts on patrol, too."

That garnered a round of silence tinged with disbelief.

"I know that wasn't Chief Fenwick's style," he continued. "I also know I have a big pair of shoes to fill, but I have my own way of doing things. Some of you might have heard the rumor I was looking for a change when I left Chicago and took this position," he said. "Well, that wasn't a rumor, it's the truth, but I don't want a free ride. Police work is my life, and I'm not planning to give it up."

He could feel the men and women in the room settle in, loosen up. "I would like to ask a couple of favors. I'm sure you've all heard the buzz about the alleged garden-gnome thief who's been terrorizing our town."

That drew a few laughs, and he joined them.

"It's likely a handful of youthful pranks coinciding with a few cases of folks putting things away and not remembering where they put them." He was sure his mother fell into the second category.

"But good police work means keeping an open mind and not letting our judgment be clouded by preconceptions, so if you see anyone skulking around residences, especially the ones in the old quarter closest to downtown, feel free to cuff them and bring them in." He glanced around the room. "You might even make it into that blog everyone's been talking about."

More light laughter.

"On a more serious note, the other favor concerns the young Daniels woman who was picked up a couple of weeks ago. She spent a week here, then she left, and now she's back and working at the Riverton Bar & Grill. She's a key witness in that triple homicide in Chicago, and I still have a vested interest in the case. If you notice any peculiar behavior, I want to hear about it, no matter how inconsequential it may seem. If you suspect she's drinking and driving, pull her over and bring her in."

Jack's request was met with a round of nods.

"That's it for me. Unless anyone has anything they'd like to add, let's get back to work, or to enjoying those days off."

After some handshakes and shoulder slapping, the officers drifted to the front desk, the report writing room or to the parking lot. Jack watched them go, then refilled his coffee cup and carried it to his office. Today, he would be keeping his chair warm while he pored over the files sitting beneath Emily's horseshoe. He checked his phone, and smiled nervously when he saw a text from her. She had gone for her first ultrasound that morning, and it had practically killed him not to be there with her. He hadn't realized until now how anxious he'd been feeling.

Bet U knocked their sox off 2day. Saw baby move. Heart beating like crazy. All's well. Em

The image from the ultrasound was attached. Jack lowered himself into his chair, not taking his eyes off the screen. He hated text messages, and this monitor was too small to reveal much detail in the gray blur. Emily's message sounded so matter-of-fact, but surely she must be excited. He hadn't even been there, and he was experiencing waves of emotions he couldn't begin to identify. Next time she had one of these appointments, nothing would keep him away. Right now, though, he had two important tasks at hand. One was learning how to run a police force, and the other was figuring out how to make sure Emily Finnegan said "yes" the next time he asked that all-important question.

CHAPTER NINETEEN

EMILY CLATTERED DOWN the stairs to the door and then dashed the half block to the Riverton Bar & Grill where she was meeting Fred for lunch. She was excited to tell him about the ultrasound, and since she'd already told Jack and sent the picture to him, she felt sharing her excitement was justified. And who wouldn't be excited? Jack was here in Riverton, he had started his new job today, everything was beginning to look perfectly…perfect.

Inside, she was surprised Fred wasn't sitting in their usual booth. Odd because he had texted to say he was already there. Glancing around, she spied him perched on a stool at the bar, which was also odd. He leaned forward, elbows on the counter, engaged in an animated conversation with the young woman behind the counter, who looked suspiciously like… Rose? What was *she* doing here?

"Hi," Emily said as she approached them.

Fred swung around, his smile wide. "Hey, you're here. I thought we could sit at the counter today." Fred already had a cup of coffee in front of him.

"But our spot is over there," she said, pointing to *their* booth. Emily always sat on the side facing the front window because she liked to see who was coming and going, and Fred always sat opposite her, facing the bar so he could keep an eye on news headlines and sports scores flashing across the screen of the wall-mounted television. They never sat at the counter, and Emily was less inclined than ever to switch up their routine.

Fred patted the stool next to him. Emily tried to think up a plausible excuse for not sitting there. Unable to come up with anything, she sighed and took a seat.

Rose handed her a menu. "Can I get you something to drink?"

"Sure. Coffee. Decaf, please. This is a surprise. It's Rose, right?"

"Yeah. Your sister Annie knew I was looking for work, so she put in a good word for me with the owner. It's my first day." Rose turned to the coffee machine, poured a cup from the orange-topped carafe, and set it in front of Emily. "Fresh brewed a few minutes ago."

"Thanks." Emily lowered her gaze to the menu. Although she could have recited every item, including prices, from memory—and she'd decided on the soup-and-salad combo even before she had arrived—she pretended to give it her full attention while she surreptitiously focused on the conversation between Fred and Rose.

"You'll like Riverton," he said. "Especially once you get to know everyone. Right, Em? Great people, great place to live."

"Mmm-hmm. Not a lot of exciting things for young people to do, though." *Young people?* She couldn't believe she'd said that. *Way to make yourself sound like an old woman.*

Fred gave her a quizzical look.

"Oh, I'm not looking for excitement," Rose said. "Back in Chicago, my life was basically boring. When I wasn't at work, I mostly stayed home or hung out with a few friends."

Emily wasn't buying it. Nothing about Rose even hinted at a cloistered kind of lifestyle, least of all her attitude, which was more big-city street kid than stuffy small-town girl, and she had the wardrobe to back it up. And now that Rose was back, Emily was once again bothered by Rose's apparent lack of identity. These days someone her age would have some kind of online presence. Rose was a mystery. And when Emily encountered a mystery, she immediately wanted to solve it.

However, today Rose had toned down her

excessive use of black eyeliner and mascara.
Her short black hair was tucked neatly behind
her ears, the long, purple-streaked bangs were
swept to one side, and her oversize silver hoop
earrings swung every time she moved. She
wore a pair of black jeans that made her look
superskinny, a short-sleeved white top and a
pink, black and white print scarf that Emily
recognized as Annie's. Was Rose back at the
B & B? And what was her sister thinking?
Helping this girl get a job here, lending her
clothes. Unless Rose had helped herself to the
scarf without bothering to ask.

Emily interrupted her own thoughts. Her
instincts told her Rose was not to be trusted,
but there was nothing to suggest the young
woman was a thief. And why would she steal
a scarf and then wear it in public, in a place
where Annie might show up in person, given
that she had helped Rose get the job?

"What about a boyfriend?" Fred asked.

And it was Emily's turn to fire a giant, silent question mark in his direction.

Rose's pale skin turned pink. She shook her
head.

Fred smiled.

Seriously? *Seriously?* He was flirting with
Rose. Emily wanted to smack him. What was
he thinking? Not only was this young woman

not the least bit suitable for him, she wasn't likely to be in town for long.

It's none of your business.

But it was her business. Fred was her best friend, and she didn't want to see him get hurt. Yes, he deserved to have someone special in his life, but Rose was not that person.

"So, Rose," Emily said. "It's Rose Danvers, right? Where were you working before you left Chicago?"

A cup and saucer rattled in Rose's hand.

Fred's eyebrows drew together. "Danvers? Didn't you say your last name is Daniels?"

She nodded. "That's right."

"Oh," Emily said. "My apologies. I was sure Annie told me it was Danvers. Maybe she was confused." As if that could ever happen. "Or I might have misunderstood."

Rose shrugged, and Emily guessed it was an attempt to look nonchalant.

You're not fooling me, Rose Daniels. Or whatever your name is.

Emily thought back to the conversation she'd had with Annie right after Rose had checked into the B & B. She had not misunderstood what Annie told her, and she was equally sure Annie had not confused Daniels with Danvers. She had her guests fill in a registration form when they checked in. However,

Annie had admitted she hadn't asked for ID
to verify the name on the form. Normally, she
would compare the name on the form with the
one on the credit card. But Rose had paid cash,
claiming she didn't have one.

Emily watched the young woman closely as
she smiled at Fred and managed to brush his
hand with hers when she picked up his cup
to refill it.

Oh, please. Bad enough Fred was showing
a complete lack of judgment by flirting with
her. Now she was flirting back. Ridiculous.

Right after lunch—if Rose stopped flirting long enough to take their order—Emily
would go back to her apartment and run an
internet search for this new name. Rose Daniels was hiding something, and Emily had a
hunch whatever that something was, it would
turn up. Then she would call Jack at the police
station and fill him in on the latest intrigue.

The door opened and the two stock boys
from Henderson's Hardware came in and settled into the booth that Emily liked to think
of as hers and Fred's.

"Be right back," Rose said.

Emily waited until Rose was at the booth,
handing out menus and reciting the lunch
specials—which she still hadn't mentioned

to her and Fred—before she leaned toward her friend.

"What's going on here?" she hissed.

Fred was still grinning. "I think I might ask her out."

"Are you out of your mind? Look at her."

"I think she's kind of cute?"

Cute? "I guess, if you go for the vampire look."

Fred shook his head. "You're jealous."

"That's ridiculous. You can go out with anyone you choose, and I'll be very happy for you, but Rose? There's something weird about that girl."

"Weird?" Fred shook his head at her.

"There is." She ran through her list, starting with her random appearance at a small-town B & B and ending with this new piece of evidence, the mix-up over her name. "None of it adds up."

"Are you sure you're not trying to cook up another mystery for your blog?"

Cook up a mystery? "What is that supposed to mean?"

"You can only get so much traction with your Riverton bandit posts. If no one catches this guy, and soon, then your readers will lose interest."

"You know perfectly well I am not making

up those stories, and for your information, I
have no intention of blogging about Rose Danvers or Daniels or whatever her name is."

"It's Daniels—she told you herself—and
like you said, you or your sister must have
made a mistake. Why would she lie about her
name?"

Good question. Emily shrugged and glanced
over her shoulder to the booth where Rose was
now coyly laughing with the two young men
from the hardware store. "If you're going to
ask her out, you'd better be quick about it."

Fred briefly followed her gaze and swiveled back to the bar. "Do you have to read
something into everything? She's only being
friendly."

Emily patted his hand. "Right. You keep
on deluding yourself. I'm going back to my
place." She stood, fished two dollars out of her
wallet and dropped it on the counter.

"What about lunch?"

She shot another glance at Rose, who now
appeared to be on the verge of pulling up a
chair. "Yeah, good luck with that. She hasn't
even taken our order. I don't think you're
going to see food anytime soon."

"Suit yourself."

Emily hated it when she and Fred disagreed—
they always ended up sounding like preteen

siblings—but she wasn't backing down on this. There was something shady about Riverton's newest resident. She intended to find out what that was, and then people like Fred and Annie would have to listen to her.

Back in her apartment, she poured herself a glass of milk, opened a can of soup and slapped together a grilled cheese sandwich while the soup heated. Pretty much what she'd planned to order at the Grill, if ordering had been an option.

Emily opened her laptop on the table, and while it booted up, she ladled soup into a bowl and set it on a plate next to her sandwich. She sat down and swallowed a spoonful of soup. Then she rubbed her hands together.

"Okay, Rose Daniels from Chicago. Let's find out what secrets you're keeping."

There were too many hits to count. The subject lines included phrases like "triple murder" and "suspect in custody." A series of thumbnail images across the top of the page confirmed she had found the right person. Emily scanned the sources, and then, with her heart racing and her hands shaking, she clicked on an article in the *Sun-Times*.

Chicago police have discovered an unexpected link between the murders of three Chicago women, who were first thought to have been randomly selected by the alleged serial killer Jason Caruthers.

Rose Daniels was connected to the murders of three women? Emily shoved her plate aside and fixated on the screen. Tempting as it was to scroll down until she found Rose's name, she forced herself to read the article from the beginning.

Twenty-seven-year-old Caruthers, from Albany, NY, is undergoing a series of psychiatric evaluations to determine whether or not he is fit to stand trial. His lawyers have filed a plea of not guilty by reason of insanity.

Emily had heard the story on the news, read a few snippets on the wire, but they didn't run articles like this in the *Gazette*. Frankly, they totally creeped her out.

Jack Evans, lead investigator on this case, says the evidence to support a conviction is overwhelming.

Jack. Of course. This had been his last big case. He hadn't said much about it, and Emily had put it out of her mind. Besides, they had plenty of personal matters to work out. But a case like this, one that involved a woman who had recently come to Riverton, a woman about whom she had expressed concerns that he had all brushed aside? Why hadn't he said anything? What was *he* hiding? She continued reading.

The murders, committed over a three-day period, took place in different parts of the city. The first victim, a social worker with the Department of Child and Family Services, died from multiple stab wounds. Her body was discovered by a coworker in the parking lot behind their office complex.

Emily shuddered. Why her? Why this woman, who had dedicated her life to helping others? This was why Emily hated reading stories like this, and one of the reasons she hadn't wanted to work for a big city paper.

The second woman was a homemaker and a PAWS volunteer who worked part-time at a nearby library. She was stabbed multiple times. Her body was found by her husband when he returned from a full day at the office. He was never considered a suspect.

The article didn't say whether or not they had children. Emily prayed they didn't. She had skimmed past these women's names. It was less personal that way.

The third victim was a homeless woman... Seriously?

...a homeless woman, fifty-one-year-old Scarlett Daniels, who was found in the alley next to the shelter where she had been spending the night. She died as a result of multiple stab wounds.

Scarlett Daniels? Was this Rose's mother? What if...? No. That was a ridiculous thought. But Rose was here in Riverton. Why? Was this more than just some bizarre coincidence?

It had to be. Jack knew about Emily's mother, and he obviously knew about Rose and Scarlett Daniels. He would have told her if there was a connection. Wouldn't he? Of course he would.

Emily tried to steady her breathing. Part of her wanted to stop reading while the other part desperately needed to know the whole story. Besides, she still hadn't found the reference to Rose, so she pressed on.

The murders initially appeared to have no motive, until Chicago PD detectives pieced together the connections. The link turned out to be Daniels's daughter, Rose, who had spent much of her life in and out of foster care. Now an adult, the daughter had befriended Caruthers, whose DNA was found at all three crime scenes.

Emily jumped to her feet, whirling in a frenzied circle, then rushed out of her kitchen and through the apartment to the bathroom. She felt sick, as though she might retch her guts out, but there was nothing in her stomach but that spoonful of soup. She splashed cold water on her face, struggled to draw a breath, and another. She was suffocating, having a heart attack, dying maybe.

"No, you're not." *You know how to do this, how to control your breathing, lower your heart rate.*

She needed to lie down, close her eyes, get herself centered. She forced herself to turn around, walk into her bedroom and lie on the bed. This was no different from any other panic attack. She could do this.

One scattered thought after another chased through her mind. Did Jack…? Was Rose…? Was Scarlett…? No. *Stop, breathe, focus.*

Within minutes, Emily's breathing had calmed, and in a few more, the tightness in her chest had disappeared, and her heartbeat had slowed enough so she was able to get up and return to the bathroom. With shaky hands, she pressed a damp washcloth to her face and forehead. Her stomach was still unsettled, but some food would help.

In the kitchen, she spooned some lukewarm soup into her mouth, bit into her sandwich. The bread had gone crunchy and the cheese was congealed, but none of that mattered because...it just didn't matter. She managed to eat the soup and half the sandwich. She washed it down with the milk that was now the same temperature as the soup.

She contemplated her laptop, debated whether or not to finish reading the article, but decided she had seen enough. Too much, really, so she snapped it shut. She dumped the uneaten half sandwich into the trash, rinsed her milk glass and soup bowl and left them in the sink with her coffee cup from that morning. Finally feeling calm enough to drive, she knew what she had to do. She needed answers, and she was going to get them. She grabbed her bag and keys, let herself out the back door and hurried down the wooden steps to her parking space at the back of the building.

CHAPTER TWENTY

JACK SAT AT his desk and opened the lunch his mother had packed for him. He desperately wanted a place of his own, but after returning to Riverton, he had decided to hold off until Emily accepted his proposal. With any luck, he thought, tracing the outline of the horseshoe with the tip of his index finger, that would be this weekend.

His mother's lunches almost made sleeping in his old room worth it, though. He was polishing off a roast beef sandwich when he heard raised voices at the front desk.

"I'll let Chief Evans know you're here," Karla said.

"No need. I'll surprise him."

It was Emily. He stood and was halfway around his desk when the door burst open, and there she was, eyes alight with anger.

"Em, what's wrong?"

"Is Scarlett Daniels my mother?"

In that instant, he experienced every cliché

he'd ever heard about having his world collapse around him. "Listen, I can explain—"

"She is! You knew, and you didn't tell me. My mother was a homeless drug addict. She had another kid. Rose is my—" The last word was swallowed up by a sob.

"I was going to tell you, but I didn't want to upset you. I was worried about you. And the baby." He reached for her.

She pulled away, tears streaming down her face. "No. I can't do this. I can't talk to you. Don't touch me." She swung around and rushed out the door.

"Emily, wait!"

He stood in the middle of his office for a few seconds, silently cursing Rose Daniels for doing this to Emily, and himself for allowing it to happen.

"Everything okay, Chief?" Karla asked from the doorway.

"Not even close." He grabbed his jacket and brushed past her. "I need to go after her. Lonnie Gable's on patrol this afternoon. Tell him I'll be back as soon as I can, and ask him to keep an eye out for Emily Finnegan."

EMILY DROVE THE short distance from the police station to downtown, fully aware she was exceeding the speed limit and not caring one bit. She wished she dared to go faster, break all the rules. Why shouldn't she? Everyone else did. All the time. And they got away with it.

She had no idea where she was going, though. Not to her apartment. That was the first place Jack would look for her. The barbershop was the second place, so she couldn't rush over there and cry on Fred's shoulder. Besides, he was probably still at the diner, flirting with Rose. What she wanted most was to go home and be with her family, but she couldn't go there, either. How could she break the news to her sisters that their mother was dead? Murdered! That Rose Daniels was their half sister? That the girl must have come to Riverton because she knew about them, and had lied to them about her reason for being here.

Jack had known all along who Rose was, and he hadn't told her. That was unforgivable. He'd known that Scarlett Daniels was her mother and withheld that, too, along with the sordid details of how she had lived and the gruesome events that had led to her death. How could he? What right did he have?

She slowed down when she pulled onto Main Street, drove past the barbershop, the newspaper office and the stupid Riverton Bar & Grill where at this very minute Rose Daniels was coming on to half the men in town.

Emily turned onto Second Avenue and then onto Cottonwood Street and then the next thing she knew, she was stopped in front of Mable Potter's place. She had known the woman most of her life, which meant Mrs. Potter had known her and her family.

Emily had never asked anyone about her mother. Somehow, even as a small child, she had known the subject was off-limits, if not downright taboo. Well, not anymore. She pulled up and parked by the curb. She had promised the elderly woman she would visit again soon, so she shouldn't be too surprised to see Emily on her doorstep. Dropping by to have an afternoon cup of tea with an old friend was a perfectly normal thing to do. And no one would look for her here.

She looped her bag over her shoulder as she climbed out of the car and gazed admiringly at Mrs. Potter's home. She loved the salmon-pink house with its tidy window boxes and flower beds. The front porch had a welcome mat that actually read Welcome. On the front door was a black sign in the shape of a dog with white lettering that read Be Aware of Dog. Perfectly normal.

Emily knocked and waited. She knocked again, but there was no flurry of footsteps, no barking Banjo to greet her. Mrs. Potter and the dog must be out. Emily tried the doorknob, and the door opened. She quickly pulled it shut again. Just because this woman seemed oblivious to the need to lock up her house when she wasn't home didn't give Emily, or anyone, the right to go inside. She went back down the steps and strode to her car. She was standing there, pondering her next move, when she spotted Banjo racing up the sidewalk with his jaws clamped around a pink plastic flamingo.

What on earth? Ken and Marthe Bartlett were the only people in town who had pink flamingos. They lived two blocks away. The dog dashed across the front yard and through the gate, which Emily realized she had left unlatched because it had been unlatched when she arrived. She carefully closed the gate and followed Banjo to the backyard. Sheets and pillowcases flapped on the clothesline, a pair of aluminum lawn chairs with faded green webbing had been unfolded on the tiny patio by the back door, and Banjo's bright yellow tennis ball lay on the neatly trimmed lawn. Perfectly normal.

The dog deposited the lawn ornament on the grass and gazed up at her, tail wagging, as though expecting a reward. Finally, the penny dropped. Mrs. Potter must have forgotten to shut the gate when she went out, and Banjo had gone out on his own. "Banjo, did you steal the Bartletts' flamingo?" Was he the garden-gnome thief? The dog grabbed his tennis ball and dropped it at her feet. As she reached for it, he snapped it up and dashed away.

"Silly dog. I'm not going to chase you." She would sit here in the sunshine, wait for Mrs. Potter to come home and find a way to ask if she knew anything about the other things that disappeared around town. Besides, this was the last place Jack would look for her. She settled into one of the chairs, leaned back and closed her eyes. Her phone buzzed with an incoming text message.

Emily, where are you? We need to talk. I can explain everything. Love, Jack

Love, Jack. Right. Because when you loved someone, you withheld life-changing information about a person's family. Jack Evans wasn't in love with her. He was in love with doing the right thing. Or what he perceived to be the right thing, including making decisions on her behalf. Her phone buzzed again.

You okay? Jack's looking for you. The guy is frantic. Fred

Great. Now he was dragging her friends into this mess. Another message popped up.

Sweetie, what's happening? Jack called and he's looking for you. It sounds pretty urgent. Call him, OK? Call me, too. Annie

Stop already! Emily turned off the phone—something she seldom did—and shoved it into her bag. She settled her gaze on the garden shed and noticed that, unlike her previous visits, the door was ajar. She crossed the yard and stepped inside.

The space was dimly lit and smelled of dust and garden fertilizer with a hint of gasoline. As her eyes adjusted from the bright sunshine to the shed's dark interior, Emily began to make out items. A lawn mower and gas can stood on one side. Next to those, a wheelbarrow. Gardening tools hung from hooks across the back wall. Low shelves spanned the other side wall, cluttered with plant pots, coiled garden hoses, an ancient watering can. On the top shelf there was a garden gnome. And another garden gnome, and another, as well as a pair of black rubber boots, a welcome mat, a trowel and a garden stake that read "Weed It and Reap." All items that anyone might expect to find in any garden shed in Riverton. She squinted and gasped. But a window-washing squeegee?

Emily picked it up and carried it outside into the sunlight for a closer look. Written on the handle with black magic marker—Gabe's Gas 'n' Go. She carried it back inside and set it on the shelf.

So, Banjo was the thief. But why would Mrs. Potter stash these things in her shed? She had been very absentminded lately, a little confused even. There was only one way to find out. Emily would wait for her to come home.

The wait seemed endless, leaving her with nothing to do but replay the devastating events of the past hour. It was too much. Rose, her mother, Jack. Her sisters and father, who still didn't know the truth.

Emily took out her phone and turned it on. Fourteen missed messages. She turned it off, leaving the messages unread, and shoved it back into her bag. She already knew who they were from and what they said. She couldn't deal with any of them right now.

From inside the house, she heard a door open and close. Banjo barked and raced up the back stairs. The door opened, and Mrs. Potter stood in the doorway, beaming at Emily. If she was surprised to see Emily, she didn't let on.

"Hello, dear. Isn't this a lovely surprise?"

"Hi, Mrs. Potter. I dropped by for tea, but you weren't home so I decided to wait. It's so peaceful out here."

At least it had been. Banjo grabbed the flamingo and raced a full circle around the backyard, then brought it back but refused to relinquish it.

"Oh, dear. Not another one. I don't know where he finds these things," Mrs. Potter said. "Would you like to stay for tea? I'll put the kettle on. Banjo, you stay out here and keep the squirrels out of the yard."

Having no place else to go and wanting to find a gentle way to broach the subject of the items she had found in the shed, Emily followed the woman inside.

"This is a lovely surprise." Mrs. Potter filled the kettle and plugged it in. "Have a seat, dear. It'll take me just a minute to make the tea. If I'd known you were coming, I would have baked you a red velvet cake."

The way Emily was feeling right now, she could devour a whole cake all by herself. After tea, she would go out to the farm, she decided. She could gorge herself on Annie's muffins, cookies and strudel, then haul herself up to her old room and curl up under the covers and succumb to a food coma.

"Your cake is always a treat, but tea will be fine."

Mrs. Potter went through the ritual of readying the teapot, setting out cups and saucers, teaspoons and the sugar bowl. She filled the creamer. This time she left the sugar bowl on the table instead of putting it in the fridge. She picked up her purse, which she had set on the kitchen table when she came home, and moved it to the counter by the canisters.

"This is a lovely surprise," she repeated. "It's been ages since we've seen each other. You should come by more often."

"I'll try to do that," Emily said. There was no point to reminding the woman it hadn't been that long since her last visit.

The kettle whistled. Mrs. Potter filled the teapot and popped a faded tea cozy over it after setting it on the table.

"How's your daughter?" Emily asked. "Is she planning another visit?" Her daughter, Libby, had followed in her mother's footsteps and become a teacher, which meant she would soon be on summer vacation.

Mrs. Potter's face darkened. "I don't know. She might, but if that husband of hers has any say in the matter, she'll try to put me in a home, and then they won't have to bother with me anymore."

"I'm sure she would never do that." Although Emily suspected that may well be the plan.

Mrs. Potter poured the tea. Emily lifted the lid of the sugar bowl and quickly clamped it down again, startled to see a set of keys inside.

"Almost empty," she said, getting up and moving to the counter, taking the sugar bowl with her. "I'll refill it for you." With her back to her host, she discreetly removed the keys and set them next to the woman's purse, then went through the motions of opening a canister and scooping sugar into the bowl. "There we go," she said, returning to the table. "So, I was wondering about something."

"What's that, dear?"

"I see Banjo came home with a lawn ornament. Actually, a number of people around town have reported things missing from their yards and gardens."

The elderly woman didn't say anything, but her expression spoke volumes.

"And I noticed you have all the same items in your shed."

"Oh, my. I was hoping no one would find out."

"You haven't heard anyone talking about it? No one's told you about my blog?"

Mrs. Potter looked confused. "What's a blog?"

"Nothing, it's not important. I just wondered how all those things ended up here. Is it Banjo?"

The woman sighed. "Yes, it's that darn dog. Libby gave him to me so I would have some company, but he's so full of beans. I don't like to go out at night but I have to let him out, you know, to do his business before I go to bed. Sometimes I guess I forget to close the gate, and the rascal gets away. When that happens, he always comes home with something."

Emily pressed her lips together to prevent her face from spreading into a smile. She hadn't allowed herself to speculate on the identity of the garden-gnome thief but if she had, Mrs. Potter's dog would not have come to mind.

"You won't tell Libby, will you? She'll put me in a home for sure if she finds out about this."

Emily's heart went out to the poor woman. She was confused, at least part of the time, and lonely all the time. As Emily formulated a plan to help the woman, she also knew she would have to contact Libby and have a talk with her about her mother. She was lucky to have a mother, so surely she would do the right thing. "I won't breathe a word, I promise. If it's okay with you, I will make sure everything is returned to its rightful owner, but you need to promise me something, too."

"What's that, dear?"

"That you will always check the gate before you let Banjo out at night."

"Of course. I'm getting forgetful," she confessed. "But I'll do my best."

Emily covered the woman's hand with hers and gave it a squeeze. "That's all anyone can ask."

But as she stirred milk and sugar into her tea, her mind flitted from one thought to another. Her own mother, who was never coming home. Mrs. Potter's daughter, who seldom visited hers. Jack, who had been keeping secrets from her. It wasn't fair, none of it.

Emily slid her hand across her tummy. Right now, this little person seemed to be her one sure thing. *I will always*, always *be here for you.*

And there were a few things she needed to do for her old friend Mrs. Potter, too. No matter what Libby's intentions were, she needed to know her mother was having memory problems, possibly showing early signs of dementia or Alzheimer's, and should be checked out by a doctor. Libby didn't need to know about her mother's involvement in the case of the missing garden gnomes, though, and Emily knew exactly what she had to do to make sure no one found out.

CHAPTER TWENTY-ONE

AT DUSK, EMILY parked her car two blocks from her apartment, sauntered nonchalantly down the alley and up the back stairs and let herself into her kitchen. She groped in a drawer for a penlight, and was grateful the batteries had enough power to produce a narrow beam. She flicked it off and felt her way through the living room, pausing to turn on her laptop and toss a couple of nuts into Tadpole's cage. Finally, Emily stumbled into her bedroom.

She closed the door, made sure the drapes were tightly drawn and switched the penlight back on. It provided just enough light to help her find the things she needed, but not enough to alert anyone who might be watching for her—particularly Jack, Fred or her sisters—that she had returned to the apartment. Not to be overly paranoid, she thought, but given that she now had more than twenty missed texts and a number of voice messages, someone was likely to be outside waiting for her to return.

She quickly shed her clothes and wriggled

into a pair of black jeans—only managing to zip them up after she lay on her back on the bed—then pulled on a chunky black turtleneck pullover and shoved her feet into black ankle boots. Her reflection in the dimly lit full-length mirror showed she'd achieved the exact effect she was after. On Riverton's dimly lit residential streets, she would be all but invisible.

Since no one had thought to look for her at Mrs. Potter's place, Emily had spent the afternoon there, silently hatching a plan to deal with the loot in the garden shed. She had been grateful for the reprieve from dealing with personal issues, and now it was time to put her plan into action.

She turned off the flashlight and tucked it into her back pocket. As she made her way back through the living room, she avoided the temptation to peek out the front window to see if anyone was waiting for her. Tadpole ran silently on her wheel, having apparently polished off the nuts. Emily quickly connected her laptop to the printer, hoping the light from the monitor wasn't bright enough to illuminate the window. She was quite certain she remembered which item belonged to whom, but just to be sure, she printed the most recent map she'd posted on her blog, folded the printout and stuffed it into her back pocket with the flashlight. Then she slunk out the back door and within moments was behind the steering wheel of her car.

At the Potter place, she knocked on the front door. She was greeted by her friend, already dressed in a nightgown and housecoat, and a barking dog.

"Hi, Mrs. Potter. I'm here to collect the box of things I packed up and left in the shed this afternoon."

"That's fine, dear. You help yourself to whatever you need." She sounded as though she had already forgotten which "things" they were talking about.

That's all for the best, Emily assured herself.

"Good night, then. I'll make sure the gate is latched so Banjo won't take off when you let him out tonight."

"Good idea. Good night, dear. Come for tea anytime you like."

"I will. Thanks."

From the backyard, Emily scooped up the box, then secured the gate and loaded everything into the hatchback of her car. Once again in the driver's seat, she pulled out the map, unfolded it on the seat beside her and shone the flashlight on it. She hadn't considered the thief might have been right in the middle of the nine-block area where things had gone missing, but it made sense now that she knew who it was.

She would start in one corner of the area and zigzag through until she had returned everything to its rightful owner. That made the most sense, and it was certainly the most efficient way to get the task done. Most importantly, poor old Mrs. Potter would save face.

Emily started with the weed-it-and-reap garden stake. She had no way of knowing which part of the yard it had disappeared from, so she simply stabbed it into the front flower bed and beat a hasty retreat to her car.

Next up was one of the garden gnomes, the one from old Mr. Jamieson's. His had been the first to go missing, and he had been irate, accusing "all those young hooligans running around town" of the theft. He had described it as having a blue shirt and a white hat, which immediately made Emily picture a Smurf rather than a gnome. Luckily, only one of the pilfered gnomes had a white hat, and he was now safely settled with his cohorts in the circular bed in the middle of Mr. Jamieson's front lawn.

This was going well, Emily congratulated herself. Easy-peasy. Piece of cake. She drove around the corner, past her next target, and parked several doors down. She was relieved to see the Browns' porch light was off as the welcome mat was theirs. She had crept halfway up their front steps when the light turned on. Emily froze, listened and heard nothing. The light must have a motion sensor. She hastily slid the mat into place and fled.

Returning to the car this time, her heart was beating a little faster, but it was an adrenaline rush. And it felt good. She was energized, like a superhero. She chuckled. How completely ridiculous. She was the least heroic person she knew. Annie was the one who saved the world, or at least everyone in her world. CJ took the world by storm. Emily used her books and journals to escape from the world. Already she was excitedly drafting her next blog post, how an anonymous tip had led to the discovery of the stolen items. In her mind, she could see a few holes in the story, but she could fix those. For now, she was happy to focus on her mission as it meant not having to acknowledge Rose's appearance in Riverton, the shocking reality of her mother's death and Jack's deception.

Emily flicked on her flashlight and studied the map. Her next stop was to return the rubber boots. She started the car and drove a block and a half. The boots had been swiped from the Redfords' backyard, but after the close call with the Browns' automatic porch light, she wasn't sure it was a good idea to venture that far. She couldn't remember whether or not the Redfords had a dog, but why take a chance?

She climbed out of the car, quickly and quietly clicking the door shut so the interior light turned off. She opened the hatchback and was lifting out the boots as a police cruiser came around the corner, illuminating her with its headlights. The cruiser pulled up behind her and cut its engine, but the headlights stayed on. Blinded by the light, she froze for a moment before her instincts kicked in and she slammed the hatchback shut.

Someone stepped out of the car and shone a flashlight beam directly into her face. "Evening, ma'am." A male voice.

"Um, hello?"

"I'm Officer Gable with the Riverton PD. We've had a report of a possible prowler in the area. Have you seen anything or anyone out of the ordinary?"

Uh-oh. Busted.

"N-no. Nothing, officer, sir." She knew everyone in the police department except Lonnie Gable, who was a young new recruit. Just her rotten luck.

"What's your name?"

"Emily Finnegan."

"Interesting. Those your boots, Emily?"

"Oh, um, no." They were huge—at least a man's size twelve—so she couldn't very well say they were.

"What else have you got back there?"

Emily was suddenly light-headed. "Nothing."

"Open the back of your car, please."

Her only choice was to do as he asked.

He directed the beam of his flashlight at the contents of the box. "Do these belong to you?"

"No, but I can explain."

"You can save that till we get to the station."

"What? No, really, I can explain everything. This is just a misunderstanding. I didn't take these things. I'm returning them."

He shook his head in a way that suggested he had finally heard everything.

"I'm afraid you'll have to come with me, Ms. Finnegan." He moved to the side of the cruiser, opened the back door.

"Am I under arrest?"

"Not yet," he said, implying she might be if she didn't comply. "The chief told us we were to bring in the garden-gnome bandit if we spotted him. Or her," he added.

This was ridiculous. However, as much as she did not want to see Jack right now, at least he would hear her out, which left her with no choice but to slide into the backseat and watch while Officer Gable transferred the box from the back of her car to the trunk of his cruiser.

And once Jack heard her out, he had some explaining of his own to do.

AFTER A FUTILE afternoon and evening spent searching for Emily, Jack sat at the island in Annie's kitchen with a cup of coffee. He had called her after Emily confronted him and stormed out of the station, and he'd had no choice but to tell her everything. She was upset, of course, and she'd decided it best not to say anything to her father or CJ until they tracked down Emily and made sure she was okay. Luckily, Thomas was out for the evening, CJ was spending the night in the stable nursing a rescued mare she had taken in, and Isaac was asleep, giving Jack and Annie the freedom to talk.

Together they had called Fred, because if she turned to anyone at a time like this, it would be him. That irked Jack more than he cared to admit, but he was also grateful the guy was staked out at the barbershop and would call the minute Emily returned to her apartment.

"I'm sorry you had to find out about your mother this way," Jack said for what seemed like the hundredth time. "I've had my suspicions for a while, but I didn't want to say anything until I knew for sure and I only just found out myself."

"Jack, you don't have to keep apologizing. To be honest, I developed a soft spot for Rose while she was staying here, and I think it's good she's back in town. Especially now that I know she's family. However, who our mother was and how she died has nothing to do with you. It's heartbreaking, and I understand why Emily is so upset, but she'll come around."

He wished he could believe that. "She was devastated. The thing is, I was going to tell her, but I wanted to wait till the time was right." Preferably after she said "I do."

"Has my sister told you much about our mother?"

"She said she's always clung to the secret hope that your mother would come home someday."

Annie wrapped her hands around her coffee mug as though she was seeking comfort. "I have better memories of our mother than either of my sisters. Looking back, I think she had some serious mental health issues. I didn't realize it at the time but as an adult, it's easier to put those memories into perspective."

"Does Emily know that?"

"If she does, she didn't hear it from me. I know she's dreamed about a reunion someday, but for a long time I've known and accepted that it was never going to happen."

It killed Jack to think the woman he loved was hurting like this, and having her turn away from his support hurt even more. "I think those feelings have intensified now that she's pregnant. Emily said she's not sure she'll be a good mother because she'd never had role model."

Annie sighed. "The truth is, Emily is going to be an amazing mom. Your kid will be reading Tolstoy by the time he or she starts school."

In spite of being sick with worry, the image made him smile. "She's an amazing woman."

"You're in love with her, aren't you? It's not just because of the baby that you want to marry her, am I right?"

She was bang-on. He nodded. "Crazy mad in love with her."

Annie beamed. "Have you told her?"

"No. I didn't think she was ready to hear it."

Annie reached across the counter, gave his

hand a reassuring pat. "You should have told her as soon as you figured it out. If you had, you might be married by now."

He wasn't so sure about that. "I think I started falling for her when you and Eric got married."

Annie hesitated, as though giving some thought to what she was about to say. "I'm going to let you in on another of Emily's secrets, but if you tell her I told you this, I will put a hit out on you."

He laughed. "I'm good with secrets."

"Emily had a major crush on you in high school. I've never snooped in her things, but I remember seeing her journal from time to time when she accidentally left it open on her desk."

Interesting. "What did she say?"

"If you want specifics, you'll have to ask her yourself."

And he might, if she ever spoke to him again.

His phone ringing startled both of them. He checked the call display. "It's work," he said. "I have to take this."

"Of course."

He held it to his ear. "Evans here."

"Jack, it's Lonnie Gable."

"How's it going?"

"Just letting you know I picked up the garden-gnome bandit."

He groaned. This was not something he wanted to deal with right now, but he didn't have a choice.

"Where are you now?"

"Taking her into the station."

Her? That was unexpected. "Who is it?"

"Emily Finnegan."

"Did you say…never mind. Put her in a cell. I'll be there as quick as I can."

"In a cell, sir? I'm not sure—"

"You heard me, Lonnie. I'm on my way."

Annie was watching him closely. "Everything okay?"

"One of my patrol officers picked up the garden-gnome bandit. It's Emily."

She stared at him with a blank expression for a full three seconds, and then she burst out laughing.

"Emily… Oh, my. This is too funny," she gasped. "My sister is not a thief." She dabbed the corners of her eyes with a paper napkin. "Will that officer…" More laughter. "I'm sorry. I'm sorry." She drew in a deep, unsteady breath. "Is he really going to put her in a cell?"

One sure thing about a well-trained police officer, he or she always followed a command. Jack nodded.

"Well, that's one way to catch a wife."

Annie was still chuckling to herself as she walked with him to the front door. Her amusement was not contagious. Quite the opposite, in fact, and as Jack drove away, he found himself hoping he hadn't made things a lot worse than they already were.

CHAPTER TWENTY-TWO

EMILY PACED FROM one side of the small space to the other. Lonnie Gable hadn't had much to say during the drive to the station, and after they arrived, he simply escorted her into a cell and closed the door. Locked it, to be precise. She'd checked.

"Am I being arrested?" she had asked.

"Not at this point."

"Then you can't lock me up. It's unconstitutional."

He had gazed at her through the bars, as though this wasn't the first time he'd heard that statement. "You be sure to tell Chief Evans that when he gets here."

"Jack... I mean, the police chief is coming to see me?"

"That's right."

"Don't I at least have the right to a phone call?"

"That'll be up to the chief."

"This is ridiculous. I'm going to hire a lawyer." She saw him smile as he walked away.

"You're not going to get away with this," she called after him.

Left to her own devices after he disappeared, Emily realized he hadn't taken any of her belongings. She still had her black cross-body shoulder bag with her phone in it. She took it out and turned it on, cringing at the number of missed messages that had piled up throughout the afternoon and evening. Even if she did feel like talking to someone, who would she call? Fred had always been there for her but she hadn't been able to convince herself to call him today. He had been flirting with Rose Daniels, for heaven's sake, and as far as Emily was concerned, Rose was at the center of this mess. She was the enemy, and Fred had no business fraternizing with her. She wasn't ready to face her sisters yet, or even talk to them on the phone. Oddly enough, sitting here by herself and having time to reflect, she realized her father was the one person she truly wanted to see. She needed one of his special hugs, to hear him say everything would be okay in that way only a father could. A mother might be able to do that, too, but Emily wouldn't know.

She rubbed her temples. This sounded like a pity party for one. And then she heard Jack's voice, and her mind went blank.

JACK STARED INTO the contents of the cardboard box that Lonnie Gable had left on his desk. He then glanced at the small flashlight and a printout of the most recent map Emily had posted on her blog. He brought up her blog on his phone and compared the bulleted list with the stuff in the box. All but three of the items were there.

"She's in the lockup?" he asked the rookie patrol officer.

"Yes, sir. I mean, Jack. And not too happy about it."

"I'm not surprised." He suspected he was in for an earful about having her put in a cell, but considering her actions today—going AWOL after accusing him of ruining her life and then skulking around town with a box of contraband—giving her a chance to cool her heels had been in order.

Officer Gable cleared his throat. "She insisted she didn't steal any of this stuff. Said she was putting everything back where it belongs."

How Emily came to be in possession of a boxful of other people's junk was of no interest to him. Right now, he had Emily Finnegan exactly where he wanted her, and he wasn't letting her go until she heard him out. "I appreciate this, Lonnie. I can take it from here if you'd like to get back out on the road."

"Sure thing. Let me know if you need anything."

The main door clicked shut and automatically locked after the young officer returned to his cruiser, leaving Jack alone in the after-hours quiet of the station. He eyed the door to the lockup. The Riverton police station had two cells, and they didn't see a lot of action. The occasional young fellow who got into a fisticuffs after the bar closed on a Friday night and needed a place to sleep it off, or the occasional kid who'd been caught shoplifting and needed to be taught a lesson. Jack knew with absolute certainty that a maddeningly meddlesome reporter pregnant with the police chief's baby was a first. He had no idea how he was going to start this conversation, but Emily saved him the trouble of having to think of something to say.

"This is ridiculous," she snapped when he walked in. "Did you really tell Lonnie Gable to lock me in a cell?"

He had, and for now he intended to leave her in there. He didn't trust her not to bolt, and he didn't trust himself not to kiss her senseless. Not confident he could talk and keep a straight face, Jack merely nodded. She was standing near the back of the cell with her hands on her hips and a menacing gleam in her eyes, dressed entirely in black from head to toe.

"What right do you have to lock up an innocent person?"

He took his time crossing the corridor, stopping mere inches from the bars.

"Are you going to let me out?"

He shook his head.

"*No?* Why not? How long do you plan to keep me in here?"

He chose his words carefully. "Until you listen to what I have to say about your mother and Rose." And because he couldn't resist, he added, "And until I find out why you're skulking around town like a cat burglar so you have something to blog about."

Her face, already an angry shade of red, turned even darker.

"I did not take those things just to blog about them. There's a perfectly logical explanation, but do you think that wet-behind-the-ears rookie would listen? No. He said I needed to save it for you."

Jack was enjoying this far more than he had any right to.

She crossed her arms. "Maybe I'll put a story about police harassment on my blog."

He grinned. "It's a free country."

"This is not funny. A friend's dog took all those things, and I was helping her out by returning them."

Right now he cared less about garden gnomes than he had five minutes ago, but maybe if he let her tell her story, she'd be more inclined to listen to what he had to say.

"And this friend is…?"

"I can't tell you." She turned away from him. "I promised I wouldn't tell anyone. She's elderly and she lives on her own. Her dog goes out at night, and he started bringing those things home. She didn't know where he was getting them, but I did because I've been blogging about them."

"Are we talking about Mable Potter's dog?"

Emily swung back to face him. "How did you know?"

"I saw him on the loose a couple of nights ago and was planning to talk to her about him."

"Oh." She was losing some of her bluster.

"How's Mrs. Potter doing these days?" Jack asked.

"I'm worried about her." Emily frowned. "She's getting forgetful, and I'm not sure she should be living on her own anymore. I'm going to give her daughter, Libby, a call. She lives in Minneapolis and doesn't visit her mother very often. I just hope she doesn't think I'm being a busybody."

"I'm guessing she'll be glad to know someone's looking out for her mother."

"Mrs. Potter won't be happy. She's afraid they're going to put her in a home. That's why I offered to help her, so no one would find out about Banjo being a thief." Emily seemed calmer now that she had shared the story. "Do you believe me?"

"Of course I do."

"Now will you let me out?"

He wanted to. More than anything he wanted to put his arms around her, but he knew she wouldn't let him.

"Emily, you need to know that I wasn't trying to hide anything from you. I was as surprised as you were when I heard that Rose had come back to Riverton, and I only just found out for sure that her mother was also—"

"No! Don't say it. I can't talk about this with you. Not like this, not here, not now. I need to talk to my family first."

"Fair enough." He desperately wished he was the one she wanted to lean on, but he understood her need to be with family. He pulled out his keys and swiped the fob over the electronic keypad. The cell door swung open. "I'll drive you out there."

"I'll call Annie."

"I'll drive you."

"My car—"

"It'll be fine where it is. I have a feeling you'll want to spend the night at the farm anyway. You can call me in the morning and I'll run out and pick you up."

"I'll figure something out, but thanks." She tried to sweep past him, head high.

"Emily," he said, catching her by the shoulders. He needed to heed Annie's advice.

"What?"

"You might not want to hear this right now, but I need to say it. I love you. I want to marry you. I want to make a home with you, and I want to have this baby with you."

She stared at him. He held his breath as he waited for her response, feeling some of her tension fall away.

"I…"

He waited.

Her voice was barely a whisper. "I really need my family right now."

"Okay." For now, he would have to be content with the knowledge that he had been her high school crush, and confident that Annie was his ally and would have an easier time talking sense into her sister than he would. Right now it was the best he could hope for.

EMILY DRIED HER eyes for the umpteenth time and tossed the soggy, crumpled tissue onto the pile in front of her on Annie's kitchen island. "I can't believe our mother was in Chicago all this time. It's not that far away. She never once came to see us, or let us know she was okay."

Her father sat next to her with his arm around her shoulders. "She wasn't okay, Emily. Not really."

"Did you know that's where she was?"

"I had a pretty good idea. She was from Chicago, and she never really fit in here in Riverton. The farm was as foreign to her as Iraq was for me."

Emily loved this home and this town so much, making it impossible to believe others might not feel the same.

"She loved you girls. She really did, but motherhood didn't seem to come naturally to her."

He squeezed Emily's shoulder and smiled at Annie and CJ, who sat across the table, both with red-rimmed eyes. Annie seemed to be taking the news in stride, though, as she did with everything. So far CJ had been uncharacteristically quiet.

Emily sniffled. "The news report I read said she was homeless, that she was a drug addict. Did you know about that?"

He nodded grimly. "I can't say exactly when it started, but I realized soon after I came home from Iraq that she was using prescription drugs. Or maybe abusing them would be a better way to describe it."

"Then her doctor must've known about it."

Thomas Finnegan heaved a sigh. "If only it had been that simple. Turned out she was driving to various towns and getting other doctors to write prescriptions. That was before the days of storing medical information on a central computer, so she was able to get away with it. We—your grandparents and I—staged an intervention and tried to get help for her. She left shortly after that."

Emily reached for another tissue.

"I had to make a choice," he said. "It was either her or the three of you, and I chose you."

That got the waterworks flowing again, and she noticed that even Annie looked a trifle teary.

"What about Rose?" CJ finally broke her silence. "Did you know we had a sister?"

"No, I didn't. Not that there's much I could have done for her. She's your half sister, but not my daughter."

"I feel so sorry for her," Annie said. "She seems like a nice kid who's never been able to catch a break."

"She lied to us," CJ reminded her. "Rose Danvers indeed."

"And our mother is dead because of some lunatic Rose was going out with," Emily added.

Annie wasn't swayed. "She was scared. And like it or not, she is our sister. Jack told me she was in and out of foster homes all her life. Can you imagine? We were lucky to have Dad to take care of us, but most of the time, she had no one."

"I get why she came to check us out," CJ said. "But I don't see why she had to move here. That's just plain creepy."

Emily agreed, and it was beyond annoying that Rose had already caught Fred's attention. "It's definitely creepy," Emily said. "And she was flirting with Fred at the restaurant today, and now he says he's thinking about asking her out."

"So?" Annie asked.

"So…she's not right for him."

Annie wasn't letting her off the hook. "Could it be you're a little jealous?"

What a ridiculous question! Except it had some validity to it. She had never seen Fred as a love interest, but she valued his friendship more than any worldly possession. "What if we stop being friends?" she asked.

"Emily, you know that's never going to happen," Annie said. "Unless you do something to put a strain on it."

Emily blew her nose and added another tissue to the pile. "I won't, but that doesn't mean I have to welcome Rose with open arms."

"Well," Annie said, "I'm going to do what I can to help her out. She found a room in town, but I'm going to suggest she come and stay here for a bit. As family," she said firmly. "Not as a guest."

Thomas patted her hand. "I'd say that's very generous of you, Annie, and I'm not surprised. You've always had a big heart. And as for you," he said, turning to Emily, "you say you've been waiting all these years for your mother to come back, and now part of her has. Getting to know Rose will give you a chance to get to know your mother, too. Deep down, she was a good person. Now that I know who Rose is, I can see some of those qualities in her, too. I know all of this comes as a shock, but I hope you and Cassie Jo will follow your big sister's example and give her a chance."

Emily laid her head on his shoulder. "I'll try." She reached across the table for CJ's hand. "We both will."

"Thank you," he said. "Now, it's late, and I'm going to turn in."

"Me, too." CJ stood and stretched. "I'm spending the night in the stable so I can keep an eye on that mare."

After they were gone, Emily helped Annie clear off the table.

"What about Jack?" her sister asked.

"What about him?"

"He and I talked earlier tonight, and he's completely devastated about this."

"I know."

"He told me he's in love with you."

"He told me, too."

"And?"

Emily sighed. "I told him I wasn't ready to hear it."

"Emily! The poor guy. How long are you going to make him suffer?"

She smiled at that. "Not long."

"Good. You've been waiting for this for a long time. It must be nice to have one of your wishes come true."

Annie was right. She collected her bag off the table. "I hope it's okay if I stay here tonight."

"Of course." Annie smiled.

As soon as Emily was settled in her old room upstairs, she would send Jack a text message. She wasn't sure yet what she would tell him, but she owed him something.

CHAPTER TWENTY-THREE

AFTER BREAKFAST the next morning, Emily still wasn't ready to go back into town. Instead, she dug a pen and a leather-bound journal out of her old desk and carried them both, plus a thermos of decaf coffee, to the gazebo by the river. She hadn't brought a change of clothes, so she had borrowed a flowy mint-green sundress from Annie and a pearl-pink cardigan, which she draped over her shoulders.

After she'd crawled into bed the night before, she had sent a text message to Jack.

I'm staying at the farm tomorrow. Will you come out so we can talk?

Seconds later, she'd received his response.

Nothing could keep me away.

He hadn't said when he would arrive, but she knew he would come, and that was enough for now.

She filled the thermos cup with coffee and opened her notebook.

Dear Hearts,
I am happy to share with you the news that the Great Garden Gnome Caper has drawn to a close.

Emily still wasn't sure how much of the story she would actually share on her blog, but she would write it all down and decide what to cut later. For several minutes, her attention was focused on outlining the unexpected and appalling experience of being alone in a jail cell until she heard footsteps behind her.

Jack climbed the steps of the gazebo. The sight of him literally took her breath away. He wore black dress pants and a dark green cotton pullover with the sleeves pushed up to his elbows.

He smiled down at her. "Good morning."

"Hi. I'm glad you're here."

"I'm glad you asked me."

"Thank you for coming." The exchange sounded ridiculously formal. "Here, come sit." She set the journal and pen aside, and patted the bench next to her.

He sat close enough to touch her, but kept his hands to himself.

She flipped the journal closed. "My family and I had a long talk last night."

"How did that go?"

"My dad and Annie convinced me to give Rose a chance, get to know her, and maybe she can tell me what my mother—*our* mother— was like. My dad says there's good stuff along with the bad."

"I am truly sorry things turned out the way they did. You have no idea how much I wanted Scarlett Finnegan and Scarlett Daniels to be two different people. I'm sorry you found out about your mother the way you did. I wanted you to hear it from me. I should have told you right away, even before I knew for sure."

"It wouldn't have changed anything. None of this is your fault."

"You have no idea how much I needed to hear that." He reached for her hand. "I love you, Emily."

She could hardly breathe, and the lump that formed in her throat stopped her from talking. He was waiting for her to say it back. She wanted to. She truly did. Was Annie right? Was this one wish that really was coming true?

Jack plucked a daisy from one of the hanging baskets, held the stem between his thumb and forefinger, twirled it back and forth. Then the spin of the flower stopped as quickly as it started. He studied it, thoughtfully it seemed, and then abruptly tugged off one of the petals and dropped it. It reminded her of their picnic and how she had recited the lines of the childish game. *He loves me. He loves me not. He loves me!*

"She loves me." Jack's words were quieter than her thoughts and far more startling.

He looked up and locked gazes with her. Oh, those eyes. Her heart thawed, just a little. Then his smile melted it a little more.

Another petal fluttered to the ground.

"She loves me not."

Not possible. Never possible. She had always loved him.

"She loves you." Emily took the flower and tossed it aside. "Now stop torturing that poor thing and kiss me."

He leaned in and touched his lips to hers, letting them linger, making her more breathless than she already was.

"One more thing," Jack said, "and this time I'm not taking no for an answer."

"The answer is yes."

He narrowed his eyes. "I haven't asked the question yet."

"Okay, fine, ask away."

He stood and pulled her to her feet, reaching into his pocket as he did.

"Emily Finnegan, will you please do me the honor of being my wife…and making an honest man out of me?"

"Yes, I will."

"Finally." He grinned. "Annie told me that having you locked up last night was an interesting way to catch a wife."

"I like this way better," Emily said.

And then he slid a dazzling diamond ring on her finger and sealed the deal with a kiss.

EPILOGUE

Three weeks later...

JACK HAD NEVER been to New York City, let alone sat in the front row of the audience of a national celebrity talk show. But here he was, watching the love of his life chat with one of America's most talked-about TV hosts. For a self-professed small-town girl, Emily was a natural. She'd had a brief episode of nerves in the dressing room, but on stage she was so poised and professional, so beautiful she took his breath away. She wanted to be a writer—she was a writer, and a brilliant one, too—but she could as easily have been a television personality.

The interview had opened with questions about her blog, why she started it and how long she'd been blogging. The next question surprised him but Emily took it in stride.

"The title of your blog is *Small Town, Big Hearts*. Can you tell us, Emily, why you decided to create a blog about life in a small town. I mean, it's not exactly exciting."

She bestowed a megawatt smile on the live audience, paused briefly for the camera, then turned to the host to answer his question. "There's an honesty and a sense of realism in small towns that you don't find in big cities. No pretense. Most people have known each other all their lives. They might not always see eye to eye but when push comes to shove, everyone rallies around to help and give support."

The host waited for the applause to quiet down before posing another question.

"Tell us about your recent series of posts. I think you called it 'The Great Garden Gnome Caper.'" A photograph of a gnome-inhabited garden filled the big screens on either side of the stage.

If Emily was bothered by the wave of laughter that rolled through the audience, it didn't show. Instead, she gave a brief but animated summary of the puzzling disappearances and how her readership had gradually increased as she wrote about them.

"In one of your final posts, you mentioned that a certain Mrs. P. and her dog were at the center of this so-called caper."

"That's right. I didn't want to identify her,

although most people in Riverton know who she is. She was alone and elderly and kept the dog for company, but I'm happy to say she's no longer on her own. Her daughter is moving back to town to live with her. They've given me permission to share their story because they want the world to know that people in small towns really do have big hearts."

And, Jack thought, because everyone liked to be part of a huge success story like Emily's. He sure was proud to be part of it.

"Now that the country's buzzing about *Small Town, Big Hearts*, you're being compared to a new generation's Garrison Keillor. How do you feel about that?"

Jack connected with Emily's brief gaze, felt the warmth of her smile. "He's an amazing writer, so I couldn't be more honored, or flattered. I try to write stories that have a broad appeal to young and old alike, and if I've accomplished that in some small measure, then mission accomplished."

There were times Jack wanted her to flaunt her accomplishments to the world, but it wasn't her style. The audience's vigorous applause showed they appreciated her humility as genuine rather than the false modesty of so many celebrities.

"So," the host continued, "what's next for Emily Finnegan?"

Jack watched the excitement light up her beautiful brown eyes.

"Thanks to my readers, the last post in my garden gnome series actually went viral. Somehow it caught the attention of an editor at a New York publishing house. She contacted me and offered a book deal."

Jack would always remember the day she burst into his office, barely coherent and excitedly waving an email printout.

"Impressive," the host said, speaking over the applause this time. "Can you tell us about the story that went viral?"

Emily's blush was visible in spite of a heavy layer of stage makeup. To the audience's surprise and delight, she described how she wanted to save Mrs. P from the embarrassment of admitting her dog was the thief, so she had set out under cover of darkness to return the stolen items. Instead she ended up being the suspect and locked in a cell at the local police station.

Jack glanced over his shoulder. The audience was eating this up.

There had been a time when he'd been sure that digging in his heels and insisting Emily move to Chicago was the right thing for both of them. Finally he'd come around to seeing that he was the one who needed to compromise. But from where he sat right now, he could see he hadn't sacrificed anything. Not a single thing. His career had taken a giant leap forward, he was going to be a father, and this talented and beautiful woman had agreed to marry him.

"Emily, what would you like the audience to know about the man who had you arrested?"

"His name is Jack Evans and he is Riverton's Chief of Police. After I was released," she said, playing along with the embellished arrest, "he asked me to marry him." She flashed another smile at the camera, then at the audience. "I said yes."

The applause was thunderous.

"I believe Chief Evans is here with you tonight."

Jack's pulse sped up when Emily made eye contact. "Right there in the front row."

His image appeared on the monitors as he mouthed the words *I love you*, and then the cameras panned to Emily as she blew him a kiss and whispered, "You, too."

The talk-show host beamed as though he alone was responsible for the wild hand clapping, wolf whistles and catcalls. "Remind us,

Emily," he finally interjected, "what the title of your blog post was."

"I called it 'How to Catch a Wife.'"

That brought the house down.

Watching her laugh with the audience, Jack knew he'd caught more than a wife. He'd captured a life.

* * * * *

*Be sure to look for the next book
in Lee McKenzie's*
THE FINNEGAN SISTERS *trilogy,
available in December 2016!*

LARGER-PRINT BOOKS!

GET 2 FREE
LARGER-PRINT NOVELS
PLUS 2 FREE
MYSTERY GIFTS

Love Inspired®

Larger-print novels are now available...

YES! Please send me 2 FREE LARGER-PRINT Love Inspired® novels and my 2 FREE mystery gifts (gifts are worth about $10). After receiving them, if I don't wish to receive any more books, I can return the shipping statement marked "cancel." If I don't cancel, I will receive 6 brand-new novels every month and be billed just $5.49 per book in the U.S. or $5.99 per book in Canada. That's a savings of at least 19% off the cover price. It's quite a bargain! Shipping and handling is just 50¢ per book in the U.S. and 75¢ per book in Canada.* I understand that accepting the 2 free books and gifts places me under no obligation to buy anything. I can always return a shipment and cancel at any time. Even if I never buy another book, the two free books and gifts are mine to keep forever.

122/322 IDN GH6D

Name _____ (PLEASE PRINT)

Address _____ Apt. #

City _____ State/Prov. _____ Zip/Postal Code

Signature (if under 18, a parent or guardian must sign)

Mail to the **Reader Service:**
IN U.S.A.: P.O. Box 1867, Buffalo, NY 14240-1867
IN CANADA: P.O. Box 609, Fort Erie, Ontario L2A 5X3

**Are you a current subscriber to Love Inspired® books
and want to receive the larger-print edition?
Call 1-800-873-8635 or visit www.ReaderService.com.**

* Terms and prices subject to change without notice. Prices do not include applicable taxes. Sales tax applicable in N.Y. Canadian residents will be charged applicable taxes. Offer not valid in Quebec. This offer is limited to one order per household. Not valid to current subscribers to Love Inspired Larger-Print books. All orders subject to credit approval. Credit or debit balances in a customer's account(s) may be offset by any other outstanding balance owed by or to the customer. Please allow 4 to 6 weeks for delivery. Offer available while quantities last.

Your Privacy—The Reader Service is committed to protecting your privacy. Our Privacy Policy is available online at www.ReaderService.com or upon request from the Reader Service.

We make a portion of our mailing list available to reputable third parties that offer products we believe may interest you. If you prefer that we not exchange your name with third parties, or if you wish to clarify or modify your communication preferences, please visit us at www.ReaderService.com/consumerschoice or write to us at Reader Service Preference Service, P.O. Box 9062, Buffalo, NY 14240-9062. Include your complete name and address.

LILP15

LARGER-PRINT BOOKS!

GET 2 FREE
LARGER-PRINT NOVELS
PLUS 2 FREE
MYSTERY GIFTS

Love Inspired.

SUSPENSE
RIVETING INSPIRATIONAL ROMANCE

Larger-print novels are now available...

YES! Please send me 2 FREE LARGER-PRINT Love Inspired® Suspense novels and my 2 FREE mystery gifts (gifts are worth about $10). After receiving them, if I don't wish to receive any more books, I can return the shipping statement marked "cancel." If I don't cancel, I will receive 4 brand-new novels every month and be billed just $5.49 per book in the U.S. or $5.99 per book in Canada. That's a savings of at least 19% off the cover price. It's quite a bargain! Shipping and handling is just 50¢ per book in the U.S. and 75¢ per book in Canada.* I understand that accepting the 2 free books and gifts places me under no obligation to buy anything. I can always return a shipment and cancel at any time. Even if I never buy another book, the two free books and gifts are mine to keep forever.

110/310 IDN GH6P

Name _____ (PLEASE PRINT)

Address _____ Apt. #

City _____ State/Prov. _____ Zip/Postal Code

Signature (if under 18, a parent or guardian must sign)

Mail to the **Reader Service:**
IN U.S.A.: P.O. Box 1867, Buffalo, NY 14240-1867
IN CANADA: P.O. Box 609, Fort Erie, Ontario L2A 5X3

Are you a current subscriber to Love Inspired® Suspense books
and want to receive the larger-print edition?
Call 1-800-873-8635 or visit www.ReaderService.com.

* Terms and prices subject to change without notice. Prices do not include applicable taxes. Sales tax applicable in N.Y. Canadian residents will be charged applicable taxes. Offer not valid in Quebec. This offer is limited to one order per household. Not valid for current subscribers to Love Inspired Suspense larger-print books. All orders subject to credit approval. Credit or debit balances in a customer's account(s) may be offset by any other outstanding balance owed by or to the customer. Please allow 4 to 6 weeks for delivery. Offer available while quantities last.

Your Privacy—The Reader Service is committed to protecting your privacy. Our Privacy Policy is available online at www.ReaderService.com or upon request from the Reader Service.

We make a portion of our mailing list available to reputable third parties that offer products we believe may interest you. If you prefer that we not exchange your name with third parties, or if you wish to clarify or modify your communication preferences, please visit us at www.ReaderService.com/consumerschoice or write to us at Reader Service Preference Service, P.O. Box 9062, Buffalo, NY 14240-9062. Include your complete name and address.

LISLP15

WESTERN (WP) PROMISES

YES! Please send me **The Western Promises Collection** in Larger Print. This collection begins with 3 FREE books and 2 FREE gifts (gifts valued at approx. $14.00 retail) in the first shipment, along with the other first 4 books from the collection! If I do not cancel, I will receive 8 monthly shipments until I have the entire 51-book Western Promises collection. I will receive 2 or 3 FREE books in each shipment and I will pay just $4.99 US/ $5.89 CDN for each of the other four books in each shipment, plus $2.99 for shipping and handling per shipment. *If I decide to keep the entire collection, I'll have paid for only 32 books, because 19 books are FREE! I understand that accepting the 3 free books and gifts places me under no obligation to buy anything. I can always return a shipment and cancel at any time. My free books and gifts are mine to keep no matter what I decide.

272 HCN 3070 472 HCN 3070

Name   (PLEASE PRINT)

Address   Apt. #

City   State/Prov.   Zip/Postal Code

Signature (if under 18, a parent or guardian must sign)

Mail to the **Reader Service:**

IN U.S.A.: P.O. Box 1867, Buffalo, NY 14240-1867
IN CANADA: P.O. Box 609, Fort Erie, Ontario L2A 5X3

* Terms and prices subject to change without notice. Prices do not include applicable taxes. Sales tax applicable in N.Y. Canadian residents will be charged applicable taxes. This offer is limited to one order per household. All orders subject to approval. Credit or debit balances in a customer's account(s) may be offset by any other outstanding balance owed by or to the customer. Please allow 4 to 6 weeks for delivery. Offer available while quantities last. Offer not available to Quebec residents.

Your Privacy—The Reader Service is committed to protecting your privacy. Our Privacy Policy is available online at www.ReaderService.com or upon request from the Reader Service.

We make a portion of our mailing list available to reputable third parties that offer products we believe may interest you. If you prefer that we not exchange your name with third parties, or if you wish to clarify or modify your communication preferences, please visit us at www.ReaderService.com/consumerchoice or write to us at Reader Service Preference Service, P.O. Box 9062, Buffalo, NY 14240-9062. Include your complete name and address.

WPBPA16R

LARGER-PRINT BOOKS!
GET 2 FREE LARGER-PRINT NOVELS PLUS
2 FREE GIFTS!

HARLEQUIN®

super romance®

More Story...More Romance

YES! Please send me 2 FREE LARGER-PRINT Harlequin® Superromance® novels and my 2 FREE gifts (gifts are worth about $10). After receiving them, if I don't wish to receive any more books, I can return the shipping statement marked "cancel." If I don't cancel, I will receive 4 brand-new novels every month and be billed just $5.94 per book in the U.S. or $6.24 per book in Canada. That's a savings of at least 12% off the cover price! It's quite a bargain! Shipping and handling is just 50¢ per book in the U.S. or 75¢ per book in Canada.* I understand that accepting the 2 free books and gifts places me under no obligation to buy anything. I can always return a shipment and cancel at any time. Even if I never buy another book, the two free books and gifts are mine to keep forever.

132/332 HDN GHVC

Name	(PLEASE PRINT)

Address		Apt. #

City	State/Prov.	Zip/Postal Code

Signature (if under 18, a parent or guardian must sign)

Mail to the **Reader Service:**
IN U.S.A.: P.O. Box 1867, Buffalo, NY 14240-1867
IN CANADA: P.O. Box 609, Fort Erie, Ontario L2A 5X3

Want to try two free books from another line?
Call 1-800-873-8635 today or visit www.ReaderService.com.

* Terms and prices subject to change without notice. Prices do not include applicable taxes. Sales tax applicable in N.Y. Canadian residents will be charged applicable taxes. Offer not valid in Quebec. This offer is limited to one order per household. Not valid for current subscribers to Harlequin Superromance Larger-Print books. All orders subject to credit approval. Credit or debit balances in a customer's account(s) may be offset by any other outstanding balance owed by or to the customer. Please allow 4 to 6 weeks for delivery. Offer available while quantities last.

Your Privacy—The Reader Service is committed to protecting your privacy. Our Privacy Policy is available online at www.ReaderService.com or upon request from the Reader Service.

We make a portion of our mailing list available to reputable third parties that offer products we believe may interest you. If you prefer that we not exchange your name with third parties, or if you wish to clarify or modify your communication preferences, please visit us at www.ReaderService.com/consumerschoice or write to us at Reader Service Preference Service, P.O. Box 9062, Buffalo, NY 14240-9062. Include your complete name and address.

HSRLP15

READERSERVICE.COM

Manage your account online!

- Review your order history
- Manage your payments
- Update your address

> ### We've designed the Reader Service website just for you.

Enjoy all the features!

- Discover new series available to you, and read excerpts from any series.
- Respond to mailings and special monthly offers.
- Connect with favorite authors at the blog.
- Browse the Bonus Bucks catalog and online-only exculsives.
- Share your feedback.

Visit us at:
ReaderService.com

REQUEST YOUR FREE BOOKS!
2 FREE WHOLESOME ROMANCE NOVELS IN LARGER PRINT
PLUS 2 FREE MYSTERY GIFTS

☆☆☆☆☆☆☆☆☆☆☆☆☆☆☆☆☆☆☆☆☆☆☆☆

HEARTWARMING™

☆☆☆☆☆☆☆☆☆☆☆☆☆☆☆☆☆☆☆☆☆☆☆☆

Wholesome, tender romances

YES! Please send me 2 FREE Harlequin® Heartwarming Larger-Print novels and my 2 FREE mystery gifts (gifts worth about $10). After receiving them, if I don't wish to receive any more books, I can return the shipping statement marked "cancel." If I don't cancel, I will receive 4 brand-new larger-print novels every month and be billed just $5.24 per book in the U.S. or $5.99 per book in Canada. That's a savings of at least 19% off the cover price. It's quite a bargain! Shipping and handling is just 50¢ per book in the U.S. and 75¢ per book in Canada.* I understand that accepting the 2 free books and gifts places me under no obligation to buy anything. I can always return a shipment and cancel at any time. Even if I never buy another book, the two free books and gifts are mine to keep forever.

161/361 IDN GHX2

Name _____ (PLEASE PRINT) _____

Address _____ Apt. # _____

City _____ State/Prov. _____ Zip/Postal Code _____

Signature (if under 18, a parent or guardian must sign)

Mail to the **Reader Service:**
IN U.S.A.: P.O. Box 1867, Buffalo, NY 14240-1867
IN CANADA: P.O. Box 609, Fort Erie, Ontario L2A 5X3

* Terms and prices subject to change without notice. Prices do not include applicable taxes. Sales tax applicable in N.Y. Canadian residents will be charged applicable taxes. Offer not valid in Quebec. This offer is limited to one order per household. Not valid for current subscribers to Harlequin Heartwarming larger-print books. All orders subject to credit approval. Credit or debit balances in a customer's account(s) may be offset by any other outstanding balance owed by or to the customer. Please allow 4 to 6 weeks for delivery. Offer available while quantities last.

Your Privacy—The Reader Service is committed to protecting your privacy. Our Privacy Policy is available online at www.ReaderService.com or upon request from the Reader Service.

We make a portion of our mailing list available to reputable third parties that offer products we believe may interest you. If you prefer that we not exchange your name with third parties, or if you wish to clarify or modify your communication preferences, please visit us at www.ReaderService.com/consumerchoice or write to us at Reader Service Preference Service, P.O. Box 9062, Buffalo, NY 14240-9062. Include your complete name and address.

HW15